THE NIGHT AND THE LAND

Book One of The Deschembine Trilogy

BY

MATT SPENCER

BACK ROADS CARNIVAL BOOKS,
BRATTLEBORO, VERMONT

BACK ROADS CARNIVAL BOOKS
mattspencerauthor.wordpress.com

Digital ISBN: 978-578-45227-2
Print ISBN: 978-578-45145-9

Originally published in 2013 by Damnation Books.
Second edition published in 2017 by Siento Sordida/Caliburn Press

"Sure."

As they walked down South Main, Rob spotted a short waddling shape. It materialized into a small, curvy female body, her round head capped in a tumble of dreadlocks. Bethany, the Hippie Hobbit Sex Goddess of Brattleboro, as Rob couldn't help thinking of her.

"Well, look who it is." He greeted her with a sly smile.

She flashed that cartoon-sultry grin of hers and poked his stomach. "I hear people have been asking questions about you, mister."

"Wouldn't surprise me. Who's it this time?"

"Oh, I don't know if I should give you that information, Mister Sketchy."

"Am I gonna have to hog-tie you and tickle it out of you?"

"Promises, promises." Her eyelashes batted.

"So, what're you up to right now?"

"Nothing much. Secret business you shouldn't know about."

"That a fact." She probably meant something to do with sex, drugs, or both. Rob's voice grew quasi-serious. "So honestly, who's saying what?"

"Oh, just a certain new stranger in town. I only saw her for a minute this morning. Just some people say she's *mighty curious* about what's the deal with you."

"Which people?"

She drew up uncomfortably like she was actually starting to feel interrogated. "Just, you know, the whole Common Ground crowd…"

"Uh-huh. She still staying there?"

"It's where she's been hanging out. Couldn't hurt to

check."

After breakfast, Rob used the diner's phone to call the Lucca Bistro and ask if he still had work tonight. Virdelle, the owner, said no. For once, Rob couldn't have been happier to hear it.

Still, he thought, *What the hell are you so excited about, especially not even knowing if you'll find her there, or if she's half as interested as you hope? Hurting for hours as you are—*

Saying fuck it, let's see what happens, *that's what. Yeah, shaking off some of this stagnation before it drives me any crazier… Maybe going a little crazier's the only way to stay sane at this point.*

There was a spring in his step as he walked out. For once, it wasn't just from too much coffee.

Two

Picking at some vegan chili, Sally listened to the Common Ground's battery-powered radio. It was tuned into some local community station, yet she still kept expecting to catch a report of the murder. Whenever they found the Pittsburgh man, the radio probably wouldn't mention it this far north. Nah, it would seem like just another big city murder, even with what had been done to the body.

Earlier, she'd helped clean. She would have helped Clover wait tables now, but the only customers were a bearded. barrel-gutted mountain man and his wife. The latter might have been beautiful once. Now the black bags under her eyes sagged halfway down her face, and her mouth drooped to show craggy stalactites and stalagmites for teeth. They took turns asking Clover personal questions like a concerned aunt and uncle. She wasn't hiding her annoyance too well, but they didn't seem to notice.

Someone trudged up the front stairs, too naturally quiet for most ears. "Hey, everybody," came a lazily sarcastic male voice. Clover waved, then shot Sally a conspiratorial smile.

Sally stood and saw Rob Coscan's face light up. "Hey you," she said.

When she went and hugged him, he lifted and spun her around.

Right then, tumbled against him, there came that melting, irrationally familiar feeling. When he set her down, she swayed and looked up. They were still by the stairs, and his height and broad shoulders eclipsed her from the rest of the place. With the light from the windows to his back, only his eyes still seemed aglow.

"So what are you up to?" He sounded like the one who'd been given a spin.

"Just waiting around, trying to think of something to do."

He smiled like he knew something he wasn't supposed to. More than ever, she didn't want to see a monster, wanted to just see the boy, the man, whatever he was.

"Wanna go get lunch?" he asked.

"I just ate."

"Wanna do something else then? I'm sure if we wander around long enough, we'll think of something."

She didn't know what she'd say 'til the words "Doesn't sound so bad" came out.

"Gonna be back later, Sally?" Clover called after her.

"Oh yeah. It okay to leave my bag here a while?"

"Sure." Then coquettishly, "Have fun."

As they stepped out, Sally felt Rob's fingers slide across her palm. His hand was slender, rough, knotted. Her own hand was much smaller, but not much smoother. Maybe this disappointed him. Oh well. As they walked in no particular direction, she kept feeling his eyes on her. How soft did he think she was in general? Did he expect her to lean on him, let him be the tough, protective man who could shield her from whatever? Either way, she noticed herself squeezing his hand tighter. Had all these hippies gotten her that overly relaxed already?

When he asked how she was getting along in town, she told him more of her impressions of the Common Ground crowd. When he laughed, she asked more about the locals. Most of his anecdotes focused on Liam and a pirate radio show the kid ran. Sally laughed at the image of those two guys high as kites, ranting maniacally in turns or overlapping on the airwaves between songs. When Rob told stories, every little inflection filled Sally's head with sharper smells, images, sounds…like he'd pulled her into his memories with him. She felt warm and safe there. Did Rob even know what his voice could do? Was that one of *their* powers, something she'd never been taught to watch out for?

"So, you feel like seeing a movie?" he asked.

THREE

Alongside Putney Road, their hands stayed locked 'til the path grew too narrow. Sally led, swaying dreamily on the edge of the steep hill, arms out like a tightrope walker. Rob watched, relieved not to have to hide how high in the clouds she sent him. When she hummed some soft, wistful child's melody, the sound nearly locked up his chest…carefree and melancholy all at once, scared of the world like a small rabbit hiding in a moment's peace, yet so full of strength. It was the kind of sound people usually only let out when no one else was around. Then she looked back at him and they both laughed. He swayed and raised his arms, mimicking her. In response she exaggerated her own swaying. When it looked like she might spill over the hillside, he stepped in and caught her. The outline of her body's heat lined up so closely with his, the electricity flowing between their palms, the smell of her hair…it all made him want to pull her back against him, push her hair aside, bury his face in her neck…

Whoa there, boy. Don't hit the gas that fast.

"What's that?"

Oops, had he just said that out loud? "Nothing."

"Hhhmmmmm…" She squeezed his hands tighter.

Emboldened, he moved closer, his face sliding up alongside hers. "You know, it's colder out here than I thought." He guided her arms inward 'til they encircled her. "Don't you think?"

"I'm not so cold now…for some mysterious reason."

He rested his face against hers then kissed her cheek.

"What are we about to get ourselves into?" Alarm haunted the edges of her whisper.

"Only one way to find out."

"Mmmmm…We should probably get along to that theatre." She let go, reached back for just one of his hands, and tugged him back into walking.

Hopefully she didn't hear his frustrated sigh. At least he didn't feel cold anymore. Especially not with his hand in hers, burning against her palm. After the narrow path, they moved side by side again, cutting through a parking lot.

"So, what are you doing living in Brattleboro, anyway?" she asked.

"It's good as anywhere. Might say the town said *come on in, stay a while.*"

"What, you mean all the people…"

"Not them so much. I mean, yeah, I've got friends here, but… places have spirits, you know? If the spirit of a place likes you, it helps you get by there. Won't make it easy for you, but if you know how to listen, it helps you find your way to what you need. See, I made friends with the spirit of Brattleboro the first time I lived here. Let me tell you, life was sweet for a while, back then."

"So why'd you leave?"

"Just…too many memories built up."

She shifted uncomfortably. "You said you were in New Orleans for a while. How'd that place *like* you?"

"Oh, New Orleans fuckin' *loved* me."

Sally edged away a little from that wild grin. "Just…too many memories there, too?"

"Nah. Just life got a little too crazy. That place offers you a lot, but it doesn't always let you refuse its offers, even when you're choking on 'em."

They stopped and faced each other. Now why the hell had he gone and told her all that? Except instead of disbelief, there was… something else, worse. Like he'd set off some unheard-of new set of warning bells.

"Where did you learn to…notice it?" she asked.

"You do too?"

"No. I've…known others who can. So how?"

"Hold up, hold up. What do you mean? What others?"

"I've known a lot of people. Just answer me. Please."

"I don't know. Just…the more life I go through, the more I notice things like that."

"What was your life like growing up?"

"Shit, where to start? I don't know. Kind of a pain in the ass, I guess. I was raised on a farm by my parents—well, actually, my dad and stepmom. I ran away when I was pretty young, like still mid-teens." He shrugged.

"You *ran away*." Her voice dropped a few octaves, slow and studious…grim. "They didn't kick you out or…abandon you somewhere."

"Uh, that's right."

"Why, then?"

"Mostly 'cause I would've killed my stepmom if I stayed much longer. That or she'd have found a way to kill me. And I hated the town we lived in. Why?"

"I don't know. Isn't that the kind of shit people ask when they're getting to know each other?"

"I guess. So what was your childhood like?"

"Not much to say, really."

"Not much you like to talk about, you mean."

"Yeah…"

"Sorry…I mean if I shouldn't have…"

"No, it's okay."

"Something about me bothers you. What, you thought I didn't notice?"

"I…don't know what I thought. Look, it's been pretty nonstop on the road for a while, y'know? I'm still pretty mixed up. A lot of things are…registering in ways that just make less and less sense. So who are you, Rob? Do you even know?"

"What's that supposed to mean? Shit, how do I answer that?" His voice softened. "Guess there's only one way you can find out. Plus I wanna find out who Sally Wildfire is, too."

She smiled and closed her eyes. His fingers slid across her cheek and through her hair. When he kissed her, her mouth slipped instantly open, their chapping lips turning to warm velvet against each other. His mouth opened and closed very slowly on hers, arms tightening around her, gliding along her back, easing her closer 'til she held him just as tight. She pressed herself against his hardon, and his arms snaked inside her coat, then back around her body, feeling the contours of her ribs and curves through the thin, ratty T-shirt. When their lips parted, the rest of them didn't let go, just hugged. He pressed his face into the crook of her neck and inhaled deeply. Her scent was dusty and flowery, in a way that drove him crazy.

Eventually, they walked on to the theatre. It was Thursday, so the place was nearly empty. Rob and Sally sat near the back, curled up close. Halfway through the show, he glanced over and realized she'd slipped into one of the deepest, most contented looking sleeps he'd ever seen anyone in, her face half-buried in his jacket. He lost himself in the sound and feeling of her breathing, then something shuffled by his feet. Both her shoes lay well shy of his, so he peered at the dark floor, trying to adjust his eyes, to pick up any more movement. Sally stirred. He was afraid he'd woken her, but she'd only snuggled closer.

When the lights came up, her eyes opened, bright with no trace of bleariness. She kissed him full on the mouth 'til an usher came in.

On the way out into the late dusk, she purred in his ear, "We're gonna get each other *in all kinds of trouble*…What are you nervous about?"

"Huh?"

"You keep looking around, like there's something you expect to see."

"Just habit, I guess."

FOUR

Puttergong scuttles out of the mopperkid's way, even though he ain't solid enough to get stepped on, yet. Still, he don't feel like pushin' his luck. After all, he's solid enough to eat spilled pufftreat bits from this here floor, and it's the second time Biter-Boy's sorta spotted him. Way things is goin', Puttergong figures he'll be solid enough to beat the air down under his wings in less than a week. Maybe sooner, dependin' on how fast shit happens from here.

The First Call came so sudden, Puttergong's still a little rattled. What he's found since ain't done much for his nerves, neither. For a while there, he was wishin' like hell he was solid enough to make the call home, say there must be some mistake.

Now Puttergong's had time to think it over, and he's got a better idea how shit's shapin' up. Might be hope for Biter-Boy yet! So obviously the boy's a straggler, some prodigal's offspring. Whichever prodigal it is, they've done a sure-shit job raisin' him out of the loop. 'Course, civilians pull that crap all the time, rearin' their brats to think they's Earth-line. Puttergong still never thought he'd see it among the Crimbone. Not that it'll make much difference. Blood writes the book, as the old sayin' goes. When it comes to figurin' shit out, Biter-Boy's barely stepped onto Page Fuckin' One, yet here he is, makin' the Calls just the same!

Man, wouldn't that be somethin'…Puttergong gettin' to familiarize a downright honest-to-Old-Lords High Natural. Truth be told, the idea's kinda rattlin'.

So, the Cabinet had better send Puttergong the homework on this here fledgling, quick. They'd better be ready for that Second Call, too. Usually the youngin's don't go makin' that 'til they's done lots more time under their Familiar's wing. 'Cept Biter-Boy just might surprise everyone. 'Course, ain't no one gonna be more surprised than Biter-Boy hisownself. Hell, ain't been two whole days since his First Call, and he's already drawin' in his First Poach.

After some sittin' an' thinkin', Puttergong goes sniffin' his way out of the show hall, weavin' an' wheedlin' between the feet of the mopperkids and marks. No one notices him, 'least not consciously. By the time he's outside, Biter-Boy and his First Poach are out of sight. Puttergong'll have to catch up later. By then, it might just be time to talk to the kid more directly like.

First, though, Puttergong's hankerin' for dinner. He don't gotta sniff long. Hell, wouldn't you know, it's right off to the side of the show hall building, where not too many marks tend to go, but where the managers and mopperkids park their big ol' cars. Yeah, that's where Puttergong spots the dead squirrel. 'Cept, well, *dead* don't quite do the critter justice by now. Damn thing's been here at least two weeks, gettin' flatter an' drier, as folks drive in and out every day. A week ago, the weather was warmer, and oh how the sun must'a beat down on the carcass then! Puttergong imagines how the critter smelled, so he sorta wishes Biter-Boy made that First Call earlier. Then maybe Puttergong would'a gotten a nice meal, at least.

Over the squirrel's carcass waddles a pigeon, hazy shimmering splotches of silver, purple, and peacock green all over them matted, dirt-gray feathers. Now Puttergong's seen fat pigeons, but if this is the kind they got in Vermont, well, he just don't guess he could look at the rest of the state quite the same. Shit, the thing don't got so much a body as a bloated sack lookin' ready to spring a leak, saggin' so you can't even see its little birdie legs. Its tiny head rolls around on that sack like the tie on a balloon, its black-pea eyes zeroin' in on one rough, fuzzy corner of what used to be the squirrel. The bird's head dips like a sewing machine needle into the dried, crusty remnants.

"Well I'll be," Puttergong muses aloud in pigeon-speak, "I didn't think you fellers was into all that carrion stuff."

The pigeon's feathers ruffle like it's about to fly off in a hurry. Then it spots Puttergong. "Oh. One of you guys."

"Ain't gonna get all fussy now, is ye? Ain't gonna go puffin' up like you too good to eat with us Crimbone Familiars?"

"I wasn't eating the squirrel. There was a piece of puffy-corn mashed in there."

"Oh, my mistake. An' here I thought, you wasn't bein'

so high an' mighty all of a sudden."

"You wish, errand boy."

Dumb fuckin' pigeon. "Whatever. Anyhow, surprised?"

The pigeon shifts its wings and upper body in what you might call a shrug. "I didn't realize you had any of your little boys and girls stashed around here."

Puttergong gives off a wheezy laugh. "Yeah. Funny damn thing, neither does this particular little boy." Even funnier, neither did the Crimbone Cabinet 'til now. Yeah, they thought Ripper-Man's kid was the last of 'em in these parts. If Puttergong told the pigeon, the damn thing'd probably laugh 'til it busted. Temptin' as that is, Puttergong figures he's pushed enough luck in the sensitive information department. Fuck it, he's already sick of this critter. He takes two big hops, so him and the pigeon face each other over the squirrel carcass. "So, you done diggin', or you think I ought'a go havin' some live pigeon on the side with my dead squirrel?"

"Fuck you," the pigeon says and flies off. Damn, them Vermont pigeons sure can fly fast. For such fat fuckin' bloated-sack-about-to-bust pieces o' shit, anyhow.

Now, if Puttergong's two tiny front paws was made more like human hands, this is where he'd give the pigeon's soarin' posterior two big ol' middle fingers. Shit, if he was solid enough, he could fly after that snot-nose pigeon and take a big ol' bite out of the rude birdie's fat gray ass. Instead he just sorta huffs and dips his snout into some squirrel.

FIVE

Sally had gone to use the restroom. Sprawled across his mattress, Rob might as well be chained helpless. They'd only been making out, and damn, he was still shaking. It wasn't just that he felt better with her than with any girl, ever. No, more like she opened something long bottled up, letting him breathe deeper, fuller…freer. When the door opened, he swore she floated over.

She sat on the edge of the mattress and stared at the faded green wall, swollen from years of water damage, all its jagged lumps and cracked lines like a three-dimensional map of a desert mountain range. "I think you said you'd tell me how you got the habit."

"One of my bad habits?" He grinned wolfishly. "Which one?"

She chuckled and shook her head, then she went serious again. "Always looking around like you're waiting for something."

He sat up and kissed her neck. "Did I say I'd explain that?"

"Sort of. Look, if you're not ready, that's fine."

"No, it's okay. I just…well, I like to keep on my toes."

"Does Brattleboro tell you to?"

"Not really."

Earlier, it hadn't been so hard, getting him to talk about his past. Most of it, anyway. Back in Harmony Lot, he'd bought her dinner in Frankie's Pizzeria. He'd been sixteen when he ran away, barely seventeen when he first found Vermont, when he'd met Al Carpenter, a film professor out of Saint Johnsbury. Al was the state's most respected independent filmmaker, running his small operation out of a home office in the summer, teaching classes at Marlboro during the school year.

Rob had been a bit of a movie nut growing up, thought for a while he'd like the film business. Maybe Al saw potential in him, because their coffee shop conversations landed him an off-the-books office job. By summer's end, Al's family had genuinely embraced Rob. Once he turned eighteen, he got his GED and finally asked about that little school in southern Vermont where Al taught. Soon he started part-time, scoring phenomenal grades. During the school year, he worked and saved, then lived and worked full time in Brattleboro that summer. He snagged some loans, accepted the help Al offered, and did one full-time year.

Two years later, and he still couldn't come up with a good reason for leaving college…One more topic he always dodged, with everyone. Until yesterday, when this weird, magic girl came along, doing all these freaky things to his brainwaves. Except now his past was the last thing he wanted to discuss, because this moment was all he gave a damn about.

"I guess I've spent my whole life feeling like I'm waiting for something," he said.

"How's that?"

"I don't know. It feels like someone delivered me a message once and told me to watch for something…told me *what* to watch for and when, and that it'd be the start of everything that would ever matter, and it had all been decided for me already." Had that made any sense? How should he know? He'd never tried finding the words before.

"Hmmm. So…do you think it's a good or a bad thing, whatever it is?"

"Not sure. I mean, it feels like I'm supposed to know, but somehow I forgot. I can't even remember who delivered the message."

Ghostly soft, she eased close and kissed first his forehead, then the bruise near his eye, then his mouth. His hand slid through her hair, to keep her around. She scratched at his scalp and back, her fingernails sending a singing tingle. His face moved dreamily down along her neck and shoulder, savoring every contour, lost in an almost ephemeral softness, the electric connection singing higher.

When he eased her back onto the mattress, she resisted playfully. "You're trying to change the subject."

"*Trying*, huh."

"Well, feel free to keep up the effort." She kissed him deeper, tugging him down on her. One of his hands played with the strands of her hair while the other ran up and down her thigh, steadily inward as her legs bent and flexed. She kicked off frayed sneakers and rubbed her feet together. Their limbs tangled, hips pressing and pumping. Going wilder, he pulled off her shirt and tasted her sweat all over, savoring every distinctive natural perfume. Damnit, their jeans were just too damn thick. As her breathing gave way to a faint moan, he cupped her cheeks, eyes burning into hers. When he tried steadying his shaking body, she rocked teasingly against his crotch. He didn't notice her unbuttoning his shirt 'til she reached his belt.

"How you doin'?" he whispered low.

"Like I'm about to lose control," she managed.

"That a bad thing?"

"It always has been for me."

He eased back. "What, losing control?"

"Yeah."

As if to prove something, he kissed her forehead chastely. "No hurry."

"Does it always have to mean…losing control?"

"Making love, you mean? Yeah."

"Making love…"

"Yeah. As opposed to just sex."

* * * *

They spent a long time just holding tight, feeling the shakes die off in one another. So was he the sort of guy to say that lightly, had to romance up all his tomcat games? Did she already make him just crazy enough to believe it? Right now, she could barely form coherent thoughts herself, and she wasn't even stoned this time.

Listening to him, though, she'd formed a theory of sorts…and it was the most insane one yet. Listening meant getting lost where his voice took her. It didn't help how fast things moved from there. His skeleton beneath didn't feel unusual, at least from what she could tell through his tight, wiry muscles. When she stroked his knotted back, he stirred.

"Thought you'd fallen asleep on me," he mumbled.

"No, just real relaxed. Drifting there, though. Sorry. Been missing lots of sleep."

"Catch up as much as you need. Want me to kill the light?"

"If you don't mind…"

They disentangled long enough for him to get up and hit the switch. There was something unique about him, and plenty of it matched what she'd been taught growing up, learned firsthand, still felt the scars from…As she pressed her face back into his chest, a sob escaped her. His hand ran through her hair, and she sobbed more freely.

SIX

Rob slipped free without waking Sally and crept down the hall to the bathroom. He'd have gone straight back, if he hadn't felt so damn restless. Feeling restless led to wandering downstairs, which led to standing in the night air, which led to fishing out an American Spirit. A fluttering sound drew his gaze to the zigzag fence around the yard. Some bird had settled on a post, round like a pigeon, too gloom-shrouded for Rob to be sure.

"I don' know what you're doin', Biter-Boy, or how you're pullin' it off, *but keep it up.*"

Rob blinked, not sure if the voice was in his head.

"Alrighty then, no need to be shy."

No, that was out loud, whatever it was. It sounded like an exaggerated West Virginia drawl, full of crackly, wheezy, malicious humor. Rob took a long drag and peered at the creature he'd first seen two nights ago.

"Well, Biter-Boy, I'm guessin' the phrase you're lookin' for goes a might somethin' like, *What in the Sam-Hell Fuck?*"

Rob blinked and wondered if anyone else could hear the thing. "Nah, that was my reaction last time. I've had time to think it over."

"Well, Biter-Boy, seems you been doin' more'n

thinkin'. 'Cause seriously, you should see how all-a-sudden I got these here wings up an' runnin'."

"Yeah, well, I've got other things to think and do now. So you're a little late." Rob climbed the porch steps. "Tell you what, next time my brain's running on empty, ready to go batshit crazy, you can be first in line for twisted schizophrenic hallucinations. Cool?"

"So, who the hell beat me to it, that ol' bong-smokin' caterpillar feller again? Oh right, your little First Poach. Y'know, I'm startin' to reckon you might actually be—"

"*What?*"

When the thing laughed, the snickering, wheezing sound pricked at Rob's guts like cold fishhooks. "Ain't never heard it put like that, huh? Least you don't *remember* hearin' it like that. Rings a bell, though, don't it? Yeah, it rings 'em all through the blood in your veins!"

Rob hopped back off the porch. "If you're talking about Sally, maybe you'd better get the fuck out of here, birdie."

"Ever stop an' ask yourself why you don't shit your pants at sights like me, Biter-Boy? Seen plenty of it, ain't ye? Nothin' sexy like me, of course, but you seen yer share o' shit."

For some reason, the first things Rob thought of were those damn vines in New Orleans. He'd first seen them when he'd crossed the levy and gone down to the riverbanks to clear his head. Among the growth, he'd spotted vines that didn't grow anywhere else, even amongst the kudzu climbing the walls in the city. He couldn't find pictures to identify them in any botany books, and they were greener than any other local flora, a shade he'd never seen anywhere else. When he'd asked native New Orleanians, no one knew what he was talking about. Maybe he'd gone crazy like his roommate Chuck, hallucinating without drugs.

Down by the river, out of the corner of his eye, he'd sworn they'd slithered left and right like snakes. Then they started growing around the house on Jena Street. New Orleans spring was hot as hell, so Rob had kept his bedroom window open. The vines climbed in so it became impossible to close it, their wavering tips twitching at him, like the swamp was reaching out, offering its hand whenever he decided to take it.

Half-sentient stalker vines were tame compared to this thing, whatever it was. Rob still answered, "Yeah, I've seen some shit here and there. So?"

"So, you ever think maybe you glimpsin' an' gettin' let in all that weird shit ain't just 'cause of that pretty face o' yours? Like maybe it's 'cause you're a little piece o' weird shit your own self? Look, I know what you wanna think, how me an' whatever shitstorm I'm bringin' ain't got nothin' to do with that nice lil' thing you got upstairs. But nope, it just ain't a nice world like that, kid, so get used to it. Then again, maybe you already thought some of that."

"It crossed my mind."

"That's okay, Biter-Boy. Your blood admits it, and that's what writes the book when you get down to it." The thing gave its sickly laugh again. "Just remember…I'm sorry in advance, I truly am. When you figure out what's really what, 'specially with your little First Poach up there, it's gonna hurt for a while. Once you get through it, I reckon you gonna feel just—"

Rob made as if to bolt at the thing, then halted like a

snake curling to strike. "Fucking birdie! Keep talking that shit, see what happens."

"Whoa there, tiger, ain't my fault. They just send me here to carry the news. And to fill you in on what's what as you need it…I like seein' it in you, though. Brass like that, I mean when you go poppin' off. That'll make it easier, help ye get through it when—"

Later, Rob wouldn't be sure he'd known what he was doing. Now he bent, groped, found a rock and threw it hard at the creature. He didn't hear a thump, wasn't sure he hit the thing, but it sprang into the air with a buzzard-like shriek. Rob didn't wait to see if it stayed. He just stormed back inside and up the stairs.

SEVEN

Heavy feet shook the stairwell and upper landing. As Sally blinked in the darkness, the bedroom door hissed open. The hallway light outlined Rob, but out on the stairs—Damn, she'd sworn it must be someone twice his size.

"What's the matter?" he spat.

Sally barely heard, just recoiled from this new evil heat fuming off him. He shoved the door shut and flipped on the light. When she saw his face, her only thought was that she'd let herself be tricked. The trap had sprung and she would die, or worse. Scrambling, she snatched her coat. The sonofabitch…High time she brushed up on Crimbone anatomy, and not like she'd done earlier. No, she'd carve all the way to his unnatural organs, have a good long—

Before she could open the blade, he cleared the room and dove, hands locking on her wrists and pushing them above her head. The blade had just started to open when he wrenched it away, grazing his thumb before he tossed it over his shoulder. He pivoted his hips, dodged a knee to the crotch, and shoved her down on her back.

* * * *

"Sally! What the fuck!"

"*I knew you were—I should've—*"

He got both her wrists in one grip and clamped his free hand over her mouth. "Calm the fuck down. I'm not gonna hurt you." Of course he wouldn't. Right? Hell, *she'd* pulled a knife on *him*. He'd defended himself, and now he felt crooked and soiled, holding her down like he meant to rape or murder her. Obviously, that's what she'd thought, for whatever reason. Now in her mind, he must be confirming the worst. He locked eyes with her and repeated, softer, "I'm not gonna hurt you. Calm down." He wanted to loosen his grip, but the volatile tension in her told him that would be a bad idea. Finally, he took his hand off her mouth. "Why did you try to attack me just now?"

In her eyes, fear melted into confusion. "I…I thought you were something else."

When he let go, she didn't bolt, so he let himself hug her, gently as he could manage with his adrenaline still jacked. Finally, her arms slipped around his neck. She'd thought he was someone else…That had to be bullshit. He'd turned on the damn light before she'd—

No, she hadn't said some*one*. She'd said some*thing*.

"What happened out there?" she finally asked.

"What do you mean?"

"How you barged in…the way you looked! You should've heard yourself on the stairs."

"So you thought I was gonna hurt you?"

"Yeah. It's stupid, I know. God, I'm sorry. See? I'm just a crazy bitch you brought in. I'll leave now if you want."

Yeah, that would be smart, just drag her downstairs and toss her out on the sidewalk. Instead he said, "God no! Not unless you want to."

"I don't wanna leave. But I'm scared."

"Don't be scared of me."

"I'm not. I'm scared of what's happening here, not just between us, but…There's a lot in my life, in my head, stuff I don't know if it's real."

"What, after everything I've told you, you think I wouldn't…Hell, you know how the old saying goes. *I've shown you mine, now you show me yours.*"

She rolled her eyes, shook her head, then tried and failed not to chuckle. "Wow…Rob, is it okay if it takes me a little longer to open up? God, I know, I'm horrible, asking that of you after I just almost—"

"That's fine. Sally, you're one crazy girl. But you know what? You've hooked up with a guy who's just as crazy. And confused."

"Don't blame you."

"No, I mean, I think we're confused about some of the same kinds of things…about ourselves."

"So where's that leave us?"

"Oh, I don't know, just maybe we're the best thing for each other. Whenever you feel okay talking about it…"

As they stared at each other, he remembered how he'd

felt while storming up the stairs. What had put him in that state? He'd gone outside, had a smoke, and then—what? He'd come back up, and Sally thought he was *something else*. It seemed like he had been, all day, all night. Anticipation, exhilaration, wild lust, wilder rage, the latter so intense it blotted out the memory of whatever sparked it. At the center, scariest of all, was this whirlwind of new feelings. He already kept catching himself, wanting to call it love.

He cradled her more gently. "I didn't hurt you, did I?"

In answer, she kissed his forehead…then his neck. Over the next half-hour, they crawled bit by bit out of their clothes. By the time his boxers went, he was crouched off the edge of the mattress, hands stroking her thighs, his tongue creating a heady scented flood between her legs. He didn't kiss his way up her body 'til her ecstatic sobs sounded close to their peak and her thighs were crushing his ears— *damn, she was stronger than she looked*. Before long, all he cared about was thrusting as hard and deep as he could into her, like he could never make her his own quite enough, no matter how tight they held each other or how savagely they kissed, 'til they flared towards climax together.

By the time they fell asleep, the night sounds might as well have been faint echoes from far across town…even the soft beat of leathery wings against the window overhead.

PREPARATIONS

ONE

Around two in the afternoon, the black Buick turned off Route Nine into Brattleboro. At a curb on Main Street, out climbed Sheldon and Sissy.

Mom leaned out her window. "How soon do you think you can know, dears, one way or another? If you discover her here, leave the rest 'til we've touched base."

Sissy ventured, "We should know by…six o'clock tonight?"

Mom nodded and handed Sissy one of the family's two cell phones.

"Where'll we stay around here?" Sheldon asked.

"That's work for your mom and me," said Dad.

"What if she's already gone?" asked Sissy.

"Then she'll have left a trail, our freshest so far." Finding that trail would be the kids' department, but in this region, the parents would want to stay closer at hand. "We'll get a fine place to hide out while we trace it. Don't worry. It won't be like the last one."

Sissy's face scrunched. "So no public bathrooms with needles all over the floor?"

Dad held down a chuckle. "No public bathrooms, no

needles. I promise."

After getting a sense of the turf, the twins found their way up Elliot Street. "Let's try here." Sheldon pointed to a sign reading *The Common Ground of Brattleboro.* "I mean, look at it. If Sally's here, this is the first place she'd check out…Sissy?"

"I heard you." She was staring up, through an alleyway, closed off by a high wooden fence covered in Earth-line political and music fliers. Pigeons flapped in and out, stopping to rest on the stone ledges. "Thought I saw something."

"Yeah, sure, great. The birds around here are all real overweight."

Two

Puttergong feels the cop-girl's eyes catch him, just for a second. Nothin' she'll be sure of, of course, but it still gives him a chill or two. Hopefully one of these here windows will make a halfway decent listenin' hole. The nasty smell hits him before he gets a good look at the opposite windowsill, or more directly the critters takin' up most of it.

"Well I do say," says one of 'em. "Look who already got his wings."

There among the pigeons, Puttergong spots his ol' buddy from the show hall parking lot. Okay, so not all the pigeons 'round here is quite as disgusting as that one. Close, though.

"Well I do say," Puttergong mimics, "look who's still a

fuckin' asshole." He settles on the windowsill of the eat hall window—or is this a drink hall? "Wonder if you'd laugh it up so good if you knew what it might mean, me gettin' up an' runnin' so quick."

"Sounds like a stimulating boy you've found. So why not laugh? It's you and your refugees who should worry about that. Well, you all, and…well…" The pigeon splays its wings at the surrounding bricks. "Those who built all this."

"Damn straight," Puttergong mutters. *I'm the one y'all had better watch your fuckin' mouths around.*

The window looks into a pissroom, so that's the main thing he smells. At first, he has a hard time hearin' through the walls.

The cop-kids is askin' questions of the guy runnin' the place. They sure is beatin' 'round the bush plenty—typical dumbass bush-bangin' Spirelights—but Puttergong still figures out *whose* bush they's lookin' for…ol' Biter-Boy's First Poach! After that one lil' look at their faces, he's got an idea why.

Old Lords, don't these damn pigeons ever shut the fuck up? The feller in charge just said somethin' about where the poach might be, Puttergong's pretty sure. If the dumbass is steerin' the cop-kids towards Biter-Boy's place, Puttergong's gonna have to figure out his next move quick.

"Seems you have competing searchers."

"Yeah, fine, whatever. Now just—*Aw, shit!*" Somewhere in there, the cop-girl just asked where the pissroom is.

One of the pigeons starts, "What's the—"

"Fuck, never mind. Out'a my way, lard-feathers!" Puttergong hustles sideways, almost barrelin' over one of them roly-poly pigeons, so it goes squawkin' and flappin' around.

As the pissroom door opens, Puttergong flips loose and flaps up to the roof. Below, all them damn pigeons go into a panic, flappin' and squawkin' everywhere like the air beneath 'em just turned into a sea of snakes. Puttergong wishes the original refugee leaders brought over some of them Deschembine magic-maker folks, the real powerful kind. Yeah, one of them old-time Crimbone magic-makers probably *could* spin live snakes from this world's thin air. Sure would be fun, watchin' some magic Crimbone-generated snakes chow down on these nasty fuckin' pigeons.

Then again, if the Crimbone did have that kinda magic-folks today, they'd probably be fuckin' pussies like the rest of the refugee Schomites, too scared to spin live snakes from air, afraid of upsettin' the equilibrium of this fragile little world or some nancy-ass shit. *Old Lords, what fuckin' good's a world so fragile, it can't handle its air spun into live snakes now an' then?*

Right under him, the lil' cop-girl opens the window and sticks her head out. Puttergong ducks back before she can spot him. Damnit, this ain't in the job description! Finally, she shuts the window and heads back to the main room, so Puttergong flaps back down to the ledge. Most of the pigeons have settled across from him, back to twitterin' amongst 'emselves, about what a spectacle he just made an' *blah-blah-fuckin'-blah!* Inside, the cop-kids tell the workin' dude thank you and good day.

Right on cue, Puttergong's ol' buddy speaks up. "Got your feathers ruffled a bit? Or maybe you would, if you had feathers."

As Puttergong looks his ol' buddy straight in its black-pea pigeon eyes, he recalls that he ain't eaten all day. So he zaps up from the ledge. Buddy-bird don't even have time to ruffle his own feathers, but once Puttergong's got him, them other pigeons sure is quick to take flight, all bustlin' and squawkin'. Puttergong tastes dirty stinkin' pigeon feathers, right before there's that stretchy, meaty rip, and he gets rewarded by a sweet rush of blood an' guts all over his face. The critter keeps bleatin', squawkin', fightin', flutterin', slams into one of the brick walls so Puttergong grabs on with both paws, kicks up his rear haunches and snares the thing with his talons. Him and the bird beat against the wall a few more times, the pigeon tearing itself apart worse on Puttergong's claws, smearin' itself all over the bricks. Puttergong digs in good and goes limp in the air. The pigeon's fucked by now, on account of its own weight combined with Puttergong's, not to mention the fact that he just ripped it a new one. Still flappin', it floats down like a jerkin', failin' hot-air balloon.

Once they settle on the concrete, Puttergong rips the pigeon wider and stabs his jaws into its heart. The bird jerks and goes still. Puttergong starts chowin' down on his meal proper. When he glances up, none of them other pigeons has hung around.

Just outside the alleyway, the cop-kids walk by. "See," says the cop-boy, "I told you she'd go into a place like that."

"Yeah, sure. We already knew she's at least been through town."

"She's still here. Let's call Mom and Dad." The cop-boy starts punchin' buttons on a phone, but the cop-girl snatches it out of his hand.

"Not 'til we get better confirmation." That's the last

thing Puttergong catches before they're too far away to hear.

Now no denyin', Puttergong's been gettin' his nerves tested on this here trip. A less sturdy Familiar might just hightail it home by now. While he's eatin', he gets to thinkin', particularly about Biter-Boy's thing with the First Poach. Why Biter-Boy ain't already killed her, why his blood's will ain't kicked him onto his proper course of action, disregardin' whatever he *thinks* he feels…well, Puttergong ain't quite got that figured. He swears, shit like this wouldn't pop up if the Cabinets regrew their balls, made this place a little more like the Old World. Once Biter-Boy's broken in on a few slaughters, they'll set to brainwashin' him into one more little Crimbone-light, barely fightin' back the Spirelights from wipin' out the Schomites. Hell, the Crimbone were already gettin' wobbly back at the end of the old days, when they let 'emselves get driven over here, across the Great Black Ocean through the Ephemeral Realms, right when they'd been so damn close to up an' wipin' out the Spirelights but good.

'Cept now the poach's family's here to get in on the action…from the Spirelight Secret Police no less. Hot damn, this jus' gets better an' better! While Puttergong enjoys his lunch, he thinks it over some more and realizes he's been goin' about things all wrong.

THREE

There weren't many kids here today, but it still seemed noisy to the stringy-haired, dark-skinned thirteen-year-old girl leaning against the pool table. It had felt too noisy before Russ started yelling in her ear. Actually, he was barking from across the table. His girlfriend and three of his guy friends stood around, shooting her sour stares.

"Hey Janie! Tha's right, bitch! Why you even come in here anymore? Yeah, I said I know it was you, pointed us out to the cops that time! Hear me, bitch? Know what I do to you, you'd fucked up my brother's probation? Yeah, 'cause you almost did. Your dead bitch faggot brother ain't gonna come 'round no more to keep you from gettin' your stupid ass whupped."

So, when would Lindsey be out of the office? Lindsey was the only supervisor here today, and she'd been in the office for almost twenty minutes. Some chick had come in ranting about a thirty-year-old man who'd date-raped her last night, venting the way most people do about flat tires. Kids either fawned with concern or told her to shut up, 'til her shivering panic nearly turned violent. So Lindsey got her into the office for a chat.

Janie shoved her ass off the pool table and headed for the door.

"Oh, what now? Gonna go tell the cops on me again? Fuck you, little bitch! You bring the cops here, an' I don't care, my whole family gonna come beat your ass!"

Janie stepped outside, beneath a sign reading *The Brattleboro Boys & Girls Club: A Positive Place for Kids, Age 13 to 19*. The air was cool, though not cold like it had been all week. Drizzly fog settled on her face. She felt like she'd brought it fresh wounds to sooth, as if Russ's voice had solidified into needles jabbing at all the right nerve clusters.

Should've just gone over and slugged him. Why you gotta be such a pussy?

She'd only been thirteen for two months, but she'd been coming to the club for almost four years. 'Til a year ago she'd hung out there with Larry on summer nights and Saturdays. After the accident, she'd wondered if they'd still let her in. When she finally dropped by, no one gave her trouble, maybe because her face was so narrow and sharp for her age, or because people had gotten used to seeing her. Then again, Larry had been twenty for the last seven months of his life, and no one had ragged on him. He'd seen a lot of new kids turn into regulars, and he'd been the same big brother to every one of them, even the bad ones. Meaning, it would have been scary just how absolutely he'd do anything for you, except you felt so safe around him…safe to really be yourself. *But man, don't be the punk who fucked with any of his little brothers and sisters.* No matter how low he sank in treating himself, how obviously it was taking its toll on him, everyone still saw that guy, right to the end. Janie still did, even as she realized what douchebags him and Dad had both turned into towards the end.

These days, she came here more than ever. Maybe it was because Larry had always smelled like the place, so Janie felt most comfortable when immersed in that smell. When she didn't have anyone to talk to, she did volunteer work like sweeping, dishes, or organizing lost or donated clothes. Sometimes they paid her in canned food, or she'd sit and read. There'd been nothing to clean or organize for the last couple hours, and no interesting books lay around except a battered copy of *The Stand,* which she'd already read enough times to get sick of. So she'd shot pool 'til Russ started giving her shit.

Outside, two kids turned the corner from Main Street. Probably just more of Russ's dumbass friends…only they didn't look old enough for the club. They seemed to argue over whether to check it out anyway. Yards back, doors slammed open.

Janie stepped smoothly into the new kids' path. "Hey, what'cha up to?" She gave the boy a spicy-shy smile. Russ or whoever might leave her alone if they saw her talking to someone.

From behind, a shrill female voice yelled, "Hey bitch, you in there talkin' shit to Russ again?" Russ's stupid girlfriend stormed forward, flanked by another guy and girl.

"I didn't say anything to him," said Janie. "He was talkin' shit to me!"

"Oh, you talkin' shit about him now, huh?"

"I'm just sayin'—"

"Bitch!" Russ's girlfriend flung herself at Janie.

Janie swatted back hard, but the girl grabbed her sweater, pulling 'til some seams ripped. Her attacker's two friends tugged at their companion. Then the new boy stepped up and shoved the bitch away. All these kids were bigger than Janie, and this new guy was at least half a head shorter. Still he shoved hard with one arm, his other hand prying the fingers off Janie's shirt. His sister tried yanking him out of the tussle.

"Get out of this, little punk!" Russ's buddy lunged at him.

The new boy's fist didn't fly with the sloppy adolescent brutality kids were used to around here, but with the force and precision of a boxer. Except faster. The other boy's nose crunched and sprayed blood, right before the new guy sent a roundhouse into his temple, knocking him sideways. Russ's buddy bounced off a brick wall and rolled limp. The two female attackers shrieked and dove, fingers out in claws. A sandaled foot drove into one gut while the other girl tackled his shoulder. Her fingernails caught his cheek right before his elbow caught her chin. The splintering jaw and teeth sounded like firecrackers.

Janie's vision spun from so much blurred, bloody movement. Three adults hurried forward from as many directions. One of them was Lindsey. The new boy panted and shook. While his sister dragged him away, his eyes met Janie's and he looked confused. The three attackers littered the pavement between them. One of the girls had flipped onto her stomach, dry-heaving while she tried to push herself up.

"I'm sorry," Janie told her psychotic little rescuer. "You shouldn't have—You guys better go."

"Janie! Janie, what happened?" Lindsey grabbed Janie's shoulders, half protectively, half in blind panic. "You okay? Janie, look at me. I know you didn't do this. You're not in trouble. Just tell me what happened."

"It was two other kids, a boy and a girl," said someone else. "They were just—hey, where'd they go?"

FOUR

Sally lay with her head on Rob's chest. She could tell by his breathing that he was still asleep. She also felt him getting hard against her leg. At first, she liked it. Then she remembered the dream.

She'd been back in one of the towns she'd stopped in. Just a few weeks ago, that place, yet it might as well have been last year. Time was funny on the road, especially with degrees of separation between spots. You could get caught up somewhere for weeks or months, then you hit somewhere else for a day or two, so by the time you reached the third stop, the first one seemed like a lifetime ago. At some point, she'd been in Indiana, and that's where the dream led her. Or was it South Carolina? Either way, she'd been with one of the friends from that town, one of hundreds of true-blue friendships, abandoned before they started. Sometimes actual danger prompted her to leave. Usually, it was something small, unimportant in retrospect, just enough to spook her.

This dream friend led her to a house in the suburbs. For some reason, Sally spoke only to answer questions. That, or she said things with no idea why, things no one else seemed to hear. She wasn't surprised to recognize the house, even though it belonged in New Orleans. Before going in, she knew she'd see vines covering everything, choking the space beneath the rotted boards and plaster. Everyone else acted like they didn't notice, even when the growth churned and twitched at their feet like heaps of snakes, guiding them through labyrinthine hallways. Sally wasn't surprised to find Talino leading the meeting. Then again, she spent half her waking hours expecting to run into him around the next corner, no matter where she was.

When he said, "We have a recovering Spirelight's daughter in our midst," she tasted the flesh of the man from Pittsburgh.

Now she was awake, so she couldn't taste anyone but Rob. She squeezed him harder, sucked lightly at his neck and ear. Muttering, he ran his fingers through her hair. She flexed her hips so he slipped right inside her, and he chewed on her neck. With a sigh, she bent her head back. Now his eyes were awake and blazing, locked on hers. He turned her onto her back, sending a sweet flare-up through her. Before long, he bolted and spasmed.

When he sighed "Hi," she giggled and ruffled his hair. "Sorry," he said. "That wasn't my best."

"You hear me complaining? That's a nice way to get woken up in the morning."

He looked at his watch. "It's the middle of the afternoon."

"Hmmm…That's fine too."

He rolled onto his stomach, pushed himself up and stretched like a big cat. "I wish. Gggrrr…I gotta go to work in a few hours."

"Where you work?"

It was his turn to giggle. "I'm a dishwasher."

"What's so funny?"

"Just…it feels weird, telling you that now. Some damn reason, I don't know."

Somehow, she didn't suspect he made a priority of telling girls his job title before getting them into bed. "Yeah…"

"Well, we don't have to get up yet." He leaned on his elbow and gazed at her. "What'd you wanna do while I'm at work?"

"Could I…maybe just stay in here?"

"I guess, if you can amuse yourself for six hours."

"I'd manage…You'd actually trust me like that?"

"You have a point, but…Yeah, I guess so."

"You're nuts."

"Glad you noticed 'em. Seriously, though, you should be less afraid."

"Maybe. So what are you afraid of, Rob?"

"What do you mean?"

"Wow. You really think I'm that dense?"

He sighed. "I'm scared of lots of things. I don't know where I'd start."

"You ever scared of yourself?"

"No. What's with a question like that? I mean, I'm the only thing I know belongs to me. Hell, how can anyone survive if they're scared of themselves?"

"I manage." When he didn't have a snappy comeback to that one, she almost asked, *what do you mean, you're all you have? You have me now!* Instead, she said, "For starters, what were you so scared of last night?"

"I remember you being scared worse." He looked guilty.

"I manage those fears too. Don't change the subject."

"I saw something…I can't say what it was, if it was just something I dreamed too vividly, or…Thinking about it now, it seems more like I was talking to myself but at the time…" His eyes seemed to plead, *Even if you think I'm the looniest sonofabitch in fifty states, Sally, don't get scared off.*

"Maybe just the spirit of Brattleboro talking to you again?" So he'd know she wasn't making light of it, she went on, "Don't try to understand it if you're not ready. Sometime I'll tell you some things about me. Maybe then you won't feel so alone."

"You already make me feel less alone." Then they were kissing again. This time when she crawled on top, he let her stay there.

* * * *

In Rob's old drunken bull sessions with Louis, women had been one of the top subjects. "When you think about it," Louis once said, "the whole idea of *love at first sight* is pretty scary. If I looked at anyone for the first time and felt a deep emotional connection beyond simple attraction, I'd be pretty weirded out." At the time, Rob had agreed. You don't gauge such feelings by time or catalogued facts, though. You could look back on it with cold logic in short retrospect, but lots of good that ever did. Right now, as far as Rob and Sally were concerned, eternity might as well have started in Mocha Joe's. Her fingertips touched his lacerated thumb. "I can't believe I cut you."

"You didn't. I cut myself when I grabbed your knife." When they started dressing, he went and picked that knife up. "Jesus, I must've got myself worse than I thought." He closed the blade and handed it back to her. Just a little too quickly, she shoved it in her pocket.

Out in the kitchen, Rob turned the sink on to wash his hands. He paused first to look at his wound. Faint crusted dots and fainter splotches speckled it, nothing compared to the smeared, dark residue he'd just seen on Sally's knife. No way had he bled so much without noticing, let alone through all that sex. Oh well, hadn't she said she had her own crazy stories? He figured he'd seen worse. Besides, if he was being honest, it was one more freakish turn-on about her. Hell, by now, what wouldn't be?

As he pawed through the refrigerator, Sally came out

and sat at the small kitchen table.

"Damnit," he grumbled. "I don't have shit for breakfast."

"What about those other shelves?"

"Those belong to my roommates. Wanna go out to eat?"

"Uh, sure. Where?"

"There's a great place I'll show you, right at the bottom of the hill."

She looked mildly embarrassed. "Uh…is it cheap?"

"Ah, don't worry about that. I've got it."

"You keep saying that, I'm gonna feel like I owe you."

"Long as you keep having sex with me, consider it even."

She stuck her tongue out and they laughed.

On the way to Linda's, they paused to stare off past the graveyard, out to the mountains flanking the town. Ragged patches of mist drifted across the slopes through the trees, like pale, ghostly brush fires. Just then, what was before Rob and Sally was the world, and they dreamed that it was theirs.

Linda's was an old-fashioned diner, occupying a former barbershop. The feisty, well-preserved old dame who ran the place hadn't remodeled much, aside from replacing barber stools with tables and chairs, plus setting up a kitchen in the back. Most of the regulars had been crusty and weathered when Linda was young. Rob had developed a mild addiction to her Eggs Benedict recipe, and he convinced Sally she had to try it. When she did, the look on her face confirmed for him that the day was officially a success.

An hour later, they parted ways outside the Bistro. "Here's the keys to the place," he said, "if you wanna go back there."

"Thanks. When'd you say you get off work again?"

"Around ten. I warn you, not much in Brattleboro stays open past six."

"What about the Common Ground?"

"These days, your guess is as good as mine. So…if you're still in town by then, come meet me here. Otherwise, just come let me in when the doorbell rings. None of my housemates should bother you. You run into the landlady, say you're my friend visiting from out of town."

"I still can't believe you're trusting me like that."

"Maybe I'm just cocky enough to figure I have you hooked."

"Maybe you're right." She kissed him slower and deeper than ever. "Okay, you'd better get to work. Tonight at ten?"

"Yeah. If I'm not out right away, come inside."

* * * *

Normally Sally would have jumped at the chance to stay shut in all night, just so she wouldn't have to be out on her feet for once. Otherwise, she'd be on the first ride she could hitch out of town.

She started towards the Common Ground, then remembered her duffel bag. Didn't look like she'd have to sleep there again. Still, she thought of her friends there: Liam, Clover, Bethany, even Jake. If she had to leave tomorrow, she'd make for Canada, maybe as far as the western regions where the feuds were weakest on this continent.

If she told Rob, he'd want to go with her. She felt guilty, having that strong a hold on someone. When she licked her lips, she still tasted him. The pleasant shiver almost chased away the painful thoughts. What if she told him not to come along? She could leave him behind, if she had to—she wasn't *that* far gone. Still, to find something like that and push it away…

Sally felt flustered and incoherent inside and out, like the first stabs of panic whenever things went bad. *But nothing was bad right now.* In fact, for once, it was great.

FIVE

Slipping off—the center of attention one minute, ghostlike the next—was just one of the skills Sheldon and Sissy had been taught since they could walk. Their elders constantly praised them, not just Mom or Dad or other Secret Police, but high-ranking members of the Tribunal itself.

"That was *so bad*, Sheldon! What were you thinking?"

Pain flickered through the bones in his hand. When he wiped the blood from his knuckles, the smear rolled off the waxy fabric of his shirt. "I was gonna ask her some questions, thought maybe she'd seen Sally. Then those other kids—"

"You should've stayed out of it."

"Yeah, well…they looked like they might actually hurt her."

"So what? If she knew anything, it would've been *good* if she got beaten up some. We could've waited 'til they left, then made her talk, while she couldn't make as much trouble."

"Yeah, but—"

"Now there'll be Earth-line cops around and we'll have to stay away from that end of the street, so we can't learn anything from any of those people. All 'cause you thought she was pretty."

"Did not! I mean—yeah, she was, but that's not why—"

"What do you even want with an Earth-line girl? You ain't old enough anyway."

"Now who's got the filthy mind?"

"Ugh!"

No one told them their present skills would last another three years at most, that they'd have to learn adult skills soon. They'd watched how other police family members acted at different ages, though, and had figured it out somewhat. What Sissy hadn't realized was that they'd be expected to start looking for mates about a year after their child detection talents failed.

Sheldon figured it out, started telling her his theories once, but she'd yelled at him to shut his filthy mouth. Good thing he hadn't mentioned how they'd be expected to mate with each other, if they couldn't find anyone from the other police families of compatible age and skill.

In Mocha Joe's, they found another description that sounded like Sally. When asked, they said they'd been separated from their big sister and were trying to find her. So far, three people recognized the description. Sorry, though, they hadn't seen that girl today. When people remembered seeing Sally—really remembered her—they almost always stared at the twins, spotting the family resemblance. There was often a trace of mystified awe, seeing these two exquisite children, remembering their equally exquisite older sister.

You are Spirelights, their grandfather used to say. *It's the kiss of the Spirah gods they see on your pretty foreheads, even those too lowly to comprehend it.* Sissy believed that more than Sheldon, or at least more enthusiastically. Whenever people offered help, tried to take the poor lost twins under a safe wing, they slipped away again.

According to the coffee shop clerk, Sally had walked out a couple days ago with some young man. The guy came in here a lot, but the clerk hadn't caught his name. Yeah, it turned out, other folks had seen him around town with Sally since. Before Sheldon could ask more, Sissy collared him and tugged him along. Before long, he was the one pulling her, chasing better descriptions of Sally's guy. She twisted loose and took out the phone.

"What're you doing? They told us to call at six."

"They said call *by* six. Obviously, she's still here. We got lucky and found out early."

"But we might *really know* how to find her. I mean…I think we might have a lead on where she's *staying*."

"That's just your nasty mind."

"No! I mean…I really have a feeling that's it."

"*Nasty mind*," Sissy chanted. "Besides, they said not to go after her. We can do all that together, later, as a family. That's what's safe." Before she could hit *send* on the phone, he snatched it out of her hand. "Sheldon, give it back!"

He stretched out both his arms, holding her back at one end, dangling the phone at the other. "We're not calling 'til six! Come on, Sissy, we can know more by then…I'm not giving the phone back, okay?"

Finally, Sissy yielded, and not because she couldn't have won out. Looking at his eyes, she was starting to believe him. Feelings like that, of a conscious willful nature, were for those mature enough to comprehend and act on them properly. Secret Police children were taught to listen to more wordless, visceral instincts, too debased for adults to live by, at least Spirelight adults. Weren't the Crimbone—and Earth-line people for that matter—perfect demonstrations why? The purer unconscious of a child was better suited to it. Except what instincts had caused Sheldon to help that Earth-line girl? Much as Sissy hated to admit it, her brother's precocious guesswork had paid off too often to ignore.

"Okay, fine," she said. "So where do we start looking?"

"Let's have another look at that funny restaurant."

"The Common Ground."

"Yeah. There."

UP NORTH

Late that afternoon in Barre, Vermont, Jesse Karn made his rounds through the office building and found his way down to the basement. In one corner, a crooked little wooden door looked like it might lead into a small closet. His nostrils flared at the air that leaked out of it. In the rafters above, he found the little key to the padlock.

He took the steep, narrow, natural staircase, into the winding network of granite caverns that met up with the massive six-hundred-foot quarry less than a mile back through the woods, towards the main road. Much of the dank subterranean trek was made through darkness, by very old memory. Ahead, a shaft of light spilled in from one of the smaller, more obscure local quarries above, into a natural underground amphitheater. An unguessed array of rare stones gleamed in rock walls like a psychedelic paint collage, catching and magnifying the light from above to illuminate the smooth stone altar that sprouted from the center of the amphitheater. Jesse now recognized the smell that had drawn him as the afterglow of the recent ritual. The centerpiece still lay on the altar, waiting for a fledgling to make the step, wherever the latest little bastard or bitch was.

As the sight set in, the cavern felt smaller and smaller, like a moldering dungeon closing tight around Jesse's tall, broad frame.

As soon as he found his way back to the world above,

he stormed straight to Zane's office. "When was the ritual performed?" His voice stayed calm, though his every muscle bulged and buzzed.

"Last night," said the scarred, bald black man behind the desk. "You'd already left when the ground started twitching, telling us we'd better get down there. When we assembled, the pieces had already arrived. You didn't feel the ground talking from wherever you were?"

"Just felt like perimeter lines sharpening to me."

"Huh. Felt to us 'round here like this fuckin' town was gonna heave up an earthquake if we didn't hoof it straight down there. Honestly, I was worried those caverns would miss you more than they would the rest of us. Like we need any more earthquakes around here. I'm surprised this is the first you've heard."

"*Seen*," said Jesse. "Did you take part in the ritual?"

"Of course."

Jesse's brick-sized fist made an echoing crash on the desk. "*Are you fucking nuts?*"

The cheap beer Zane had been swilling vibrated all the way off his edge of the desk. He caught the bottle as it fell and swigged from it. "It's this world and the way it moves that's nuts, or seems nuts to us. You should know that better than anyone."

Jesse straightened upright. He only glared for a second. "So Coscan's boy is this far into the game? When the hell did he get brought up to speed, huh?"

"No one knows exactly—Quit looking at me like that. Actually, the Cabinet's been wondering how much you know about it." When Jesse didn't answer, Zane shrugged and continued, "He sent the First Call the night before last.

Then the piece showed up yesterday…or *pieces*, rather. That freaked everyone out. I'd have told you, if I'd been able to find your ass."

"I was out and about. So, why didn't you tell me later?"

"Other things to do by then."

"Fuck you." Jesse grabbed Zane's beer and swigged deep.

"Anyway, we weren't sure at first who the pieces were for. Word came last night from the Familiar that the moment of the Second Call will be soon."

"Could you repeat that?"

"Yeah, I know, fucked up, right?"

"Get a good look at those *pieces?*"

"Yeah." Zane stood up—tall as Jesse and broader across the shoulders—long enough to snatch his beer back.

Jesse might have asked all sorts of questions, pointed out no end of ominous implications, made every accusation that went with them. "So there's basically two possibilities— and no, I don't know about that first one. As for the second…Damn, this *would* happen with Coscan's kid, wouldn't it? We know the Familiar?"

Zane looked as close to awkward as he ever got. "Puttergong."

"Coscan's kid might be a High Natural. And he's got Puttergong as a Familiar. Figures." The energy in the room changed. Jesse knew he'd caused it, tossing off two words no one had yet dared speak aloud.

Zane cleared his throat. "There's more." He reached into his desk and brought out the latest intelligence-correlation report.

Jesse read the first paragraph. "Why are you showing

me this?"

"I'm not." Zane winked. The rest of his face stayed blank.

Jesse couldn't decide if he was grateful for the favor, or pissed because Zane wasn't straight up backing him before the Cabinet. Probably both. Oh well, he'd put it aside 'til the next time they stepped into the boxing circle. For now, he read the rest of the report. Rob Coscan was little more than a footnote, but his address was listed. Jesse jotted it down, saw to the day's final business in Barre, and took off for Brattleboro.

Vermont might have lost its neutral status, but the Cabinet liked it peaceful, which was why they didn't instantly call in a pack to take out every patter of Spirelight activity that came through. Jesse would agree, at any other time.

COMMENCEMENT

ONE

Jake stirred baked beans on the gas stove, then walked out onto the main floor of the Common Ground. They'd served several lunches today and gotten some nice donations from tourist families. Jake loved Brattleboro life as much as the next townie, but he'd never figure out how the place drew tourists, except in skiing or leaf-peeping season. Most of the foliage had come and gone early this year. Hopefully they had another month before the first big snow. Anyway, the Common Ground was slowly but surely creeping out of the red. Half the locals apparently thought the place was totally dead, and the other half hardly tipped for shit.

In a booth sat Sammy, a squat, greasy, hairy dirtball of an old unemployed regular missing half his teeth, hunched over the table, swilling a forty of Newcastle.

"Chief, you can't have that in here," said Jake.

"Okay…I'll go pour it out in the bathroom…"

Of course, he'd chug most of it and pour the rest into that mug he snatched on the way. Then he'd splash it with coffee as camouflage. Jake couldn't look down on it too much, considering how much weed the workers regularly smoked here after hours.

From the bathroom, Sammy shouted, "Holy shit, Jake, come have a look."

When Jake entered, the first thing he saw was the empty forty on the toilet seat lid. Ignoring the mug in Sammy's hand and the thicker fumes on his breath, he followed the bum's gaze through the window.

"What the fuck you call that?" said Sammy.

"Pretty nasty, that's what. I think it used to be a pigeon."

Lumpy blood and viscera decorated the brick wall across from the window. It started in a big splat, running downwards in a glistening smear. Feathers clung to the smear like bugs on flypaper. None of the usual live pigeons were around.

"Wha'ya suppose got it? A hawk?"

"I don't think hawks usually hunt in alleyways."

Besides, hawks weren't even around this time of year. They didn't leave such a mess, either. The lumpy stain looked like something that had been hit by a grenade. Out in the restaurant, someone sounded up the stairs. Jake headed back out.

"Hey," Sammy groaned behind him, "what'cha gonna do about that?"

"Nothing. That's the building next door's walls it's all over."

Out in the main room, there stood that weird drifter girl. "Hey," she said. "Is Clover around?"

"Yeah, around town somewhere. She'll probably get here soon. Hey, I think some people might've been here looking for you earlier. You have family in town or something?"

Her face went frosty. When she next spoke, her voice was so flat, it almost sounded robotic. "No. I never heard of this town 'til this week."

"Right. Sorry. They must've been looking for someone else."

"Who?"

"Just some kids, looking for their big sister. Sounded like it might be you, and they seemed like people you'd know."

"What's that supposed to mean?"

"Hey, nothing. Besides, who cares?"

"Yeah, whatever." The weird girl went behind the counter and hoisted the big bag she'd left there.

As she wandered back towards the stairs, Jake felt bad for working her nerves. "Hey, you want some beans or anything?" he called.

"No thanks." She didn't look back. "I'll come by later when Clover's around."

"Yeah, but I don't know when she'll—"

She halted halfway to the door, her body bracing as though arctic winds had just blasted out of the stairwell. Face livid, she turned. "Hey, can I use the...The bathroom's back that way, right?"

"Uh, yeah." Oh wait, Sammy was still in there, staring out the window at the shredded bird. "Someone's in there, though."

"I'll wait, then." She hurried into the hallway.

A moment later, the front door creaked open, and a chill tickled Jake's bones. Then up came those two weird kids. He'd guessed before that they were twins, just from how they related to each other. Now he stared at their faces, particularly the girl's. Yeah, there was definitely a strong family resemblance, and not just to each other, either.

"Hey." He tried to smile. "How've you guys been?"

"Fine," they said in unison. Their faces beamed with carefree childlike joy. Jake wanted to feel stupid, getting spooked by a couple of kids. When he looked in their eyes, though, they didn't look like kids at all.

"Has our sister been in again?" the boy asked. The girl rolled her eyes and huffed in frustration.

"Uh, no, I don't think so. Look, I really don't think your sister's been in here."

The boy whispered something in the girl's ear. "I know," she hissed back. "That doesn't matter. C'mon, let's call—"

"Hey Jake, sure you don' wanna get someone to clean up that splattered bird?" It was Sammy. "'Cause I tell ya, that's a real nasty fuckin' sight, someone goes in there to take a piss, happens to look out an'—Oh, hey, kids!"

Somehow, Jake guessed he'd known shit was about to hit the fan. He didn't see exactly what was happening, didn't realize why the boy had snatched a stray coffee mug. Then the boy cocked back his arm and chucked the mug like a fastball. It hit Sammy square in the forehead, cracked clean in two, then clattered in either direction. A gleaming dark line rolled down Sammy's forehead and forked on the bridge of his nose, and he toppled like a bowling pin.

"Holy shit, you little asshole!" Jake lunged at the boy. "What—"

The boy's hand shot forward. Something glinted in his fist. A cold, narrow bar of pain lanced Jake's midsection. His knees buckled. Somewhere, the girl screamed. Then Jake was on his back. He felt the knife flex in his gut so his back arched.

"*You lied,*" the boy yelled in his face. "Sissy, go lock the door."

"Sheldon, you idiot! Stupid idiot!"

"Doesn't matter. It's started. Go lock the door before someone else comes in."

The stairwell echoed as Sissy thundered down. When Jake tried to move, Sheldon manipulated the knife handle again, locking up his body with pain.

"*Where's our sister?*" Sheldon whispered in his ear.

"I told you, I haven't seen—"

The pain intensified. "I can tell if you lie, so don't."

"Okay, fine…but she's not here, *really, I fuckin' swear!*" On top of everything else, his throat was already dry and raw from shrieking. His words sounded and felt like he was hacking them through sharp gravel, so he just tried to blurt them out as fast as possible, hoping like crazy he wouldn't be forced to say anything else.

The knife twisted, sending the strongest rush of pain yet.

"Sheldon, stop it!" came Sissy's voice from far off.

"He's lying, Sissy. He's seen her, today. Go check the bathroom."

Without further protest, Sissy's feet padded off. Her voice sounded back, "She ain't here, Sheldon. *Holy crap, you really messed everything up now.*"

The back stairs…So that's where the big sister had been headed. As if reading Jake's mind, Sheldon shouted, "*Sissy, check for a back door.* If there is one, have a look out through it."

After a few seconds, Sissy called, "Okay, I checked, she's not out there."

"Fine. Now lock it. Now mister, you're gonna learn to talk with a knife in your stomach."

TWO

Sally thundered down the back stairs, her heavy bag thumping against her shoulders, threatening to send her spilling forward. She hit the landing in a run, straining her back. Desperately, absurdly, she wished she'd thanked Jake. Because he'd waited around to get killed, bought her cowardly ass one more escape—

No. That's not how they do things. He'll be fine. They aren't stupid enough to pull a stunt like that. They'll question him and maybe he'll spill what he knows—or maybe he's smart enough to get creeped out and clam up—and they'll go somewhere else.

Either way, here she was, running again.

But you just felt *them, close by. Somewhere you got sloppy, and they've traced you here, and now you know that you still have some detection-feelings left in you. What for, so you can act like you always have when it comes to your own kind, like a damn little coward?*

But what else could she do? What would happen if she faced them?

You know damn well. Oh, you think you've gotten so badass, 'cause you can handle your weak little self out in this weak little world. When it comes to where you're from, you'll always bend the same way.

No. I'm stronger now.

Yeah? What, 'cause you've managed to kill a few starved, crazed

Crimbone here and there over the years, and one Earth-line pig lately? Yeah, sure, just keep telling yourself that.

By now, she'd circled the Common Ground, back to Elliot Street. A sleepy-eyed redheaded girl walked towards her from Main Street. "Sally-girl!" Clover flung her arms open.

"Hey!" Sally forced a smile and hugged Clover. Realizing where the girl was headed, she thought fast. "So what's up with the Common Ground today?"

"I don't know, but I was just headed there. Why?"

"I just came from there and it's locked, both the front door and back."

"Really? What the fuck?" She looked Sally over. "You got your bag back, though."

"Yeah, I was in there earlier, too. I grabbed it then. Just still haven't had a chance to stash it anywhere else yet today." *Wow, could that sound any more like obvious bullshit?*

"Huh. I bet business was so shitty, Jake decided not to bother anymore today."

"You don't have your own key?"

"Jake's got mine on him. Asshole."

By the time Clover discovered the lie, Sally would be long gone, busy covering her tracks. For now, let them have their last good time together.

"So…have you found someplace else to crash, or what?"

"Yeah. Yeah, I have. I just haven't had a chance to drop my bag off there yet." Sally smiled, then walked and gestured for Clover to follow. "What other fun hangout places are there?"

"Huh. At this hour? I don't know, wanna go to Mocha

Joe's?"

"No, not there." That was just the sort of place the twins would think to look next. "Back to your place, maybe?" Hopefully she didn't sound too pushy. Clover's place was Jake's place, and Jake didn't seem like someone who'd give the directions to strangers, definitely not to a pair of creepy, nosy little kids. At least Sally could get out of the line of sight while she planned her escape.

"Yeah, I guess we could. C'mon, I'm parked this way."

As they headed up Main Street, Sally said: "Could we…go by Rob's place? I need to drop something off." A jolt of pain shot through her, which she did her best to hide.

Clover's face lit up. "Rob Coscan? So that's where you been staying?" She read the answer on Sally's face. "Wow. You and Rob, huh?"

"Yeah…" Sally smiled weakly.

"Oh, my God, I knew it! Huh. Gotta admit, I always sorta wondered, y'know, things about that crazy bastard…"

"Hey!" Sally grinned. "Hands off."

"Oh, you know what I mean. Don't think I ain't gonna grill you for details, though."

On the way, Sally let Clover grill her. It always felt good, pretending she had a future in a place. In Brattleboro, it felt better than ever. When she dreamed like this, her survival procedures went on auto-pilot. Later, she'd live out her life here in her daydreams—on buses, boxcars, hitched rides—until another place claimed her. Once she left that spot, her daydreams would be for whatever life hadn't happened there. Likely Rob would spend a while swearing no one would ever eclipse her. She imagined him drinking excessively for a week, smoking too much tobacco and weed, sure she'd come back or that he'd figure out how to find her, think of something she'd said or left behind that gave him a clue to follow. Then he'd wake up some morning with some girl from the bar, and he'd admit to himself that yeah, it was possible to recover from one sweet, wild night with a crazy drifter girl he barely knew.

There were three doorbells on Rob's porch, one for each floor, labeled in masking tape and black marker. Sally rang the one marked *2nd flr*. What if no one was home? Hell, she had the key. Why not just go in and drop it off? That felt wrong. She could drop by his workplace, hand his key back personally. Imagining his face, she shivered and hugged herself. When he'd hugged her, everything else had fallen away. Missing that, she shivered deeper. Somewhere upstairs, movement sounded. What if she didn't run? Maybe it was time to—

Shit, this place really is turning your brain to jelly, isn't it? Oh hell, screw the town. It's got nothing to do with the town, and you know it. Still, she couldn't hide behind Rob Coscan. Together, maybe the two of them had the strength to—

No. Her family would kill him. She rang the bell again.

Unless he kills them. Think about it. Think about Rob. He has it in him, doesn't he? You've only gotten a glimpse of it, but that ought'a be enough for you by now, right? Remember last night when he saw you with the knife? How many Earth-line people can move like that?

Inside, a slow set of feet clumped downward. Sally flinched. The first time she'd run away from home, she hadn't hated her family. She'd just known she couldn't stay with them. When they'd found her, she'd been desperate to be back with them—not like she'd been in any state to argue, exactly. By the time she ran away again, she'd learned to hate them just fine. On the road since, she'd spent nights thinking about how to fight them off. Suppose they were dead. She imagined herself disposing of their cooling bodies, like everyone she'd seen die because of her, people she'd sniffed out for them, based on a thousand little preternatural characteristics they'd trained her to notice. She'd spotted every one of those characteristics in Rob Coscan.

The door opened and a stringy, hunched, sleepy-eyed man droned, "Heeey."

Rob had described his housemates for Sally in an amusingly manic litany. She couldn't remember their names, but she recognized this guy as *the sprout man.*

"Uh, hey, I'm, uh…Rob's friend."

"Aaahhh." The sprout man probably remembered sex noises from last night. "Wooowww…I don't think Rob's here right now." She thought of some seventies drug culture comedy skit a lot of young Earth-line people liked to quote—*Daaave's nooot heeere right now, maaannn*…and she almost laughed. "Yeah, Rob's like, at work at some…restaurant…Heee never talks much about it…" The sprout man seemed only incidentally aware of her. "It's funny, 'cause, like he aaaalwaaaaaays hangs out with Darren, and Darren's like, the other really young guy who lives here, and they both work in restaurants, and they both come home and drink a lot and—"

"Right. But you'll be here when he gets home."

"Huh? Uh, Rob or Darren?"

"Rob," Sally said through her teeth. When Rob had mentioned regular thoughts of strangling this guy, she'd assumed he was joking.

"Uhm, yeah. You…want me to give him, like, a message?"

Sally almost said, *No, that's fine. I'll come back later.* Then she dug the keys out of her pocket. "These are his. Could you let him in whenever he gets home?"

"Uuuhm, sure."

She handed the keys over and hurried back to the car.

"You okay?" Clover asked as Sally climbed in.

"Huh? Yeah."

"You look like you're about to break down sobbing."

"Just a little overwhelmed." She gulped.

"Why? Hey, what happened with Rob, anyway? Is everything… okay? I mean…"

"*No*—Yeah. Everything's really okay, just…I really like Rob. A lot. Already. And it's weird."

"Wow, that was fast…But…Yeah, I guess I sorta know what you mean. So why don't you drop off your bag while you're here?"

"Maybe later. I don't know if I'll sleep here tonight. I mean I want to, but I might need to think things over, get my head straight before this goes any faster." Yeah, there went her little fantasy life talking, telling all its pretty lies.

THREE

Business was dead for a Friday, the type of dead night that normally left Rob bouncing off the walls. Tonight, the place didn't feel so bad, though, which probably meant Rob was crazier than he'd figured.

Crazy with love…No, love had *stopped* him from going crazy. Probably just in time, too. Except there were still things like little talking bat-like creatures, at least in his world. *No, Rob, you aren't the one who goes crazy. People meet you and they think you're nuts, 'til they're the ones losing it thanks to what you bring to the table.*

For the first time in a while, he thought of Chuck Sawyer. Chuck had always thought Rob was nuts. Then again, Chuck had started ranting about how the FBI was constantly watching him, over something to do with telepathic contact with extraterrestrials, the day Rob moved in. Chuck had died getting ready to put a gun to the back of Rob's head. He'd probably gone out calling it dumb fuckin' luck, standing on Carrollton Avenue, bit by a poisonous snake that must have crawled all the way from the swamp. Maybe it actually had been dumb luck and Rob was the crazy one for thinking otherwise…even as he'd stayed calm the whole time, pretending he hadn't known the bastard was trailing him, 'cause the voice of city—the swamp—of New Orleans had told him to hang tight and trust it, manifesting from a dozen directions at once that couldn't possibly have just been voices in his head…which, in Rob's understanding, was exactly how voices in your head played you, just like ol' Chuck's FBI and extraterrestrial pals.

Mickey the bartender brought back two stouts—one for Rob, the other for Joe the cook. The barman liked slipping drinks to the kitchen staff, enough that Rob could chug 'til he was too drunk to mind the grease and soap smells seeping into his hands, or other dishwater chemicals pickling his skin.

"Virdelle come back yet?" asked Joe, a heavyset Asian

guy who always showed up stoned halfway out of his skull.

"Ha," barked Mickey. "You kiddin'?"

"Any new people out there?"

"Yeah, a Mister Jack Shit, and his family from Fuck-All."

"So Virdelle *is* back," Rob threw in.

Lately it had become an unexpected treat if the manager showed up to unlock the place on time in the afternoon so no one had to break their necks scrambling to have their stations set up in time for service. When he did, it was usually with his wife and four-year-old son. Often, he and the wife disappeared to the bathroom for who knew how long, or cuddled in a booth, leaving the toddler—who spoke no English—to run shrieking through the kitchen. Near as Rob or the cooks could figure, Virdelle assumed they'd gladly accept baby-sitting as an extra responsibility, never mind the scorching pans and sharp knives they constantly juggled.

Thinking about it, Rob remembered why this job had been tipping his restlessness ever closer to the nuthouse. Every night here, a little more of his life seemed closer to the drain, right along with the business, surrounded by people who apparently couldn't imagine why he'd mind. He'd stood still for it, played nice with them, because…Why, because they kept feeding him free beer and a shitty paycheck, just enough to keep him docile and compliant?

I've known the open road. I've tasted the thrill of life and death beneath the naked night sky. No, I never expected that to last forever, but how'd I slide to a stop in this dull rut? Hell, how have I managed to stay still this long?

Yeah? So, where'd you expect that to take you? Down the Yellow-Brick Fucking Road?

There it went, burning and twisting his mind again…That flash of almost remembering, positive it was nothing less. Except how could he remember the truth? No one had ever told him in the first place.

Sure, great. Yeah, you were about due for one of those episodes.

Not this time. It's closer than ever. 'Cause I'll tell you what else, there's always this smell on the air, real faint, for just the split instant of almost remembering, what you're supposed to be doing with all this weird shit in your brain that won't leave you alone. Over the last couple days, the smell hadn't faded. If anything, it just kept getting thicker, the longer Sally Wildfire was around. It smelled delicious.

After chugging most of his beer, he asked Joe, "Wanna come have a smoke?"

"Nah, just had one a few minutes ago."

Rob shrugged and headed up the back stairwell to Flat Street. Well, now he knew he hadn't imagined it, that better, stronger self…because out of that same night, there'd stepped a girl who embodied everything he'd ever found wild and beautiful and forever mysterious in life…everything that was *more than* himself, calling to him in a language he was still learning to understand. She wanted him, needed him, *trusted* him…

"An' I told the guy, he should'a jus' stopped while he was ahead, that he ought'a jus' collect the winnings an'…" Some random guy walking by on a cell phone, but it was the first thing Rob heard as he stepped outside.

As he lit a smoke, a stray newspaper page fluttered along the sidewalk. A scrap of headline read *Dangerous Road*

Conditions.

Across the street at the local teen center, one cluster of punk kids yelled taunts at a smaller group of the same. "…So you better watch which way you walk, motherfuckers!"

Rob connected the dots, as it were. Brattleboro spoke more frankly than most places. Just that Weathered Old Vermonter's No-Bullshit ethic, he figured.

"Hey Biter-Boy! When you gonna stop listenin' to all them pussies, start heedin' them who knows what they talkin' about?"

Rob stepped back into the doorway. Up in the rafters, the creature hung upside down by its hind legs. Rob saw it better than before, though it stayed in shadow. It looked bigger now—or at least fatter—gnawing on something clutched in its front paws.

"Fuck," he grumbled.

The thing let out its wheezing laugh. "You the one doin' all the fuckin' lately, stud. You wanna keep doin' it, though, you'd better quit all this crap about, *Oh, my little flyin' buddy ain't really there. I just ready for the loony bin, is all.* I tellin' you, Biter-Boy, right now I'm the only thing keepin' you an' your cute lil' Sally-Girl's asses in one piece, so you better start mindin'!"

"Sally too, huh? Last night, it sounded like you were about the last good thing for her."

"Keep your voice down. Want folks walkin' by to think you're some kinda crazy dude?"

"Right. Like that'd stand out around here."

"Look, I know what I said last night. Turns out I was mistaken on a couple details. See, I spent all day checkin' out lots o' shit, stuff you gonna find out soon enough, one way t'other."

Gray tufts kept floating down, like the thing was molting. Rob peered up harder at it through the gloom. Silky black hairs dusted its body, but nope, still no feathers. When it took a bite of its snack, he realized where the tufts were coming from. "What kind of shit am I gonna find out, birdie?"

"The real important kind, been creepin' along behind you yer whole life, finally gettin' ready to jump out an' bite you in the ass. Now you gotta be ready to grab it by the balls an' twist!"

"Last night, you called Sally my *First Poach*. What's that mean?"

"Never you mind! I just done told you, I was mistaken."

"Could you just cut to the fucking chase? C'mon, birdie, what do I need to know?"

"I can't go tellin' you all that right here, right now. There's too much. We'll catch up later, at your place or somethin'. Right now, I better go find out more shit we'll both need to know." When the thing spoke again, it sounded sad, condescending. "Guess you might as well get back into your lil' restaurant an' wash them dishes, kid."

A bird wing fell at Rob's feet, bones picked clean. Above, another set of wings beat the air. The thing had dipped beneath the arch, into flight. It disappeared above the rooftops across the street.

As Rob headed downstairs, its words sank in. Reaching the dining room, his heart raced and his nerves jangled. Half of it was fear for Sally, not to mention himself. The rest had nothing to do with fear, except that he'd let his life stagnate in it for too long. He'd spent his life learning to sense the things in the outer dark, listened as best he could, understanding their language just well enough to get what he needed. Except he'd never let himself follow it into those shadows, to the heart of their secrets. Now a messenger had stepped out to invite him in…implying he belonged there, that his strengths and gifts would flourish as this dull surface world never allowed. The exhilaration made him loathe his workplace more than ever.

Business was still dead, and Virdelle and his shrieking spawn remained absent. "Hey dude, it's dead," Rob shouted to Joe. "I'm just gonna put this last little pile of dishes through and go punch out, okay?"

"Uh, yeah, I'd be fine with that, but I don't know, Virdelle might—"

"You know what? Fuck it. I'll just come in a little early and finish up whatever's left; how's that?" Rob had already fished his time card from its slot. *From here, for all I know, I might not even make it back for the paycheck.* When he stepped outside, fear for Sally tempered his anticipation. Where would she be right now? He tried the Common Ground, found it locked. If she wasn't back at the house, he'd look around some more, then go back to the restaurant at the planned meeting time.

All the way home, pigeons cooed in agitation. If they carried more personal messages from the town, Rob hurried too fast to hear.

WINDING, RISING ROADS

ONE

The cell phone rang half an hour early. Syless Wildfire sat up in the bed he and his wife had lately christened. They'd chosen a house across the river in New Hampshire, at the end of a long driveway, half a mile uphill from a gravel back road. It was two stories plus a basement, the giant living room looking out through a picture window, the countryside spilling down and outward for miles. The owners—a young married couple—now lay in the basement, segmented into several bundles apiece, all wrapped in several layers of garbage bags. It would hold in the smell 'til Syless and Ella got around to burying them in the woods.

Before snapping the husband's neck, Syless had learned the pair had no children. Of course, the man might have lied, theoretically could have kids sleeping over at friends' houses or something. Both Syless and Ella had long since outgrown skills like brain searching. The wife had been pregnant, maybe five months along, though that was hardly relevant now.

Syless switched on the phone and didn't wait for anyone to speak. "Is she in town?"

"Yes. We've got leads on how to find her. Big leads."

"Where are you?"

Sissy named the spot then described the surroundings, right in the middle of town.

"Good job. We'll be there in a few."

"There's a back stairway to the place. You'd better use that."

Syless's guts churned. "Why don't you just wait outside?"

"I'd rather not. Dad, could you just come knock on the back door?"

"Sit tight." Syless switched off the phone. Ella was already up, hunting in the dark for her clothes.

They found the parking lot still fairly populated, but no one paid them much attention as they climbed the back stairs. Of course, neither of them looked around to make sure, but they'd developed a sense for such things over the years. When Syless made the practiced knock, Sissy answered, holding a lit flashlight. Behind her was ratty storage space. Once they stepped inside, she slammed the door. That was sloppy, noisy, not like her at all. In the flashlight's glow, the dining area and the kitchen all looked like one room, divided by a small counter.

Ella clicked a light switch up and down. Nothing happened. "Interesting," she said.

Almost ceremonially, Sissy turned the flashlight on Sheldon. He stood by the counter with four lumpy garbage bags piled at his feet. Syless sniffed. There'd been two corpses, originally.

"I didn't plan it," Sheldon said. "One of 'em started catching on, then the other—"

"He didn't suspect a thing 'til you started acting weird,"

Sissy chirped. Sheldon shrank inward but held his ground. "*He* was the one acting weird—"

"Then we should've just left and called right then."

"But then he'd have gone and blabbed about us maybe."

"Sheldon," said Syless, "you remember your instructions. That, and nothing further."

Sheldon stepped forward, half desperately, half excited. "You couldn't have known we'd find this. You should hear how much I got this one to tell." His foot nudged the smaller pair of garbage bags.

The back of Syless's hand struck Sheldon across the face like lightning, with as much emotion. The boy's body lashed and his head struck the edge of the counter, which let out an echoing thunderclap to complete the effect. He slumped to the floor. Outside the Spirelight Secret Police, a boy of his age and size would have been knocked unconscious, maybe killed. As it was, he was extremely dazed.

"We should really get these out of here." Sissy nudged the garbage bags.

"Did you leave any mess when you broke them down?" Ella asked.

Sissy beamed. "I found some old newspapers and set those out before we cut them up. A lot of newspapers. Once we finished, I put the papers in the bags with them."

"Was there any…initial mess?"

Sheldon pulled himself up. "The first guy…Yeah, he was a clean kill." His voice slurred a little. "The other guy bled on the floor while I made him talk, but I got all that up."

"You left the boards all stained, though." Sissy beamed at her parents again. "Don't worry. I found cleaning fluids and fixed it."

"Did you finish before it got dark?"

"Yep. You can see the spot with the flashlight if you want."

"No need. We'd better get these bags down to the car, fast."

"I really did find a lot." Sheldon held onto the countertop and steadied himself.

"You can tell us back at the house." Syless didn't look at him.

"We got a whole house?" Sissy chimed. "What kind? How big?"

Syless ignored her. "Sheldon. Do you have your head together enough to haul the bags to the car?"

"Sure, Dad…Yeah, I can haul 'em fine."

Once all four bags were in the trunk, Sissy ran back up the rickety stairs and made sure the door had locked behind them. As Syless drove, Ella glanced in the rearview. Sheldon's eyes fluttered. "Sheldon, hon, what did you learn from the man in the restaurant?"

"Let him rest 'til we're back at the house." Syless had been keeping an eye on Sheldon through the mirror, too. He was starting to worry that he'd given the boy a worse knock than he'd intended.

When Sheldon mumbled, Ella and Syless caught the names Clover Waits and Rob Coscan. The second name brought worried looks.

"I listened to what the guy said, too," Sissy said. "Sounds like Sally made friends with those people. Clover

Waits is the girlfriend of the guy from the restaurant. We got her address."

"I think she's with Rob Coscan," Sheldon droned. "You know…*with* him…"

"That's what the guy thought," Sissy added. "He'd heard rumors. I don't think it's true. Plus he didn't know Coscan's address." When they reached the house, she bounded out. "Whoa, this place is so cool! Hey Mom, after we find Sally, can we stay here a while?"

"I don't know, dear. We'll probably have to leave for the nearest homestead soon."

Sheldon climbed out and wobbled. Syless put a hand on his shoulder. "Sheldon. You did well at getting the information. But you have to learn to take things a step at a time. Jumping ahead of the game like that can jeopardize everything. And not just the goal of a mission."

"I know, Dad," Sheldon said groggily. "I just…Could you give me a few minutes?"

"Go rest. Sissy can fill us in on the rest of the details."

Sheldon went and lay down in the spare bedroom the parents had found for the kids. Alone in the dark, he wished Sissy could come and lie down with him. Earlier, he'd been mad, had wanted to hurt her for getting him in trouble. Now everyone else was downstairs in this cool big old house, talking about what they'd do next. He wanted to be down there, planning with them. Sissy relaying his information wasn't the same as stealing the credit, but that's how it felt. Then again, when Sheldon remembered the last time he'd seen Sally, he wasn't sure he wanted to be there when they found her. In fact, he had his own reasons to be terrified of the reunion.

Sally wouldn't tell what I did, even if they do manage to rehabilitate her. Would she? Before long, he fell asleep to these thoughts.

* * * *

Out in the hall, Syless Wildfire stood by the door. He glanced in now and then, watching his son sleep, trying not to worry too much. Once they had Sally back, he'd ask the Tribunal for a few months off before their next assignment. Of course, he and his wife would need time to rehabilitate Sally—as they hadn't managed the first time—but he also wanted a stretch of peacetime to spend with his son. Syless's frequent stomachaches, caused by Sheldon's rashness, were equaled only by his amazement at the boy.

Syless had been an only child, and he'd been scared shitless when his parents started sending him off to search alone. He'd not only survived those silly childhood fears, but had raised one of the most respected Secret Police families in generations. Neither Sissy nor Sheldon ever seemed afraid, and they showed three times the skill he'd had at their age.

Sally had always been another matter, even before she'd first run off. Sometimes Syless was almost afraid to send the kids into the field, wanted to tell Ella that the three of them should keep close, do all the investigating together. Had anyone known about such cowardly thoughts, they'd say he'd paid too much attention to the Earth-line ways, been weakened by his love for his family like an Earth-line parent.

By allowing the Earth-line world to grow so strong around them, the Spirelights had invited it into their own. The children paid for it in how they came up, the part that world played in shaping them. No matter how much Syless loved his oldest daughter, there was no denying she was the most damning result.

Ella entered the hallway. "You should come down. Sissy's already told me what they got out of the restaurant man."

"I think I might have hit Sheldon too hard."

"He disobeyed and you disciplined him. Will he be able to function for the rest of the mission?"

For a moment, Syless flared. They were looking for their daughter, not chasing down Crimbone. Recalling that name Sheldon had dropped, though, he wondered…"We'll see in the morning. What did Sissy have to say?"

"We have an address. There's a chance Sally's there."

"Then I guess we'd better head that way."

"That's the idea, except I think just Sissy and I should go. As in, maybe you should stay and keep an eye on Sheldon."

"If he gets—" Syless forced the lump out of his throat. "If I think he's hurt bad, I'll go ahead and call the nearest homestead."

"If you have to. Let's keep this small, for as long as possible. If Sally's not there, we'll find out what Clover Waits knows about Rob Coscan."

Two

"Fuck." Rob glared at his keys. When he looked up, Gus recoiled. "What else she say?"

"Well, uuuhm, she diiidn't really saaay anything else…"

"She just handed you the keys, then took off. Not another word."

"Weeelll…yeah. I think she, like, seemed like she was in a reeeaaalll hurry to get out of heeere, though…Just sorta hurried off the porch without looooking back, then jumped in a caaar with this other chick who drove ooofff."

"Yeah? So what did the other one look like?" Sally had mentioned her little fling with Bethany, but she'd made it sound like a one-time deal that didn't affect things between her and Rob. Great, now he felt jealous on top of everything else…stupid anxiety, he knew, but now that his blood was heated, it was hard to curb. He looked around like he expected to see a better answer written on the walls.

Gus shrugged timidly. "So, like, whyyyy'd you give your keeeeys to this girl, anyway?"

"Why the fuck you think?"

"Aaahh! Wow! So you guys are, like, whaaatt, together, or something?"

"Thought so." Rob headed towards his room.

"Sooo, liiike, how long had you twoooo…known each other?"

Rob unlocked his room. When Gus kept droning out questions, Rob spun back and got right in his face. "I'm not fucking talking about it to you, okay?"

"Oooooh. What, soooo you guys like, broke up, or whaaatt?"

Rob slammed the door in time to punch the wall instead of Gus. Pain screamed from his hand to his elbow. His scraped knuckles slid from the fresh hole. Green plaster chips sifted loose and pattered the floor. He spun and kicked the closet door. The straining, cracking wood, the impact vibrating through his boot, up his leg…Yeah, that was satisfying.

"Fucking bitch," he growled through his teeth. *"Goddamn lying backstabbing little cunt."*

His keys were still in hand, the ones Sally had handed to Gus before running off. All night at work, he'd replayed their moments together, staying high on them. Now he searched for any little warning sign he might have missed, whatever he might have said or done wrong to give her second thoughts. They'd been having a great time together, hadn't they? Hell, more than great! They'd only made love a few times, but to him it felt like losing his virginity all over again, recharging his libido beyond anything he could have been ready for, after draining it on years of too many drunken, hollow flings. It had been more than the sex, right? Looking in her eyes had been like glimpsing a world of secrets. Not just hers, but things about himself that had baffled him all his life, reflected back at him, laid bare and simple, or just plain irrelevant when they held each other.

Waking up after a lifetime of sleepwalking…Hadn't he been doing something like that for her, too? It had felt like they had all the time in the world to figure it out. Okay, fine, one more of life's bitter little pills of disappointment…The more he tried to shove all this into that corner of his brain, though, the crazier he felt inside. He squeezed the keys 'til the edges nearly broke skin. Then he chucked them across the room. They bounced off the wall and landed on the center of his bed like some sick joke.

Watch, probably right in the wet spot stain.

"Goddamn you," he hissed. "God, I'm such a fucking moron, trusting one more flighty little…" He sat and rubbed his temples. Okay, now was a good time to go out for a smoke, calm his nerves.

As he stepped outside, a voice that no longer startled him sounded from the shadows of the porch. "Heheheh…Man o' man, Biter-Boy! That sweet thing sure did get you wrapped around her lil' finger pretty quick, huh?"

Rob advanced. He spotted the thing's outline, surrounded by stacks of boxes and old newspapers. "Where the fuck is she, birdie?"

"Hey Biter-Boy, I'm on your side. You'll find your own way back to that Sally-Girl of yours, but first there's shit I gotta straighten you out about."

"Fuck that. Either tell me where she is, or see if you can get off this porch and fly away before I get a hold of you and rip your Goddamn wings off."

"Ain't you listened to a thing I done said?" The creature sounded more amused than scared…though there *was* real fear in that smug, craggy voice. "'Cause if you had, you might reckon you're jumpin' to conclusions."

"Fine. So what's the real deal?"

"Your girl's off runnin' scared, hidin' out…but not 'cause she's flakin' out on you. There's nasty shit on her trail, same shit I'm here to tell you about. She don't want you gettin' mixed up in it, 'cept that ain't exactly in her hands."

"Fine. What kind of nasty shit?"

"As in, folks out to kill her for what she is. What she don't know—or at least she ain't sure—is that you and her is the same thing. Well, more or less, anyhow."

"Yeah? So what kind of *things* are we, birdie?"

"Now don't go jumpin' the gun on me, Biter-Boy. To

explain that, we'd have to go all the way back to the beginnin'."

"The beginning of what?"

"Of your life, farther back than you usually let yourself go. All that shit about your daddy an' who he really was before you was born, what you always sensed but he'd never tell ye 'cause he didn't want you growin' up into all of it. See, your momma kicked off 'fore she could tell you, and your dumbass stepmom sure as fuck never figured out shit. But you...*you clever lil' dickens, you*...You still figured it out, didn't ye?"

"No. I never figured anything out. I just try to go by what the lands tell me."

Chuckling, the thing waddled into the porch light. Its body resembled a bat's, like Rob had thought, but its head was more lizard-like, except for the drooping, dog-like ears. The mouth was shaped adequately for human speech, though there was nothing human when it opened to reveal the jagged teeth, the grinning jaws, that eel-like tongue slithering across purple gums. It reminded Rob of a horse's snout, only...well...demonic. It had definitely grown, to about the size of your average dog. Its wings were partially folded, but when spread, Rob could tell, their span would be impressive. It waddled forward on three-taloned feet, a potbelly hanging between its truncated legs. The voice sounded male, but Rob spotted no genitalia, so he went on thinking of the creature as an *it*.

"Okay, Biter-Boy. You said cut to the chase, so that's what I'm gonna try. You ain't of this world, boy, not strictly speakin'."

Rob looked on dully. "Of this world. As opposed

to…"

"Why, the land of Deschemb. The place where all the big secret magic in this world came from and mostly fled back to, same place where the real ancestors of the human race came from."

"What, you're saying I'm descended from aliens from outer space?"

"Heheheheh, nah, nothin' like that…not from anywhere in the same *time* or *space* of this here world…*outer* or otherwise. In the terminology of the world you know, think of it sorta like inner-die-mentionable travel or however the fuck you say it."

The land of Deschemb…Rob thought over different world mythologies he'd read. There came that blaze in his head again, like someone lighting a match under a memory, trying to wake it up. Like there was a connection he already had, asleep on the job. Somehow, he steadied his hands to light a smoke.

"Now, dependin' on how stupid it's made you, growin' up in the dark about all this, bein' raised like one of them soft, stupid kids of this world, you might be thinkin' *Oh golly-gracious! My little birdie-friend there's gotta be pullin' my leg! No holy-hell-stinkin' way am I descended from no inner-die-mentionable bein's!*"

Rob exhaled a big plume of smoke. "No, actually, that'd explain a lot. Excuse me if it doesn't sink in right away."

"Heh. *Ain't sunk in*, the Biter-Boy says. He don't really believe it, he means, even with all that crazy, singin' blood been wakin' up in his veins. That's the real reason you ain't havin' a fuckin' conniption fit, ain't it, Biter-Boy? 'Cause ye really jus' don't believe a word I'm sayin'. Well, it can sink in later, 'cause the reality of it's gonna hit you in the face real soon."

"So quit fucking around. Where is she? What enemy? What do I have to do?"

"That's the spirit! Hey, I'm thinkin' you might be a genuine High Natural after all."

"A what?"

"We'll get to that. Hey, this is hard on me too, believe it or not. See, most times, critters in my line of work, we get assigned to help youngin's like you into the game. The difference is, Biter-Boy, most youngin's like you spend your lives knowin' it's comin', not to mention gettin' brought up with an okay idea about what you really are. But you're cut off from your own kind 'til you're ready, after a certain age anyhow. That's when you make yer First Call, when yer mind sends out the signal, to the Ephemeral Realms all yer kind's still connected to, so it sends along your Familiar— that's me—to get you, well, *familiarized* with the whole shebang."

Rob sighed. "Familiarized with what?"

"Yer heritage, that's what, line of Crimbone fighters, nastiest motherfuckers in all the history of Deschemb. Maybe your brain never knew it, but your *blood* sure did, 'cause it always does. Chances are you've heard your blood screamin' at ye all your life. 'Cept ye never knew what the hell it was sayin'. Sure would explain why you can't sit still anywhere, huh?"

"So, all this has been going on for fuckall knows how long, right under the nose of this so-called normal world, and I'm supposed to be some kind of warrior, is what you're saying." Rob waved his cigarette hand in a mock-grandiose gesture.

"*An' he's quick, too, boys an' girls.*"

"So, who am I supposed to be fighting for, and who am I supposed to be fighting?"

The thing's voice grew grave and reverent, which was weird to hear. "The Crimbone is the line of warriors from the Schomites, first race from the land of Deschemb to secretly colonize this here world, way back before the folks who was already here even figured out how to keep track of their own history. Reckon that's how all yer ol'-timey ancestors was able to get so good at blendin' in amongst the stupid fuckers. But that ain't what you gotta be worryin' about, right here, right now. As Crimbone, you're sworn, boy. Sworn to hunt down and wipe out them called Spirelights. Them's the second race from Deschemb to show up here to do colonizin'. The Schomites came over here to get away from them pain-in-the-tail Spirelights, not to mention their pain-up-the-ass-without-lube gods. But the Spirelights followed. Ain't managed to haul their gods along, but they brung the old wars with 'em, sure enough."

"I'm not *sworn* to fight for anyone," said Rob.

"Yeah? What do you call that *First Call* of yours, done brung me here?"

"You tell me."

"I just did."

"Just tell me where Sally is, or I'll—" Rob checked himself and thought fast. "These…Spirelights. They the one's Sally's running from?"

Again came the high, wheezing laugh. "You fuckin' Crimbone boys an' yer pussy, I'm tellin' ye. Can't say's I blame you, though. She's a hot little number. Well, son, I'll spin it for you quick. You wanna get the girl, you gotta go kill you some monsters first. That's right, jus' like out'a some fairy tale. Now you can sit around with your thumb up your ass while the monsters is out huntin' down an' gobblin' up your Sally-Girl, or you can start listenin' to your blood."

"These Spirelights. Why are we…at war with them?"

"Biter-Boy, them's ain't questions for a Crimbone to ask his Familiar. You go up against a Spirelight, your blood'll tell ye all ye need to know, about why you wanna fight it and kill it. 'Cept I reckon for now, you got all the reason you really give a shit about."

Rob smiled grimly. "So, if I'm some kind of badass monster-killer, where are my weapons?"

"That's for you to decide, Biter-Boy. You call your own weapons to you, when you decide you want 'em bad enough. Just like you decided you was ready to call me up."

A long disorientation cleared from Rob's brain…not from the thing's words, though the thing's presence fueled it. It was like a song, one that his whole being sang. The song of his own blood…Crimbone blood, truly awake for the first time. No room left for skepticism or hesitation, then. That *other* Rob Coscan would have felt those things. If he still had anything in common with the guy, it was what he wanted, what he'd reclaim. He would make Sally Wildfire safe, and he'd kill to keep her that way, with him. Sharp little tingles danced through his muscles, building to a thirsty throb.

"So, what's your name, anyway, birdie?"

The thing smiled a strange, sick smile. "Call me Puttergong."

Rob tried not to laugh, failed, but the thing didn't seem offended. "Okay, Puttergong, point me at some fucking monsters."

THREE

Before too much longer, Sally would have to hike to the main road to hitch a ride. She doubted she could handle being stoned while she tried to get out of town unnoticed, so she passed on the bowl Clover offered. Clover shrugged and took another deep hit. The movie was something called *Meet the Feebles*, about a bunch of puppet animals running a shady cabaret. Sally sort of saw how it would be more amusing while baked, enough to make the smell from Clover's pipe a little more tempting.

"Oh, you gotta see this," Clover had insisted. "It's like *The Muppets* on crack."

Sally didn't mention that she'd never seen *The Muppets*, in fact hadn't seen many movies at all. The other day with Rob had been her second trip to a movie theatre, ever. It took her a while to figure out what was so *on crack* about this flick, though it made her think some about stories she'd heard of the Old World. When she'd first watched a Bugs Bunny cartoon, she'd been too young to realize it was a silly fantasy for Earth-line children. It was kind of strange that every other word out of Bugs's mouth hadn't been stuff like *Fuckstick* or *Cuntface* or *Rimjob*. Rabbits, in Sally's experience, were fairly uncouth critters, and she'd never met one with Bugs's cunning or brass.

Meet the Feebles had more verisimilitude, except the animals dressed like Earth-line high society and handled things like microphones, golf clubs, machine guns, and automobiles.

Clover cackled insanely at it all, paused to pack another bowl. "This movie ain't too strange for you, is it?"

"Nah. It's sort of cute, I guess."

Clover giggled. "You're a strange one, girl."

A fox was belting a showstopper about the joys of sodomy when the doorbell rang.

"God…" Clover headed for the living room. "Watch, Jake lost his keys, and his dumb little bitch on the side had to give him a ride back here."

Sally would later wonder if she'd gotten a contact high, because the feeling didn't hit 'til just before the door opened.

There was silence from the front room, 'til Clover said, "Uh… hi. You folks okay?"

"Hello." The woman's voice was amiable, deeper than Sally remembered. "You're one of Sally Wildfire's friends, aren't you? May we come in?"

"Uh, sure. Yeah, she's here right now, actually."

Clover, you dumbass. Where was the back door? Could Sally make it through a window before they got in here? She could shake anyone easily enough in the woods, except—

Clover's feet sounded back towards the room. "Hey Sally, someone's here to see you."

Except that left Clover here, with them.

Well, fuck that! Sally stood up. She had to be tough enough by now, right? Whatever happened, at least she wouldn't have the blood of anyone from Brattleboro on her hands. First, though, she slipped into the kitchen.

She heard Clover reenter the living room, followed by two more sets of feet, one heavy, one soft. "Hey Sally, where'd you go? Huh. Must be in the bathroom or something. I, uh, thought she said she didn't know anyone around here."

"We just got to town today. I'm Sally's mother. This is my other daughter, Sissy."

"Wow. Sally's folks, huh? Hey Sissy, I'm Clover. You know, your sister's really nice."

"*Whoo!*" Mom whistled. "Smells like you girls have been partying tonight."

"Well, I have. Don't worry, she's been good."

"It's okay either way, as long as you're responsible." Mom chuckled in an *I was young once too, you know* voice.

By now, Sally had found what she wanted in the kitchen. It was time to go welcome the family. She kept the kitchen knife out of sight—not the biggest she'd found, but the sharpest—wrist curled inward, flat side pressed against her forearm. There was still the pocketknife, but she didn't trust herself with it.

It was the knife Dad had trained her on from age five, the one she'd used ever since. To open it was to stab or slice, swift and lethal. Hell, she hadn't been able to curb the instinct with Rob, though that was a whole separate can of worms. She'd only use the carving knife if they threatened Clover.

Sally stepped a few feet out of the kitchen. Mom looked a little more rugged, but otherwise not a day older.

Damn, how old would Sissy be? She had the same child's face, but on a taller, leaner body.

"Oh, there she is!" said Clover.

"Hey, Mom. Hey, Sis."

Mom came and hugged her tight. "Sally!" Her voice stayed sweet, but with a note of smug certainty of how all this would turn out.

Sally put her free arm around Mom, the knife still hidden at her side. Sissy stood too close to Clover, eyes unreadable, so unlike the Earth-line children Sally had gotten used to. Sally cursed her thumping heart, knowing Mom could feel and hear it.

"How have you been, dear?"

"Good, Mom. I've seen a lot of the country."

"Sissy hon, would you stay in here and talk to Clover? Sally and I need to step outside and have some private words."

"Mom, whatever you have to say, you can say it in front of Clover."

"Well dear, if you must be difficult…Sissy, would you please help me with your sister?"

The little girl blurred across the floor. Two small palms collided with Sally's stomach, strong even for a Secret Police child. Sally's back slammed into the wall. Sissy batted her wrist, not hard but precise and strategic, so the knife clattered at their feet. As Clover screamed, Sissy snatched the knife, then darted back and kicked her legs out from under her. With a shriek, Clover crashed and sprawled face first. Sissy straddled her, twisting her arm up behind her back and pressing the knife to her neck.

"Stay against the wall, Sally," Sissy yelled, pressing the edge down harder.

"Clover, whatever you do, don't fight her!" Then Sally saw

those bulging, shaking eyes and knew Clover had more than figured that out.

"Whatever *you* do, Sally, don't run and try to pull Sissy off," said Mom. "From here, it looks like your poor little friend's throat would open like a trout if your sister's wrist moved suddenly." She met Clover's eyes. "Now Clover, I'd assume you're not too stoned or scared to understand what I'm saying, but just in case…If you understand, tap twice with your free hand."

At first, Clover's arm only twitched with terror. Sally's guts clenched, then Clover swatted the carpet twice like someone tapping out of a wrestling match.

"Good. Now, you were very polite, Clover, and you've obviously been very nice to Sally. Once we're gone, I can tell you're not someone with the ingenuity or far-reaching motivation to try to find us yourself. If you call the police and give them our descriptions and they find us…people will die. You've obviously been conditioned to be soft, so you're probably horrified at the idea of causing anyone's death, even those not of your coterie, whatever the circumstances. Would you risk it? Tap once for no, twice for yes. Remember, both your own life and those of others hang on your honesty."

This time, Clover's hand shook a lot worse when she lifted it. It kept quivering after slapping.

"Oh, excuse me, Clover, but was that meant to be one slap or two?"

Sissy turned the blade ever so slightly, so a long, ice-white fold of flesh pinched up against the edge. Clover's next swat was a duller thud, but it was definitely just one.

"Good. Now Sally and I are going outside for a few

words. After a few minutes, Sissy will release you and come join us. I suggest you stay planted 'til you hear our car drive away. My Sissy has very sharp little ears. If she hears any trouble or fighting from your porch…well, I trust her to decide whether or not she's needed out there, but if she does run to my assistance, she couldn't well leave you unattended, so she'd probably kill you. If you give her any trouble when she lets you up, she'll still kill you. You believe me, right?"

Clover gave the carpet two more slaps.

Out on the porch, Mom said to Sally, "Get yourself together, dear, then speak to me."

Sally took several deep breaths of night air. "What do you want?" She already knew the answer, but that's what came out.

"I just want my oldest back." Holding Sally's gaze, Ella Wildfire spoke the secret language taught by the Gods of the Spirah Pantheon, long ago to their first worldly children. "No one's angry with you, Sally. You're a gifted young woman, and the good people need you. But you've been traumatized, not just physically and mentally, but spiritually. We never finished your healing, and clearly you still need it. Tell me, have these running years done anything but left you more confused and frightened?"

Hearing these words—that language, spoken aloud after all these years, by her mother—Sally felt dizzy. Mom was offering the only safety there'd ever been. All the running and fighting and bare survival had been nothing but a search for that safety. Gods, were those her thought patterns already sliding back into the rhythm of her people's language? She thought of Rob, of what she'd just seen happen to Clover. Then she recalled what Mom meant by *healing*. "Oh, what's that, you think you can still pull some *I know you better than you know yourself* bullshit? You don't know a fucking thing about me."

"I know I can't imagine what you've been through." Mom spoke Earth-line again. "But I *am* your mom. Come on, dear, please, let your family help you find your way back to yourself. That road will be painful, yes, but has anyone offered an effective alternative?"

Sally felt herself shaking her head. *The answer is yes.* That's why she had to get them out of town, as quickly as possible, before they stumbled onto Rob. Even if she escaped again, she could never come back here. There were only two places she'd ever felt like there might be peace or answers, and one of them was right here and now, no matter how much she hated it. If they realized they had competition, they'd have it killed faster than she could blink.

"Let's go sit in the car and wait for Sissy," Mom said.

Moments later, Sally watched through the Buick's front passenger window as Sissy skipped through the front door and off the porch. Thinking of Clover, Sally imagined the worst. No, even Sissy couldn't be that carefree right after killing someone.

"Everything cool?" Sissy asked as she climbed in.

"Everything's wonderful, hon." Mom beamed proud and joyful. "Now kiss your sister."

Sissy leaned over the seat and kissed Sally's cheek. "I missed you, Sally."

Sally only nodded.

"Sally, did you miss your sister?"

"Yeah." Sally's voice was distant. "Of course I missed

you, all of you. I'm just…Mom, I'm really mixed up…scared."

"I know, hon. We'll head for the nearest homestead tomorrow morning, then we can start putting things back together."

It won't be like last time. You're not a weak, broken fourteen-year-old anymore.

The drive through town was silent. When they passed South Main, Sally barely held back tears. Once Main Street turned into Putney Road, she broke down sobbing.

"Sally?" Sissy sounded worried.

"Let her be," said Mom. Then later along the winding, vacant stretch, "Sissy, did everything go well with Sally's friend?" When Sissy squirmed sheepishly, Mom looked glumly through the rearview. "Oh no, Sissy…"

"Well…I was getting the feeling she wasn't scared enough, that maybe she was thinking of fighting…Well, I thought she might not take me seriously enough. So I told her I'd already killed two people today. I know it was Sheldon who killed 'em, but, well…I thought she might take me more seriously, you know, if she knew some specifics, so…"

"Oh, Sissy…"

"I couldn't help it! I told her about the one guy, the one we got her address from, and it was like she…stopped being scared. She started fighting. I tried holding her still, but her neck jerked against the knife. Then there was blood everywhere, she was thrashing worse and worse, and…Look, I couldn't help it, okay? I swear!"

Everything drained from Sally except raging self-loathing. She stopped sobbing. Instead, she jerked and twisted, fighting the seatbelt. When her hand shot into the back, Sissy didn't have time to recoil. Sally caught a handful of hair and jerked the kid squealing forward. "*You bitch! You fucking nasty little beast!*"

"Sally!" Mom pressed the brakes.

Before the Buick could slow to a stop, Sally grabbed and jerked the steering wheel, so the car swerved towards a ditch. Panicked, Mom yanked the wheel the other way. The car screeched through the opposite lane, then over a steep embankment. A thump rolled through everyone's asses, shaking their guts into their throats, after which they slid sideways through mud and weeds. A tree smacked Mom's door, and they spun the rest of the way downhill. Twisting metal roared, shrieked and barked. Cracking glass hissed and spat sharp, glimmering dust. Everything on the hillside turned into battering rams, tag-teaming the car from every direction, 'til it slid mangled across a patch of gravel. Mom dangled sideways, the seatbelt holding her like a sling, a red-speckled spiderweb crack in her window. As Sally's head cleared, she couldn't tell whether Mom was dead or unconscious.

A shriek split her ears, and Sissy's arm locked around her neck. Flailing, Sally's elbow smashed over and over into Sissy's face. When Sissy's grip tightened, Sally's free hand found the seatbelt buckle and pressed the release button. Then she yanked her whole body forward, pulling Sissy with her. Sissy tumbled over the top of the seat, fell across Sally's lap, flailed and lunged, fingers hooked to claw out eyes. She got Sally's front knuckles in the face for her trouble, three times. The second one snapped her nose at the bridge. The third smacked her skull against the dashboard. She slumped into Sally's lap, then thudded limp on the floor.

At first the door seemed fused shut, so Sally drew up both legs and kicked hard. It groaned, resisted, then swung open. Sally tumbled out onto the gravel. Cold night air made her more lucid. So did colder stones, sharp against her palms. She had no idea how bad she was hurt, but she managed to stand either way. Through the trees on the road above, a few cars zipped by. If any of the drivers had seen the wreck happen, none of them bothered to stop.

Someone walked along the roadside, still far off, coming at a maniacal clip. At first Sally thought the figure was hurrying towards the accident. No, they stayed pointed straight ahead, striding single-mindedly towards wherever. The gravel stretch ran back out to the road, meeting at the base of the hill. Sally guessed she'd lingered in the car for a while. If the pedestrian had been in time to see it go off the road, they'd have come running by now, right? She didn't want to get anyone else sucked into this mess, so she was about to let them pass. Then a shaft of moonlight caught the profile and her heart leapt.

She ought to recognize that shape. After all, she'd spent enough hours recently exploring it thoroughly, up close and personal. She tried shouting, "*Rob*," but it came out as a soft squealing whimper. Scrambling uphill, she tried another shout, but it came out even weaker.

By the time she was almost halfway up, he was still many yards away. Surely she'd reach the top before he passed. Either way, she'd make enough noise that he'd turn and look—

At first, she thought she'd walked into a thick tree branch. Then heavy, leathery wings beat at her shoulders, while some bulbous animal's body thumped her in the face, muffling her cries. Her arms went up, but her feet went out. As she tumbled backwards, she got only an instant's glimpse of the big bat-like shape. Then the landing's blunt smack went off against her skull, rolling through her brain like a gong.

Sally had no idea how long she lay there, floating through a garden of supernovas behind her eyelids. When she managed to stand, she had to turn around several times before she figured out where the hell she was. The knock on her head pulsed, burning her eyes. The slope seemed to rise forever. Rob and the flying thing were gone, but the mangled Buick was still there. Inside, Mom and Sissy lay motionless. In the distance, sirens blared. It had only been a matter of time before someone drove by, spotted the wreck, and called 911.

Sally watched from the nearby shadows 'til the ambulance and cruisers pulled up.

FOUR

For some reason, Rob thought about Louis all the way into town. During the year they'd shared at Marlboro, Rob had spent a while dead set on a girl named Natalie. Louis had taken an interest in her too, but he'd stepped aside to let Rob have his shot…out of worry for their friendship, which was so stupid, Rob didn't know where to start. So maybe they'd have punched the shit out of each other—as they'd already sometimes done, just for fun—then they'd have gotten over it.

Anyway, Rob and Natalie shared a fun little fling in the library religion room. The romance never got any further, but a close friendship formed. Then she hooked up with another guy, one Herbert Udale, who it just happened Rob couldn't stand. As always, Louis provided a patient ear for Rob's venting. Then they caught rumors that Herbert was getting abusive. Rob had already been suspicious, spotting faint bruises around Natalie's neck that didn't quite look like the hickeys she insisted they were, noticed her acting uncharacteristically awkward and reserved.

At some point, through circumstances that were anyone's guess, Louis had acquired an authentic police billy club, which he left lying around in his room as a conversation piece. They'd been chilling out one night when a friend dropped by, all flustered. Natalie and Herbert had gotten into a loud argument in the dining hall, and Herbert had flown off the handle and hit her. Everyone watching had just stood around like idiots, not knowing what to do or say. Rob had listened silently then waited for the visitor to leave. Then he pulled on his boots, snatched up the club, and stormed across campus in the dark, planning to bash Herbert's skull in. Louis followed, listing reasons why that was a bad idea. Rob couldn't remember what Louis finally said to talk him down. He'd probably suggested some alternate means of justice that wouldn't lead to incarceration.

As Rob crossed Canal and headed along Main Street, he thought of all his reasons to rethink things now. He could almost hear Louis listing them off.

"So tell me something, Lou," he said on the corner of Main and Flat. "If I'd gone ahead and splattered ol' Herb's brains all over campus, you'd have helped me hide the body, right?"

He practically heard Louis's defeated sigh. *Of course.*

"And you know, even if you were here in the flesh, you couldn't talk me out of this for all the Tequila in Mexico, right?"

Sure.

"And you'd still help me kill these motherfuckers I'm after now, right?"

Yeah, obviously.

Rob twitched, startled. That had sounded a lot more certain than he'd have imagined. Finally, he muttered, "Good to hear it."

Hey, you know, came Louis's old melancholy, pragmatic tone, *it's not like either of us would really have a choice.*

Rob blinked. For the first time since his initial conversation with Puttergong, he wondered just how crazy he'd really gone. The windows still glowed in Sam's Sporting Goods.

When he went in, a clerk said, "We're closing in about five minutes."

"That's fine," said Rob. "I'll be quick."

Rob went straight to the glass case of pocketknives. The one he wanted had a three-and-a-half inch black grip, with a press-down lock mechanism at the base. It was nearly identical to Louis's old one… and to Sally's. Wow, how had Rob missed that 'til now? He called the clerk over and pointed out his selection.

Outside, he felt the closed knife in his pocket against his hip. "Would've been a blast to really have you along, ol' buddy. Didn't I always say we'd have adventures together some day, just like those guys in those fantasy drawings of yours?"

No answer came. Instinctively Rob's eyes darted upward. Puttergong perched on the roof of the Latchis building. Then the creature flapped and flew off. Rob didn't see it again 'til he reached the end of Main Street. High above, wings beat the air. Rob saw the bat-like shape leave the roof of the library then disappear into the blackness above Putney Road.

The night was cold, but Rob's blood raced too fast to mind. Where the sidewalk ended, he took the narrow dirt trail he and Sally had walked yesterday, to the movie theatre. The road forked off onto a broad gravel drive. Down to the left, he spotted what looked like a nasty car wreck. Yeah, someone had gone off the road and plowed clear down the hillside. Scattered glass shards glittered like stardust on the surrounding gravel, with larger knocked-off car chunks here and there. Whoever was in there, they were probably damn lucky not to have flipped or gotten wrapped around a tree. It didn't look like anyone was moving over there. Oh well, car wrecks happened all the time. Rob had monsters to go fight, and they stood between him and Sally.

Further uphill, he spotted the skid marks, then where the car had torn up the brush. Frantic rustling sounded from downhill. Rob's fingers trailed the edge of the pocket with his new knife. When a crash sounded ahead, his step quickened. As he neared the spot, Puttergong flapped up from the shadows.

"Jesus, birdie, you scared the shit out of me."

"Only just now? Damn, kid, you must be more fucked in the head than I thought." Puttergong hovered at eye level.

How the hell did those wings hold up that huge, sagging, speckled gut?

"What were you doing down there, anyway?"

"Keepin' you on your toes is all. You're doin' great!"

Puttergong flew on ahead again. Rob followed. At the far end of Putney, the creature perched out on the grassy space of the rotary like a centerpiece gargoyle. To the cars zipping by, it probably registered as nothing but a big bird. By now, cold air seeped through Rob's jacket. How far did he have to go? There was the bus station on the left. Was this about to turn into a road trip?

Puttergong flew off to the right. The streetlights fell away as Rob followed down another unpaved hill. The only light came from the cloud-blurred moon, sending blue shimmers across the blackness of the Connecticut River as he crossed the great iron bridge. Jesus, the damn critter had led him all the way into New Hampshire.

At the end of a dirt road, Puttergong perched on a stop sign. "You just keep surprisin' me, Biter-Boy, I tellin' ye."

"How's that?" Puttergong didn't answer, but Rob became acutely aware of the knife in his pocket, as if the creature had flown over and pressed a claw to the spot. "Is it much farther? It's getting cold."

"Heh. Biter-Boy, you get through this, you gonna have nights where you sleep bare-ass in snow with no blankie. Hey, ain't so bad. I mean you got it in you, I can tell. C'mon, ain't that far now."

Again, Rob followed the beat of wings through the darkness. The dirt road wound onward between a steep, deep ditch and a sharper embankment, the thickening forest blotting out more of the night's faint glow. No cars passed now.

Except for the babble of a downhill stream, the trees might as well have formed two solid towering black walls. The sky was a dim, jagged line, flickering indifferently through skeletal branches. The road rose steadily, otherwise unchanging for a mile. Rob's blood pumped hot, blotting out the cold 'til sweat broke out all over him.

"Okay, boy, stop here. This is it."

Maybe the creature was hiding in the trees, but its voice sounded close. To the right, a paved driveway cut upward, a glow barely piercing the brush. It could have been a porch light or the moon.

"Is Sally up there?"

Puttergong didn't answer. Rob sensed he wouldn't hear from the creature again 'til he found out exactly what he was here to do and did it. He thought of Sally, and that was enough to cut through his fear. Even without those thoughts, anticipation of whatever else awaited him would have kept him going…anticipation, and these deeper new instincts. They centered his senses, magnetizing them towards some point not yet in range.

The point where you can sleep naked in the snow and not even flinch…Yes, that's what this feeling is, something leading you to that kind of power within yourself, and wilder abilities besides. Once you unlock it, nothing will stop you from keeping Sally or anyone else safe.

For the record, if you ever had a chance to turn tail and run, I believe you passed it back there somewhere.

The driveway seemed longer than the rest of the walk, but Rob no longer minded. His joints ached and he loved even this, so he walked faster. He wanted to break into a run, but he figured it was better to move quietly. Finally, the house came into view. Only one light burned, through windows that revealed a living room. Rob inched forward, keeping clear of the spill. Spotting no movement within, he crept close as possible without straying from the shadows. Finally, he made it beneath a stretch of porch. He hoisted himself up, first onto the ledge, then over the railing, then pressed himself against the wall. He listened hard. Within, boards creaked underfoot. The impulse was to look through the window—

No, not to look…to go in and see, to—Wait, no, more than that even. Some new pull had taken hold, a magnetic link between him and whoever—or whatever—awaited him inside. They had something to give him, or something he had to take. The hunger wasn't unlike lust…but it wasn't Sally. Whoever was in there, Rob knew he'd never seen them before. Yet in this weird new way, yes, he *lusted* for them, body and soul. The footsteps grew louder, definitely in the living room now. Rob went down on his stomach, below the window's range, and crawled across cold boards. With this strange new sense, he tried to probe the rest of the house, find out if Sally—

Except whoever he felt, wasn't there something of Sally about them, some of her inexplicable uniqueness? *No, you idiot, you're imprinting her everywhere, because you're obsessed. These are your enemies.* Yeah, he felt sure of that, as if his new senses told him so…which, he realized, was the case, like a reptile flicking its tongue, tasting predators and prey on the air, and instinctively knowing the difference. *You and Sally's enemies…One way or another, you have to get through them to get to her.*

As the feet paced, Rob got right up next to the front

door. Keeping low, he drummed his boot toes on the boards. The enemy halted, then drew near. The door creaked open. Out stepped something blinding, except for the pair of sandaled feet at the glow's center.

What the fuck was this? When Rob inhaled, he could literally taste the glow. He wanted to dive into it like a swimming pool and drink it dry.

He sprang, and his arms locked around someone's ankles. As that someone crashed to the hard wood floor, Rob shot through the doorway. The figure started up, but Rob got on top and pinned it down, slamming his fists over and over into a lean leathery face.

He didn't punch like he had the drunks last week at McNeill's, but pistoned everything he had through his arms onto all the tender spots. Whatever was in him, there was more of it than he'd ever noticed, and his head would explode if he didn't get it out through his fists. Cartilage crunched as flesh tore, blood squirting and spattering his knuckles and wrists.

Seeing it, *smelling it*, he didn't want to punch anymore…No, *he wanted to rip this fucker's face off with his fingers, 'cause that's where the glow was, and he needed to suckle it like marrow from a bone.*

A leg kicked up and a knee thudded against his spine. He pitched forward, felt his palms and knees bruise as he rolled through it and sprawled, then scrambled around. The man was already up, closing in. Rob ducked a swing that would have broken his jaw, then head-butted the man's abdomen, barreling forward 'til they crashed into the wall.

The thunderclap rolled through both of them before sheetrock collapsed in the shape of the man's head and back. The bastard flailed as if to throw more punches, but Rob grabbed his shoulders and spun him around. This guy was a hell of a lot stronger than Rob, so the latter had to press harder than ever. Every muscle strained and shrieked, threatening to pop from the bones. The man's ribcage slammed against the wall.

Before the guy could try another mule-kick, Rob slammed his knees into both calves, then kidney-punched him over and over. When the man started to buckle, Rob held him up, twisting one arm back, pressing his free forearm against the neck, pinning the head to the wall.

How much more force would it take to snap the neck? Rob pressed harder, harder…

The man panted, "What do you—"

"Shut up!" Rob waited 'til he was sure the man heard. "Okay. Good. Now answer my questions and pray I don't think you're lying. First, where's Sally?"

"What are you—"

"You don't ask." Rob pressed harder. "I ask, you answer. Got it?"

The man nodded as best he could. If someone had described this scenario in advance, Rob would have expected to be more afraid. He'd still been scared on the driveway, but not now. No, he hadn't been scared even when it seemed like he was about to get his ass kicked to death. The last of his fear had vanished on the porch, overwhelmed by this new, intangible hunger. The victory rush surged, so he jabbed and twisted crueler.

"Okay. Good. Now tell me where Sally Wildfire is. If you've done anything to her, if she's hurt in any way…well, you'd just better hope to hell she's not."

The man managed, "How do you know Sally?"

Something in the voice made Rob pause.

Good God, what am I doing? I've never even seen this guy—this old man—*before. I just attacked him in his own living room before even getting a look at his face, because—*

Oh, cut the moralistic whining. You already know damn well it's more than—

Rob's grip must have slackened, because the man's head snapped back, knocking his arm aside, bashing him in the face. Eyes stinging, Rob let go and staggered. Then came the brick-like smack of a fist.

Oh well, so much for healing from that last black eye. Through blurred vision, Rob's last sight was the man coming at him again. *No way in hell that bastard should be able to stand, let alone fight. Look how I mangled his face. He's gotta be at least half-blind from that broken nose.*

But the guy wasn't even limping. Another blow caught Rob's temple. Before losing consciousness, he thought, *Motherfucker, I should've used the knife.*

FIVE

In Harmony Parking Lot, a red van sat off next to some dumpsters. All the glass was bulletproof, and the frame hid sheets of rare metallic armor that would shame a tank. The inside was still and quiet, except for the old CB radio coughing out local police and ambulance frequencies. Jesse Karn sat still as a corpse in the driver seat, except when his arm moved to turn the dial back and forth. He picked up what he needed and correlated what he could. Catching the reports of the wreck on Putney Road, he wished he'd talked Zane into coming along after all. Not that he'd need backup, but now was around the time they'd usually start placing bets. The thousand dollars in Jesse's wallet said the mother and child who were pulled from the wreck would be gone from the hospital within the hour. Of course, the mother would have a fake ID, with matching registration in the glove box, but no one would have a chance to question them.

With a little luck, one or both would have enough broken bones that he'd only have to deal with however many more Spirelights were in town. Beyond that, he didn't feel so lucky tonight. Death had occurred recently in the brick building across the parking lot. It hung on the air, and Jesse tasted its agony, like meat from a beast that had lived and died miserably in an Earth-line slaughterhouse. He'd be willing to bet the mother and daughter had been involved. Jesse probably could have gotten a Cabinet go-ahead, but there was no time for the red tape. They'd probably let him off the hook, once he explained how he'd prevented their cock-up from exploding in everyone's faces.

Coscan wasn't home, didn't seem to be anywhere that anyone knew about. So Jesse sat in the van, listening in on Earth-line police transmissions, dreading the next sign. Things needed to get pretty severe for the Cabinet to consider retiring a Familiar, and Jesse couldn't figure out why Puttergong had been left breathing this long. All because of the damn thing's *honorable history*, its accomplishments in the old times, in the Old World…one of the few Familiars left from back then. If anyone asked

Jesse, maybe that was the problem.

Wasn't there a bar up Elliot Street? It occurred to Jesse that he hadn't been to Brattleboro in years. Well, it was worth a shot. By the Old Lords, he'd earned himself a drink if ever a man had. He climbed out and pulled on his brown duster coat, hiding the long knife of black metal strapped to his belt. It felt good to stretch his legs. Even the big van felt cramped after a while. As he headed up Elliot, he saw not one but two bars, directly adjacent to each other. Folks stood around outside both bars, bundled up against the cold, sucking back cigarettes.

That Bob Seger song *Down on Main Street* floated out from the first place's jukebox, while some drunk fuckwit hooted, "Well hey, whaddyaknow! Looks like we got us a real cowboy here tonight. What'cha here to do in town, cowboy? Got you a couple sixshooters under that big ol' coat?"

For some reason, Jesse turned.

The man was round and stumpy, nearly bald. Something about him reminded Jesse of a big waddling, yapping toadstool. "Here for a showdown, cowboy?" He pointed both index fingers like gun barrels. "Gonna stand on *Main Street* at high noon, take ten paces, draw an' shoot?"

The fuckwit's companions let off big hyena laughs. Still, Jesse saw them tensing for trouble. He stepped back off the stoop and walked back past them.

"Aw come on, man," the toadstool man's voice trailed after him. "I didn't mean nothin' by it. We're all friends here. Why don'tcha mosey on back, have a sarsaparilla! You drink sarsaparilla, cowboy? *Hey motherfucker, I'm talkin' to you!*"

Jesse shrugged so the toadstool man would see. The

man's companions kept letting off their hyena laughs, mostly at their companion's buffoonery. Jesse got half his satisfaction knowing he could relieve this man of several fingers and have his knife sheathed and hidden again before the hyenas noticed he'd pulled it. The other half came from suspecting the toadstool man would provoke some lesser, sufficiently humbling punishment before the night was through, probably from one of the hyenas.

Bob Seger sang on about *Main Street*. "Fine," Jesse muttered, "I get the point." He hated that song anyway.

He reached Main Street and looked left. The coast was clear, except for one other human shape, about a block and a half away…lined in the familiar glow. Jesse's knife hand itched and his mouth watered. As he walked towards the glow, he made out the shape of a young girl…the one the CB had mentioned, maybe? No, there was no way in hell that girl could have made it this far, this fast, even if she'd already slipped out of the hospital. The radio had specified a kid, estimated age nine to twelve. This one looked like a teenager. She moved as if she'd taken some kind of punishment, like maybe she'd been in that wreck too. Jesse didn't assume her injuries gave him an advantage. He walked faster towards her. In the next few seconds, she'd spring, and they'd have a little dance.

Instead, she nearly buckled when she saw him, turned and hobbled off quickly. She probably meant to lead him into a trap, except she was the only one he smelled nearby. As he neared her, he realized there was something strange about her glow. His step quickened, his hand brushing the duster back from the knife handle.

The girl hobbled faster, rounding the corner. When

Jesse reached the turn, he spotted her sort of darting, sort of tumbling into a doorway. By the time he reached her, she had a pocketknife out, the kind the Spirelight Secret Police trained their young on. Except shouldn't she have outgrown a weapon like that by her age? One hand brandished it while the other tugged at the locked door. Blood caked the back of her head.

Old Lords, how far had she come like this?

Pity and admiration flickered through Jesse, or as close as he could feel towards a Spirelight. The glow still tugged at his gut, at his soul, to let his blade drink deep, let his inflamed blood drink her death—

No, it wasn't that simple, not with this one. Her glow was fainter, even if his inner response was as strong as ever. It was also a *tainted* glow. Tainted twice over, yes, first by something far in her past, then something else, more recent…

For now, Jesse made himself look at her not as a Spirelight, but as an injured girl. He pulled the duster back over his knife and leaned towards her.

When she slashed at him, he caught her wrist, the blade less than an inch from his windpipe. If she'd thought he'd drop his guard, he was glad to disappoint her. He plucked the blade from her hand, closed it and slipped it into his duster pocket.

Her gaze was distant and glassy, almost indifferent. "Guess you'll say I'm a worthless coward if I try bargaining for my life…"

"You can bargain, but I haven't decided to kill you." He carried her back to Harmony. As he'd gambled, the last of the fight had gone out of her, for now.

After setting her in the van, he dug his medical kit from the clutter in the back. She'd taken quite a knock to the skull, along with plenty more scrapes and bruises.

"Talk," he said in old Deschembine, "then I'll treat your wounds."

Her eyes squeezed shut and her face tightened. Then she answered in English, "Don't care about others…the others like me I mean… mostly…just don't care…just wanna be with…" She was fading, but she was a tough one.

"Mostly, huh."

"Help me…gotta find him…he doesn't…God…he'll find them, or they'll find him, and they'll…Help him, please…"

Jesse perked up, more aware than ever of the strange taint to her glow. "Help who?"

"Rob…"

"Rob Coscan?"

Her physical reaction was answer enough.

"Don't say anymore. You can pass out now if you need to. I'm going to treat your wounds and give you some drugs that'll stabilize you. Later, I'll give you more drugs that'll get you lucid faster. Then you'll talk."

SIX

In the ambulance, Ella willed her body to pull itself together, so to speak…not a true recovery, but rather letting her spiritual self—the essence of the gods within her—convince her physical self that it was fit to get them out of this. It would last until they were back with Syless and Sheldon. For now, she'd rather not think of the state she'd find herself in when the self-hypnosis wore off.

As they tried to settle her into a hospital bed, Ella sent herself into hysterics, wouldn't cooperate 'til they told her exactly where her daughter was. Finally, one of the doctors relented and gave her Sissy's ward and room number. They shot Ella up with sedatives, which she shook off through more self-hypnosis. After sneaking out, she found Sissy sitting up in bed, waiting patiently.

Now it was harder for either of them to be patient, crouched between two parked cars in the hospital lot. Finally, along came an Earth-line mother and daughter, probably to visit someone, close enough in size. Ella let Sissy handle them but stepped in to make sure they were only rendered unconscious. You could only report so many corpses as last resorts before you started to look silly.

Dressed in nondescript Earth-line clothes, they found a convenience store on Canal Street that let them use the phone. Syless sounded urgent when he picked up. "Ella? What's going on? I kept calling, but—"

"We don't have the cell phones anymore." The cells were still in either the totaled car or the clothes the medics had exchanged for hospital gowns. "Your voice is strained. Did you get hurt too?"

"Don't worry about that. Have you found her?"

Ella squeezed her eyes shut. "Yes, but there've been— Look, we got in a wreck. Don't worry, Sissy's fine." While the clerk pretended not to eavesdrop, Sissy wandered the aisles, swiping snacks. Ella would have to break her of that habit at some point.

"What about Sally?"

"She's…not with us right now. What's happened back there? You've found out something. What's—"

"I don't know what I've found. Things have gotten pretty strange. I don't think I have time. Get back here as quickly as possible. Do you have a way to get here?"

They'd already scoured their new pockets for loose change. "I don't think so. Listen, how much cash do you have?"

"A few hundred dollars."

"Will that pay for a taxi?"

"Yeah. I think that's a little more than enough." His nervous amusement might annoy her, but she sensed he needed all the relief he could glean right now.

"Okay. I'm going to call a taxi. I love you."

"Need a cab?" said the clerk as she hung up. "Here you go, Brattleboro Taxi Company, already got the number pulled up right here for you…"

"Thank you. Sissy honey, are you ready to go?"

Sissy scampered over, pockets bulging. Oh well, at least they'd have snacks for the ride.

THE SECOND CALL

ONE

The grass had gone soggy red, the sopping splashes thickening underfoot the higher he ran. Behind the ivory dome of the Spirelight temple, the sky was a solid sheet of white-hot tin. He sprang and bit and tore, as one with the pack as they cleared the slope and plunged towards the temple. Soon they'd all howl as one, too. For now, the mountain howled, blessing their victory. The Spirelights had spurned and trampled their lands and fellow Deschembines, in favor of their decadent shining gods. So the mountain had no more use for them, save their blood to drink. The Crimbone spilled it gladly, so long as the mountain shared.

These weren't the Spirelight police anymore, for the pack had well since broken those defenses. Still, packmates fell with bashed skulls and torn bellies, to roll and slide back down the slope, sloshing in the muck against his legs. Wind whistled off a broken club that swung at his head. He ducked low, one of his knives skewering the enemy's arm while the other shredded viscera. His head bobbed up, mouth agape to catch the splatter. Damn, he wanted to linger on the kill, to savor it…but he shoved the body aside, felt it thud against his leg as he bounded forward. The others spilled past him, and he had to catch up. So many glowing founts to quench his blades and his soul…

The last Spirelights pushed at each other to get through the great stone door. Then the pack was on them, decimating, barreling over the mangled remains. So many more inside…

Rob had thought he was the last through the door. A falling Spirelight woman caught on his left knife, by the collarbone. His other blade rose to slice off her head, but someone caught his arm. The woman slid off his point and thudded uselessly on the marble.

Rob wheeled, ready to slaughter someone else, then saw Louis. "Man, don't fucking do that!" Since halfway through the battle, he'd wondered if Louis was still alive back there.

"You have to fall back now, Rob."

"What are you talking about? We've won. Look."

"You haven't figured out it's a trap?"

Inside, the pack slid to the floor, beneath the range of a high stone partition. In the next instant, a volley of arrows streaked the air. Rob ducked out of the doorway, yanking Louis with him. Arrows whistled close, plinking off the walls.

"If that's a trap, the Spirelights are even worse strategists than fighters."

What about Sally?

"The Spirelights didn't set this trap."

Inside, the great glow swelled then flickered, screaming from many dying mouths.

I don't know what I've found…Get back here as quickly as possible.

The glow flared so Rob felt its heat on his face. He lunged and felt it recoil. Everything blurred and blackened. His neck felt stiff and strained. His head lulled in pain, his torso strapped to cold metal. He licked blood from around his mouth, but it no longer tasted like sweet, screaming Spirelight death. More like someone had taken a sledge to his face. His teeth screamed in his gums. He ran his tongue across them to make sure they were all still there. The lower left row leaned and creaked like fence posts.

"I love you, too. Get here soon."

A table lamp's glare burned Rob's eyes. Where the glowing temple had been, the man who'd knocked him out slipped a cell phone into his pocket. The man's face was bandaged in places, swollen black and blue in others. Nylon cord looped Rob's hands and torso to a folding chair. Another cord strapped his ankles to the chair legs.

"Hurting much, Rob Coscan?" The man took a few steps forward, only limping a little.

Rob did a double take.

"I thought so."

Goddamnit, he'd been tricked into confirming his identity. How'd this bastard known to expect him? Rob snarled and bucked, felt the chair jump and totter.

The man watched, then said, "Crimbone."

Rob groaned and blinked. "What, you mean you think I'm one of those?"

"On any other day, there'd be no doubt in my mind."

"Quit playing games and ask what you wanna ask."

"Fair enough. My daughter. Sally. What do you want with her?"

"Huh?"

"You said her name. You obviously know what Schomites are, and the Crimbone, so I guess you know about Spirelights, too. Heard of the Spirelight Secret Police?"

"Will you quit fucking around? It ain't gonna work."

"What won't work?"

"That bullshit about you being Sally's dad. Where the fuck is she?"

"I hoped you'd know. And I'm not bullshitting you. I am Sally's father, and I'm here in town to find her. So far you haven't made a good case for yourself, not when it comes to my daughter's well-being, or anyone's for that matter."

"I'm not trying to hurt Sally."

"I figured that much out. That's why you're still alive. Considering where the rest of the evidence points, that doesn't make a damn bit of sense."

"Sally's my…friend. I—"

"Your lover, you mean."

"Fine. Yeah. I fucked your daughter. Several times. Wanna ask about what positions?"

"I don't know how you'll feel to hear this, but it doesn't shock me that my daughter has a sex life. She was quite a few years younger when I last saw her, and she was already fast becoming an attractive young woman. Did you know she'll be turning nineteen next month?"

Rob's eyes rolled. He hadn't known that. It felt obscene to learn new things about Sally under these circumstances, from this man. "Sure."

"You believe yourself to be in love with her."

Rob's eyes flickered back to the man. The weird,

leathery, dickless fuck was reading him, sifting his emotions like a cop or parent or teacher back in high school searching his book bag. Now as then, all he could do was watch helplessly. Except now it was his fucking brain, and he was tied to a damn chair.

"In—What the fuck! I just met her two days ago, and—" He stopped. Sally's dad eyed him, as if looking up from an illicit journal entry. "Okay, fine, so what if I am. I hear she's in trouble. Someone told me to come here if I wanted to help her, so that's what I did."

"Someone? Who?"

When Rob tried to remember, it was clear at first. The more he tried to sort through details, though, the less real anything seemed. "I'm…not sure."

"Well enough. Are you Crimbone?"

Rob started to answer, yes, no, maybe, go fuck yourself, whatever. "I don't know."

"Well then." Sally's dad nodded. "I'm not sure how that happens, but it explains a lot."

Puttergong's words—the reality of Puttergong, such as it was—started to solidify again. Of course, Rob wasn't going to tell this guy that. "Like what?"

"You don't need to know. In fact, it's your ignorance that's bought you a chance to live."

"That mean you're gonna untie me now?"

"No. I'm still not sure you wouldn't try to kill me."

Smart man. "So what's you guys' deal with her?"

"I told you. She's my daughter. The rest of her family and I have been trying to find her for a long time. We're here to collect her."

"*Collect* her?"

"She's a very disturbed young woman. Whatever you are or aren't, I'm not the only reason you're lucky to be alive."

"I know she's disturbed, and I don't care. Well, I *care*, but…you know what I mean."

"I'm afraid so."

"Look, man, you've gotta believe me, I've found something wonderful with your daughter. When I'm with her, I can tell I make her happy, and that feels better than anything I can remember since… I don't know when. Look, I know she's got issues like crazy. I'll tell you straight up, I ain't the world's most well-adjusted motherfucker, either. But since meeting Sally…I feel for the first time I can remember like I can really get past all that, 'cause all of a sudden, I'm with someone who's worth working through it for. I can help her get past all her shit too. I mean we can work through it together, and…" He trailed off. Forfucksake, he was playing the starry-eyed, blithering sap for the guy who'd tied him to a chair. "Look, I know I'd never hurt her, okay?"

"I don't doubt you believe it, which really is too bad. If you two weren't…If the world, if the universe, *if the nature of our existence* were different, you'd be great for each other. I can tell. But with things as they are…Son, there's so much you don't understand. If you press forward, it won't stop with your ruin, or even hers."

"So what the hell are you gonna do with me?"

"I'll have to keep you restrained until I have my daughter back, and my family and I are ready to leave with her. Then I'll decide. You know, it's blasphemy that I've let you live this long. But part of me feels it would be equal blasphemy to destroy something so…unique. In a way, the very state in which you exist—that my daughter's beauty has so properly humbled you—is an affirmation of everything I live and fight for. For that, thank you. If I let you go, I suggest you take this unique chance you've been given."

"What chance?"

"To go on living whatever life you've made for yourself, as a simple young man of this simple world, as you know it. If you've gone this long that way, you still might make something of it without falling to what else is in you."

Rob's eyes were wide and bright, and not because Sally's dad might still decide to kill him. "What about Sally?"

"It's only a matter of time before my wife and I have her back."

"I mean what if she doesn't want to go back with you? Ever think of that, fuckstick? You gonna force your daughter to stay with you against her will?"

"I won't have to. She'll come with us freely. That's how things are with the Spirelights. Our blood binds us to one another. So say the pettier creatures you've lived amongst, no doubt. The Earth-line people have no idea what it really means, *the ties of blood.*"

In the end, Biter-Boy, it's your blood writes the book.

"*No.*" Rob jolted against his bonds. The chair tottered and the cords tightened on his wrists and ribcage. The man flinched, then kept looking at him with condescending sadness. That was just how Rob wanted him to react. While they talked, he'd had a chance to get his mind together. With clarity, there returned that exhilarating certainty. He was also getting a feel for his bonds, how they were woven with the chair. For a while, he'd been feeling out his own weight, mass, flexibility, figuring out how to play these points. The cords were well tied, but not as thoroughly as they could be. Behind his back, his hands were still securely fastened, but the rope had shifted along the chair beams and his hands were now a couple inches farther left. Somehow, he didn't suspect Sally got her brains from Daddy's side of the family. Obviously, the guy wasn't used to holding prisoners, either.

Yeah, Rob's hands were closer to his left pocket, closer to his knife. He bucked again, throwing his ass sideways, twitching his shoulders. The rope crawled on his chest, burning him through his shirt.

"Think it over while you're here. When you see Sally rightfully—willingly—leaving with her family…I'll be watching your face."

You ain't as good at reading people as you think, asshole. You watched me plead. First you raped my mind, just stood around and had a casual little look at my soul. Then you stood and let me show you more of it for nothing. You saw what your daughter's taken over, and you threw it back in my face. You'll bleed for it. I promise.

Once the door closed behind Sally's dad, Rob started working towards his pocket again. If the man still heard the shuffle, hopefully he'd assume it was more futile struggling. If the man caught wise, Rob figured he was fucked. By now, though, he had the ropes pretty well figured. If he could shift, jerk, balance, just right and for long enough, relaxing then working his muscles at all the right moments without tipping over and knocking himself unconscious, he might make it. Before long, his ass hung halfway off the side of the chair. The other half was going numb, and the back of the chair still blocked his right arm from moving much. With one more powerful shift, the chair tilted. He froze up and held his breath, before the two right legs thumped back against the boards.

From the front room, Sally's dad called, "You'll kill yourself bucking around like that."

The rope felt ready to splinter Rob's ribs. He sucked in a deep breath and twisted once more. Almost there…Again, he thrust his shoulders hard to the left. The right one strained, then his body sagged left, down along the rail. The cords were high on his wrists, the skin raw and stretched. His cold fingers flexed violently, willing circulation back through them. He found the edge of his pocket but couldn't get his fingers more than a nail's length inside. He pinched the cloth between thumb and index finger then tugged, pulling out more and more pocket lining. Wow, his face must be turning purple by now. Finally, the butt of the knife brushed his fingertips. After a little more tugging, it tumbled into his numbing palm.

From there, it was relatively easy to pry open the blade and slide it beneath the loop on his right wrist. He sawed fast 'til the rope slithered back and he spilled forward. His feet were still bound, and he tumbled onto his face, smacking his chin, gasping. The chair toppled after him, thudding against his lower calves.

"Rob Coscan? If you've knocked yourself over, I'm not setting you back up. Maybe the floor's knocked some sense into you…Rob Coscan?"

The piece of dog shit's feet thumped towards the room. Rob doubled up to reach the foot ropes. He cut quickly, leaving a light scar on his right boot, then he scuttled away from the chair. The footsteps drew closer. His whole body felt rubbery.

When the knob turned, Rob sprang, caught and held it. The man on the other side cursed. The knob twisted frantically against Rob's grip. As he pulled himself up, the door flung open, sending him staggering. His free hand caught a wall for support. The man entered. For a moment, he only looked on with dull shock. Then the fury on his face mirrored Rob's, and they shot at each other. Rob never knew if Sally's dad saw the knife. He just lifted it with the right timing and let the guy run on it, maybe deliberately, maybe a reflex. Probably a little of both. It didn't matter once the blade punctured cloth and hide, sank through tough meat into the hot, writhing jelly of guts. The man's face bled white, eyes still locked with Rob's. For a moment, Rob's own lower torso tightened. A wet chill formed at his core, lanced on the cold, hard finality of this killing union. Then he glared and yanked the blade free, slitting the wound wider. Now his enemy's face pleaded…futile, desperate pleas, in eyes that had been so smug 'til now. The man's arms convulsed around Rob's neck. Rob's free arm locked around the man's waist like they were dancing. He stabbed again.

"You can't have her back! She's mine!" On the third stab, the knife's edge scraped bone. The arms around Rob's neck tightened, forcing him closer to the shaking, paling, gurgling face, 'til he could feel the prickle of the man's whiskers. *"You hear me?"* He twisted the blade, yanked it sideways. Something slick slithered against his palm's edge. The man quivered worse, and those thick, solid arms weren't loosening. In fact, Rob was dimly aware that it was getting harder to breathe. His neck and ribcage strained like they were ready to go like rotted kindling. Hot dampness spilled over his shirt. He stabbed higher. *"You fucking hear me, asshole?"*

Really, the old bastard seemed more preoccupied with his own mutilated body than family disputes, but he wasn't laying off on Rob either way, like a drowning man bent on pulling his killer to the bottom of the darksome depths with him. Somehow Rob forced his free palm between them, shoved back the guy's chin and gashed the side of the neck. He dragged the blade across so the spray drenched his face and chest. After seconds that seemed like minutes, the legs buckled, but the arms didn't loosen, even when the pumping gouts sputtered weaker and weaker. Rob's spine felt damn near wrenched in two. His knees smacked the floor, and he still couldn't breathe. He couldn't even tell if the pale bulging eyes still saw him.

Finally, he noticed the barest slack around the crooks of the elbows. He hunched, slid out of the grip, took a long, croaking gulp of air, and flung the body back. It hit the doorframe, slumped and lay in the archway, the head half severed, the rent shirt sagging like a hammock beneath a bulge of entrails.

Rob teetered, panted and snarled. Blood trickled between his lips. He licked absently and got a nice, full-body shiver from the unexpected tang. Beyond this moment's sensation, there wasn't much he was aware of…just frenzied flickers of the dream, the marshy red hillside, the glistening temple, the blazing sky…It was the closest he had to a frame of reference. In waking life, he'd never tasted anything like the blood that now ran down his throat, or what it awoke within him. For a while, he was too overwhelmed to move, his senses one great red swirl with a clear pounding light at its center. It drew him inward…*No, not just a light*. The blaze of his kill still pulsed, ever so faintly. No, it wasn't what he saw. The only blaze was *within* him, biting at his innards, screaming for fuel.

Fuel. Yes. That's what it was, what he needed. As far as he was concerned, it was the only reason his victim had ever lived. Dropping to his knees, Rob drove the knife through the dead man's breastbone. The ribcage gave one ripping crack as he twisted, then another as he reached in and tore it wide open. His fingers slipped into the muck, around the still warm heart. It twitched twice against his palm. When he wrenched, it broke from its cables with a groaning pop. When he lifted the heart overhead, sweet rubies splashed on his tongue. He hadn't planned what he did next, couldn't have explained the impulse. It just came naturally. He pressed the heart down against his scalp 'til it burst, then he smeared its juice and pulp through his hair.

Rob stood up and tore open his shirt to smear the gore against his skin. Next thing he knew, he was peeling off his jacket, then yanking his shirt the rest of the way off. He wanted to be naked in his elation, clothed in the spilt life of his kill. The flame had been fed, and by now it felt like it had burned through his every pore and limb. He wanted more, wanted to feed the flame higher 'til he blazed wide enough to consume this whole house.

Yes, more fuel. All of them, fuel! After all, he'd been starving for this his whole life.

"I'm ready," he purred. "Yes, ready. I understand. Let it continue. Let it go on *and on and on and on and on*."

Rob sniffed and caught aromas from all over the house. Somewhere low, in a basement or something, there was more death, but it was old and cold. Even in life, he sensed, it wouldn't have been what he wanted. He sniffed again. Ah, yes, there was more here…a smaller concentration, sure, but so much fresher than the old man. He stalked towards it and found himself at the foot of the stairs. It grew stronger as he climbed. This one would be well and strong, probably wouldn't be caught off guard like the last one. That was exactly what Rob wanted…

Outside, a car sounded in the distance, too close for the road, climbing the hill. Whoever it was, they were too far off even for his newly awakened nose. Some other sense told him on an even clearer level: Yes, it was more of the fuel he wanted, needed, in an even stronger concentration. By comparison, whoever he smelled upstairs seemed weak and uninteresting. He walked back down to wait for the new arrivals.

In the middle of the living room, he stopped and stared at the coffee table. Amidst the papers and decorative trinkets, something shimmered blackly. He walked cautiously towards it. Had that been there a moment ago? Somehow, he knew it didn't belong to his enemies, and it definitely hadn't belonged to the people they'd killed for this house. It was a pair of large knives, encased in hard scabbards, strapped together by a thin black leather belt. The handles were wrapped in black cloth, capped in little silver knobs stamped in a symbol he recognized. *Two curved, vertical slash marks with serrated outer edges, either blades or flames.* Another slash, crescent-shaped, streaked the center.

"*Magur Sevi*," Rob heard himself hiss. Hadn't he also seen the symbol on a champagne bottle somewhere?

To them, we just look like wolves.

Rob still felt the blaze, felt its hunger, but it had narrowed, leaving his brain less frenzied, like maybe it had found a straighter path to its calling. He put his pocketknife back in his jeans. Then respectfully, almost cautiously, he lifted these two new knives by the scabbards, felt his new sense of purpose intensify.

Then he knew the truth, erasing all notion or memory of ignorance. *They're mine. They're here because I made them come.*

Headlights spilled through trees outside. Pressed to the wall by the window, he peered out sideways. The night looked brighter, though there were no more stars than before. It was a taxicab pulling in. The lights weren't on inside, so he couldn't see the passengers. That didn't matter. He already had all the sense of them he needed. His hand curled around one of the knives. The scabbard gave good, sturdy resistance, and the blade slid free with a singing hiss. The metal was black, and Rob could tell it wasn't paint. He couldn't say what kind of metal it was, was pretty sure he'd never seen it before. The blade stretched the length of a small machete, the lower half notched with saw teeth, the upper half curving, sharper than a razor.

He drew the other knife and set the scabbards down reverently. Then he walked out into the center of the room, hands finding the proper grip of their new extensions… which is exactly what they felt like. He was ready to swing, wanted to feel the blades cleave something. Somehow, it seemed he already knew…how that perfect weight would feel against his palms when they cut through the air, then whatever else was in their path. Oh yeah, he remembered that feeling, running up a hillside towards the ancient temple, cleaving and drinking deep. He wanted to feel it now. He could wait by the door, take these new enemies by surprise as they walked in.

No, he'd rather see their faces as he rushed them. Maybe he'd even get a real fight, boil their blood a bit in their own battle joy.

Either way, they'd be surprised to see him.

TWO

Sheldon woke to the sound of the beast roaring downstairs. Then Dad cried out. Before long, the beast's roars assaulted all Sheldon's senses, as though it were on him now. Then this passed, as though the beast had let off something of itself into the fabric of the air, something that flooded the house then drifted on. The chill lingered in Sheldon like a violation. He bolted upright in bed. His head swam, and he remembered Dad backhanding him into the table at the Common Ground.

Now Dad was downstairs fighting the beast. Sheldon had to get down there and help. He still hurt like crazy, and the chill of the beast's projection was still in him, so he felt even more dazed. Straining, he remembered…He'd tossed his clothes near the lower left corner of the bed. In his pants pocket was his knife. When Sissy had told on him, he'd been scared Dad would take away his knife as punishment.

To someone Sheldon's age, the gift of the blade was a symbol of self-reliance, of the first degrees of battle readiness. If you used it unwisely enough to have it confiscated, you were back under the full *care* of your elders and betters, under the *protection* they owed a *child*. Dad hadn't mentioned the knife. Maybe that meant their current danger was so great, they couldn't compromise the team by leaving someone unarmed.

Now that danger was downstairs, roaring at Dad.

Sheldon made it to his knees, inched towards the bed's edge, then spilled and rolled across the floor. The thump of his landing sounded loud, and he was scared the beast would hear. It was still roaring down there, and he couldn't hear Dad yelling or fighting anymore. Sheldon wrestled down his dread and crawled through the darkness. It felt like the beast's roars let off their own floating energy. Sheldon felt colder, nausea filling his gut. Finally, his fingers brushed waxy hemp cloth. When he lifted it, the familiar weight sagged in the pocket. He pulled the pants on quickly, dug out the knife and managed to stand. Now he had to run downstairs fast, help Dad fight the beast. The dark room tilted and swam.

He knew he was close to the door because of the hall light leaking through at the bottom. As his fingers fumbled for the knob, the nausea flared up his throat. Vomit splattered off the door, flecking his legs. His feet slipped out from under him, and his head struck the door, so he fell back into darkness and silence.

THREE

"Mom, what's wrong?" Sissy's words came out swollen and slick, through the caramel snack she'd been munching, but she didn't really have to ask. Mom's self-hypnosis was thinning, reminding her how badly she'd been hurt in that wreck.

The house was in sight through the trees, so Mom would be able to rest soon. Sissy's nose, right eye and cheeks stung. Her limbs felt stretched and crushed. Before, she'd felt bad for Sheldon getting hurt, even though he deserved it. Now, though, she envied him, getting to lie in the dark and sleep through this mess. She really should save some candy for him. He would have had the time of his life tonight. For all Sissy knew, he might even have gotten Sally to cooperate. For now, though, Sissy just wanted to join him in sleep.

The cab driver asked lots of questions about where they came from and what they were up to in town. At one point he mentioned his name was Clyde. Sissy sensed he found them strange, was trying to feel them out, get himself comfortable around them. Sissy had never ridden in a taxi before. Were all cab drivers this nosy?

"You say your husband'll have the money ready?"

"Sure." Mom sounded sleepier. "Park behind the SUV."

"Thought you said you didn't have another set of wheels."

"It's broken down," Sissy volunteered.

They hadn't found car keys on the married couple. In fact, they hadn't thought to search either corpse for much of anything. Probably should have.

FOUR

Clyde watched the mother and daughter walk towards the front door. When the daughter waved goodbye, Clyde smiled and waved back.

Cute kid…Strange, but not as bad as her mom. He glanced in the back. Goddamnit, the brat had left candy wrappers all over the seat. When he looked forward again, he noticed something weirder. When they'd climbed out, it had looked like the mother was pulling the kid along. Now the former was limping, holding on for support. She hadn't been in such bad shape when he'd pulled up at the Shell station. If anything, she'd looked on sight like one high riding bitch, mean-eyed and tight-assed, the kind where you were surprised if her kids didn't march behind her like whipped little drones on an invisible leash. As they neared the door, though, the daughter looked more like the one with all the control, while the mother grew increasingly dependent.

They started through the front door…and froze in their tracks. Instinctively, Clyde's hand slid to the glove box that held his .45. He'd worked as a cabdriver in Boston, where a quarter of the cabbies he knew carried, regulations or no. When he'd moved his family and his trade to Vermont, he'd stopped for a while. After a few of the freaks and junkies that got rides around here, though, he decided a gun wasn't such a bad idea in these parts, either.

In the doorway, it looked like the mother regained her strength quickly, so much so, in fact, that you might call it magic. They both shot forward…and a slender dark shape barreled out of nowhere into them. One lean arm pinned the mother's chest to the door frame. The other caught the kid under the chin and hoisted her skyward.

Clyde hadn't seen the knife get the mother—too quick—but he saw the other blade jut through the top of the daughter's skull. She jerked twice and dangled. The arm bucked as if cracking a whip, and the dripping rag-doll shape flopped on the boards. The other knife wrenched out of the mother, who slid down the wall and toppled sideways next to her daughter. Clyde's fingers fumbled in a panic at the glove box. As the gun fell into his hand, he reached for the door handle. The figure jumped off the porch and ran at the cab, still brandishing those big, ugly, dripping knives.

Clyde had thought there'd be time to get out and hold the guy off—no, fuck holding him off, he was gonna blow that piece of shit away. Except—

Oh, hell no. Impossible, had to be, even if the guy had taken a flying leap from the top step, cleared it by a yard and hit the ground running. *Holy shit, it was a Goddamn werewolf or something.*

One of those knives swung up and caught Clyde's arm, clean at the elbow. The slice didn't hurt like he'd have expected, at least not at first…just a quick sting, like being jabbed by a glass sliver, even when it sheared through bone. Then there went his arm and his gun, bouncing off the cab, thumping in the gravel somewhere. Then the first shock wore off and white-hot pain bloomed. As he opened his mouth to scream, the other blade flashed.

FIVE

The cab driver's head bounced off the hood and rolled in the gravel. Rob's arms fell to his sides, clutching the knives tight. His heart pounded like it wanted to bust through his ribs. There hadn't been time to savor those last two kills. Something had interrupted him.

What was he doing here? Oh, he knew exactly what he'd been doing, and why—*could anything be simpler or more obvious?* He squeezed his eyes shut and tried to think. Where the hell had he been before all this? Oh, that's right…on another mountain, far away. It had been daylight, and he'd run uphill with the pack, his blood on fire with the thirst, so many bodies falling at his feet, the mountain screaming for him and his brothers and sisters to—

No, that had been a dream, long ago in the Old World. In fact, he'd never seen the Old World in his waking life. How many generations of Schomites had passed since anyone had?

Are you Crimbone?

I don't know.

That's what one of the Spirelights had asked, the first one he'd killed, and that's how he'd answered. Had he been humoring the sonofabitch, or had he actually felt uncertain? Either way, he felt almost disgraced, indulging a captor like that. Of course he was Crimbone. He barely remembered what it had been to live without that knowledge, like he'd lived his first twenty-two years imprisoned in some other young man…*just another confused, callow son of this refugee world,* unable to grasp or feel purpose, because someone had hidden his true purpose from him. Now he'd beaten the bastards who'd thought they could keep him in the dark, beaten the enemies they'd thought he needed protecting from.

Rob spotted the headless body, blood still seeping from two stumps, spreading through the gravel towards his feet so the stones got smaller and smaller like tiny islands.

Where the hell had that guy come from? Rob saw the taxi light on the car's roof, and he remembered. He'd been killing Spirelights, drinking the glow, replenishing himself with strength and life. Then he'd smelled someone else in the night, smelled panicked self-righteous malice in their sweat, smelled the metal and oil of the gun before they drew it. One more of those weak, crude, muddy-headed people of this world, the ones who'd held him down, convinced him he had no option but to be one of them, playing by their rules. The man had seen him alive and free, tried to buck him back down like—

To his left lay the severed arm, still clutching the gun. The finger had already slipped through the trigger guard.

I should be back in the house, feasting on my kills. I should be feasting on this one here.

Except no, he shouldn't. Because this man didn't glow, hadn't even in life. He'd died because he'd been stupid enough to intervene. Cold night air licked Rob's naked chest and arms, colder still in the wetness of the kills. Why was he so cold?

Maybe 'cause you're standing outside with no shirt on, up on a New Hampshire mountain at night, and you're drenched in blood, jackass.

A moment ago, though…oh, God, he'd been on fire!

Now the blaze was fading, so some old awareness crept back—that stupid kid, the other Rob Coscan who'd been his shell, his mask for so many years. The motherfucker was trying to make him see the event like some soft-bellied Earth-line twit would, to destroy him with shock and guilt.

Because you just massacred a family. You killed this cab driver, because he saw you do it and reacted like anyone with balls would.

At first, he stood fighting the little bastard, struggling to hold this new awareness, this new certainty, this new *life.*

It was too cold out here. He ran back in, passing between the Spirelight mother and daughter slumped on either side of the doorway. The smell of their fading light was the same, except no longer sweet. Where something had burned and pumped with the fire of life, there lay two dead things, cooling and shitting themselves on the floor, the remains of Sally's family turning the place into a big, polished, richly furnished outhouse.

Sally…Now Rob remembered. He'd been up in his room, fuming…*over a fucking Spirelight.* He'd known it was true from the moment her dad told him. Because he'd seen not just the physical resemblance, but so much more, so much he couldn't before—

Oh, he'd seen it. Yeah, just the other night, when he'd come into his room and she'd pulled her knife.

You didn't follow through, though, did you? Now she's led you into this trap somehow.

Except you know that's not true, right?

More than anything, he wanted to believe it wasn't Sally's fault. She wasn't like her family. Rob still remembered the Spirelight glow, the pull to slaughter and consume…If he ever saw Sally again, would he feel like that towards her?

Was that what he'd felt this whole time, the truth of his maddening need for her, deluded by self-ignorance and social temperance?

He squeezed his eyes closed, shutting out this house of murder, wished he could shut out the smell, the lingering taste. "No, not her…She's not like them."

He looked down at his knives, knives his heritage demanded he use on Sally if he ever saw her again. He almost wanted to cast them away, but he found he could no more stand that idea than the notion of using them on his love.

What was going on with him? His whole life, he'd never given a damn about heritage or traditions or the prejudices they demanded. Far as he'd cared, you were no more, no less than what you'd made of yourself, from whatever the world had dumped on you to work with, what it had taught you along the way, and that's what your views and decisions should rely on. Towards people who needed their race, class, or other incidental social trappings to feel proud or sure, Rob knew only contempt. What good were you, if you couldn't figure out your own nature or worth without looking back to bullshit you'd had nothing to do with? So now what, he'd gotten a few surprises about himself, and he was thinking like another drone? He barely knew what a Crimbone was, except that it was a particularly nasty breed of Schomite, which he knew even less about. He knew less still about Spirelights.

Sure I know. Spirelights come to keep Schomites in their place or kill them, and Crimbone kill Spirelights and grow strong from their life essence.

"It doesn't matter." He opened his eyes. "I'm still Rob

Coscan. I just know what Rob Coscan is now." Yeah, and whatever Rob Coscan was, whatever Sally Wildfire was, they'd been the ones who'd found each other, who'd chosen each other.

Yeah, sure. Except you just murdered her whole family.

Fuck that. They'd tried to take her away, tried to kill him. They'd killed this house's owners, and God knew how many others. They hadn't managed to kill him, though. So now Sally had him instead of them. If his own people, his own heritage, tried to deny what was between them, he'd fight all that too.

Rob looked around the living room. Hadn't there been someone else, the scent of another Spirelight in the house? If so, he couldn't smell it through all the death. Besides, if there were more Spirelights, they'd have shown themselves by now, right? Sooner or later someone would come, either the cab company tracing their missing driver, or someone who knew the original tenants… maybe more Spirelights. If they found him here, he'd be fucked. That, or he'd fight. There'd be nothing but more fighting and killing 'til someone took him down, no future for him and Sally even if there still was now.

Rob found his jacket. The blood on his skin had hardened to moist clumps and patches. The coat would keep him warm enough, so long as he kept his limbs in motion 'til he was back indoors, someplace safer than this. There might not be time to clean up completely, so he splashed the excess gore from his face and hands at the kitchen sink. His dark jeans more or less hid what had splattered there. Still, he'd better cut through the woods to get home. At the other end of town, there was another bridge leading back over the river, close to South Main. By now, it was late, close to one in the morning. He could slip across easy enough in the dark, then he'd cut through more woods.

Rob pulled off his old belt and put on the one that had come with the scabbards. Somewhere on the way, he'd get rid of the old belt and the ruined shirt. Once home, he'd have to keep the coat closed while in the light. Some of the blood would still show. If he ran into any of his housemates, he'd say he'd been in another fight. He'd figure everything else out from there.

He skidded to a stop before the mother and daughter lying in the doorway. *Sally's mother, Sally's little sister.* When they'd stepped inside, he'd stared in shock. Just a lady and a kid, and they'd obviously been just as surprised to see him. Then they'd rushed him, sliding gracefully into the unmistakable body language of practiced killers, and their glow had overridden all other sensations.

Rob's right arm ached. When he'd skewered the mother, he'd felt the blade puncture the door frame behind her. He hadn't known how deep it had stuck 'til he'd wrenched it free. Now that they didn't glow as fuel, he really saw their faces. One was Sally years younger, features softer and more innocent, the flesh around the eyes not so sunken and dark. The other was Sally years ahead, her face tightened and roughened with more strife.

Meet your future mother-in-law, see how your girl'll look in twenty years, went some saying, or something like that. Sally in twenty years looked like a gutted corpse shitting itself. Both bodies slumped like limp sentinels, flanking a path back that had closed to him. Rob almost turned away, but he made himself keep looking.

"Neither of you are her. You never could've appreciated who she is, and now you can't take it away from her. She's better than you ever would've been, little bitch, and she's better than you deserve the honor of having pushed out of your crotch, old bitch."

Rob darted out and headed for the trees. The forest drew him in, and he felt its assurance of safe passage.

RUNNING BLIND

ONE

She tried to sit up, fell back.

"I wouldn't if I were you. You're in pretty horrible shape." The Crimbone's voice was a deep gravel rasp.

Sally's head fell to the side. Her vision rolled around the motel room. She guessed she'd expected to die on Main Street, but she frankly hadn't had enough energy left to be too scared. She sure was now, though. Her head was bandaged, along with a few injuries she hadn't noticed before. Lights dimmed and rose like someone was playing with a dial-knob lamp, and everything had a weird purplish tint. From the bed's edge, the Crimbone regarded her curiously. His tiny pale eyes weren't cruel. If anything, they were thoughtful, but they definitely let you know not to fuck with him. The narrow face and pointed nose seemed unnervingly out of place, atop possibly the thickest, hardest shoulders and chest she'd ever seen. What such a sharp, assessing brain could do with all that brute strength and raw ferocity, she didn't want to know. He was bald except for his gray goatee. A web of scars braided half his tree-trunk neck.

"Why are you doing this?"

"What, saving your ass?"

"Yeah, pretty much."

"For starters, you aren't a threat, and I don't think you're with the people who are."

"I don't want to be with them…I hope you kill them all." Those words tasted harsh. Hours ago, she couldn't have been more certain of anything.

"That why you asked to bargain for your life?"

"I tried that?"

"Yeah. Did you think to lead me to them?"

"Probably. I can't remember saying that."

"Can you still lead me to them?"

"I might…Can't think straight right now…Ask me later."

"Who are they?"

"My family."

Had he just winced? "But you *are* a Spirelight."

That wouldn't be a question, but she answered, "I don't know."

"Are your parents Spirelights?"

"Yeah."

"That'd make you one, then, wouldn't it now? It doesn't automatically mean I'll kill you. About that, though, you're lucky you ran into this particular Crimbone."

"Am I?"

He rolled his eyes. "No, I don't plan to rape or torture you, either."

"You're looking for Rob?"

"If you mean Rob Coscan, then yeah."

"Why?"

"He's a Crimbone fledgling who's just made his First Call. Word goes, he's already close to his Second Call. I have reason to think he's about to land himself deep in a world of shit in the process."

*Rob, a Crimbone…Rob, in deep shit…*Sally let out a muted sob, not sure which notion was worse. She almost spoke, but she drifted in and out.

"Hey, you there. None of that shit." The Crimbone tapped her forehead hard with one finger, like he was beating one letter on an old typewriter over and over. "I say you could sleep yet?"

"Where's Rob?"

"I hoped you'd know. What's your story with him?"

She shut her eyes again and made another soft sound.

"*Shit*…Okay, then. Gotta hand it to you, I didn't see that one coming. What's your name?"

"Sally…Sally Wildfire…"

"Wildfire? As in Syless and Ella Wildfire's daughter?"

Her eyes snapped wide. "How'd you know that?"

"I like to keep up with who's who on both sides. Don't blame you for wanting 'em dead."

Her eyes closed again. "Yeah, well, you're Crimbone."

"I was taking that into account. If half of what I've heard about those assholes is true, I still don't blame you, their daughter or no. Sally, my name's Jesse."

"Hi, Jesse. Are you gonna protect Rob?"

"Gonna try. Listen, you've got some heavy drugs in your system. Crimbone medicine. Once it wears off a little, let's see if we have anything more useful to say to each other."

Crimbone chemicals in her body…Sally might have panicked if she'd had the energy. Then she remembered, this man said Rob was one of them after all. Sally tried not to let her thoughts go there. Instead she hugged herself, wishing she were hugging Rob, chasing the other craziness away. She wanted Rob here kissing her, so she could taste and feel that he wasn't one of the Schomite's monsters. What if she held and kissed Rob again, and she felt and tasted the truth of Jesse's words? Hadn't she already sensed, hell, known it, tried to deny it?

"Sally?" It was Jesse.

"Can I go back to sleep yet?"

"If you're able to, sure. I'm gonna make a phone call now."

Sally hugged herself tighter and lay quiet. The Crimbone was dialing a number on the motel room's phone. Why didn't he use a cell? Oh right, same reason she'd never carried one on the road, aside from having no way to pay for it. The Crimbone didn't leave electronic trails like that, hadn't dumped so many resources into buying off the Earth-line communication networks like the Spirelight Secret Police had. No, the Crimbone just devalued the investment, by keeping their movements *off* such networks. So Sally had never really made it off the Spirelight grid. She sure as hell had now, because she was right smack in the middle of the Crimbone's.

Two

When Jesse called the Barre office, a very sharp voice said, "Hello? What the hell's going on?"

"Byron?"

"Jesse! Are you in Brattleboro?"

"Is Zane there?"

"We don't have time for your bullshit, Jess. There's a giant fucking crater where a third of the building used to be."

Had Byron said *crater?* Jesse rubbed his temples. "So whose cock-up can we thank for this?"

"I repeat, are you in Brattleboro?" Jesse heard Byron talking through clenched teeth, imagined sweat saturating the scarred yellow face and bleach-white dreadlocks. "What the hell have you been doing with that damn fledgling?"

"Now why would you wanna know so bad about that?"

"The kid made his Second Call an hour ago. The chapel's not there anymore. Neither are the rest of the caverns for a mile around. The astral draw caved them in, and it took the chapel office into the ground with it."

"Whatever it was, I guarantee you, it wasn't anyone's Second Call. Seriously—"

"I know what that kind of astral draw feels like. Fire alarms are still going off all over town. What's left of our building is still vibrating. We don't have a damage report yet on structural damage to Earth-line property."

"What about Earth-line civilian casualties?"

"Fuck those assholes! It's enough of a bitch keeping the wool over their eyes without 'em coming knocking, whining about how we're disrupting their happy horseshit tourist-trap town. You got any idea what it'll take to smooth this one over with their authorities?"

Guess it's time to take your teeth out and gum it some more, bear-fucker. Yeah, Jesse heard that reverberation echoing up through the line. "How the hell does this happen?"

"What, you don't know?"

"I haven't found the boy yet."

"Then you *are* in Brattleboro."

Sometimes Jesse wondered if Byron was really of the Crimbone line, if there hadn't been some mistake. If he hadn't seen how the man moved through hot situations, he might have looked into it. "Yeah. So the kid made his First Call three nights ago, and now you're saying he's already made the Second Call and it caved in the chapel."

"Not to mention we're short a third of the building."

"Whatever. My point is, the kid's going at a speed you and I have only read about, there's only one explanation I've ever heard of, and I haven't managed to find him yet. Oh, and just to calm your nerves a little more, his Familiar is Puttergong."

"I think I'm starting to piece it together."

"With my luck, one of you idiots has already gone and blabbed to the Cabinet, and now I've got goons on the way to deal with, on top of everything else."

"No, we've been too busy with local Earth-line cops and reporters. Lucky you. Now find the fucking kid."

"Let me talk to Zane."

"We can't find him. We think he might have been in the building when…"

"Fine. Whenever you drag the bastard out of the rubble, shove a phone in his hand and have him call me."

"Okay, so what's the number we can reach you at?"

"You know, on second thought, fuck it, I'll call you back when I've got the kid."

Jesse hung up. He didn't need Byron working his nerves, not while he was alone with a Spirelight glow he'd consciously decided not to drink. His nerves were already twisted aplenty, just from prying halfway decent communication out of the little bitch.

She muttered, "Rob's in deeper shit than you thought?"

"Yeah, and if I don't find him quick, I'm in even deeper shit. Could be we all are."

"You'll bring him back here, right?"

From the doorway, he looked back at her. She'd sat up, staring with the bright, wide, stoned eyes of a silly kid in love. Spirelight or not, Jesse couldn't hold his guard against it. "Yeah. If you ever want to see him again, stay put." He locked the door and headed for the van.

THREE

Rob made plenty of noise at first, trampling through underbrush, over rocks and low hills, along sloping forest trails. Then he noticed his own racket and moved more quietly. He'd mastered the skill during a childhood surrounded by wilderness, but he'd fallen out of practice. It didn't take long to pick it back up. Crouched low, he followed the sound of the river downhill. He took a flying leap from one rocky embankment, caught another one yards out, pulled himself up, and found his stride again almost instantly. Damn, he'd kept in pretty good shape, but when had he gotten this well off? Below, through the trees ahead, he spotted a narrow dirt road. Yeah, the bridge was close.

"Aw, maaan, Biter-Boy, what you gone an' done back there…*That was fuckin' great!* Knew you had it in ye. What I tell you? Natural Born Spirelight-Killer, all the way!" Puttergong perched on a rock, at eye-level two yards away.

At first Rob was too bewildered to answer. Then he remembered how he'd found his way to that house. "You lying little sack of shit, get out of here. I'm through trusting you."

"I'm the only one you s'posed to be trustin' right now, Biter-Boy! Jus' look at what I brung out in ye. You ain't gone to that house, you'd still be sittin' around with your thumb up your ass, wondering *where oh where did yer little Sally-Bitch go*, waitin' for them Spirelights to come pick up your head."

"What did you do to Sally, birdie?"

"Nothin'! I keep tellin' you, that's your job. 'Sides, weren't you listenin' to nothin' her daddy said? Biter-Boy, all I told you was what you needed to hear to get you off your ass. Weren't one damn thing you done with it that weren't *all you!* Now forget that fuckin' Poach-Girl. Mark my words, whenever you set eyes on her again, all woken up to what ye really are, to the world ahead you're here to help carve out…heh, only way you'll wanna eat that pussy again is so's you can chew your way through to her—"

Rob would never be sure why he didn't go for his new blades. Instead, he sprang roaring, arms out. Puttergong squawked and started for the air. The thing didn't get high, because Rob caught hold. Wings smacked his arms hard enough to bruise, but he held fast. Shit, those wings were broader and thicker than he'd thought. The thing must be growing fast. Even at its new size, how the hell was it this strong?

"Fuckin' punk-kid Biter-Boy fledgling gonna beef with the

Familiar? Boy, you ain't shit yet! You ain't shit that fights a Familiar! Biter-Boy, I show you what ye fuckin' with!"

As Puttergong barreled forward, Rob held fast, yanking to rip the wings off. They kept beating, and the leathery, bulbous body kept buffeting his face. Brush and branches tore at his back, the sloping earth and rocks dragging and spraying around his boots. Then he didn't feel the earth at all, just the beat of wings and the wind at his back, along with the smack and scrape of higher, thicker branches. Then cold air off the river blew through his clothes.

Puttergong's haunches kicked up, talons shredding Rob's jacket, raking his bare chest. One claw nicked his chin, snapping his head back as twin razors sliced all the way to his forehead. Two clean lines split through his cheek, and blood stung his left eye—or had the talons caught him there, too? Then he didn't feel any of that, because he no longer gripped Puttergong's wings. There was only the upward rush of wind as he plummeted downward. The splash felt like smashing through a smooth diamond surface.

Icy water sucked him deep and held his limbs, pulling him lower, lower, lower. It filled his nose like ice trying to eat his brain, but he kept beating against it towards the surface. His limbs were like hard beams of pure cold, pure pain…so he made that pain his energy. His jacket slowed him down, had shrunk tight around his arms and chest, so he fought his way out of it. The coat slid off into the current.

Then Rob's head was above water and blood was filling his face again. Water spilled into his mouth, through his ragged cheek. His good eye saw the shore, the bank of the island in the middle of the river. He swam for it, beating the water like it was one great enemy. Beyond that, there were no thoughts, just freezing pain and fighting, with no real notion left that either would ever end.

FOUR

Puttergong soars out over that big ol' river. Yep, Biter-Boy's off to a great start. Them boys back at the Crimbone office is probably pissed as all hell, but fuck 'em. Puttergong's got a feelin' about where Biter-Boy's headed. Once the Crimbone see it, they won't have much choice but to give Puttergong the biggest ass-kissin' thank you this side of the Great Black Ocean.

Right now, he'd love to stick around, watch what Biter-Boy does next. Instead, he flies back to the house in the woods, to the cop-kid Biter-Boy missed. Landin' in a tree across the paved stretch from the house, Puttergong listens, watches an' waits. This don't gotta be a setback…nor even a loose end. Nah, just be one more chance for Biter-Boy to work out them new blades. With the idea Puttergong's stirrin', it might be a way to knock Biter-Boy a few notches higher. That's assumin' he don't decide to splatter Sally-Poach after all. Honestly, at this point, Puttergong kinda doubts it.

Inside, right on cue, the last little cop-kid's just wakin' up. Puttergong's strong enough by now to smell the risin' fear, even smell a few thoughts. That cop-kid, he don't realize it was Biter-Boy's Second Call that knocked his ass back out. Nah, he figures himself for a little pussy who couldn't keep it together jus' 'cause his daddy knocked his brains halfway out of his skull earlier, or somethin'. By now, his head still hurts like a bitch, and he don't realize how long he's been out, still figures he'd better get downstairs quick, help his daddy fight that mean ol' Biter-Boy.

Now the cop-kid's gettin' a big ol' eyeful of the mess Biter-Boy made. Here comes the part where the little snot starts losin' his shit, thinkin', *oh why, oh why couldn't he get down in time, an' now it's too late, and he's all alone, an' it's all his damn little fault, an' blah-blah-blah.*

So, Puttergong sits real quiet in the tree 'til the kid comes runnin' out. Sure enough, there's that little knife out, ready to do some stabbin' an' guttin'. Then the cop-kid sees that there headless taxi-man an' he's flipped out an' confused all over again.

"Well I'll bet you feel pretty stupid right about now, little Cop-Boy." Puttergong lets off a big ol' wheezin' laugh. He waits for the cop-kid to look around frantically, makes sure Cop-Boy don't actually spot him.

"Where is he? Where's your beast?" Cop-Boy's eyes is all big an' bright with tears, and his voice cracks every other word. His body don't shake, though, and Puttergong knows he can see clear and fine as ever through them tears. He'll have 'em out of his system before he finds his next fight. If the fight finds him first…well, it probably won't make him any less of a deadly little pain in the ass.

"*My* beast, huh?"

"I know what you are, you cowardly Familiar." The cop-kid lifts the knife like he still expects to spot Puttergong any second. On the off chance he does, Puttergong'll have to hightail it. He knows better than to think a Spirelight cop-kid can't throw a knife that far or high or straight if it really, really wants to. "Go tell your beast he missed one. Tell him there's still one Spirelight alive back here, and this one's ready!"

Puttergong glides left, settles several trees over. Down there, the cop-kid's eyes ain't moved, ain't spotted shit. "Ready for Biter-Boy, huh. Hell, maybe so. But ye think you're ready for who's got his back?"

"There's more than one beast? Fine. Bring 'em both on."

"Ain't no beasts in this town but mine, Cop-Boy. Jus' you go back in there, though, have a look at the carcasses of yer sister an' mamma, you'll notice he didn't do it alone."

Cop-Boy freezes and stares. His eyes don't fall anywhere near Puttergong, but Puttergong still takes the silent stretch to glide to another branch.

"Tha's right. See, you dumbass Spirelights, you came waltzin' on into town, thinkin' you was gonna be all badass, just snatch your little prodigal back up like some lost baggage. But your prodigal don't want ye no more. Matter of fact, she hates your fuckin' guts, and she's figured out she got her a big ol' itch for beast dick."

"Shut up! Get out of here!"

Puttergong cackles. "Tha's right, you little shit. Right this second, your sweet ol' big sister's celebratin' the slaughter of your mamma, daddy, and little sister, that she don't need to worry about you dorks tailin' after her no more. Wanna know how she's celebratin'? By hunkerin' down on a big ol' beast bow-bow, that's how!"

"No! Shut up! Get lost or come out where I can see you. Bring your beast with you."

"Right now, my beast's busy makin' the Biter-Boy with Two Backs, and that other back is your sweet ol' sister. Don't believe me, Cop-Boy? Well, soon as yer done blubberin', go back in and have a look at the carcasses of your mamma and other sister. Oh sure, that's my beast's blade finished 'em off, but I reckon you'll spot all kinds of other bashes and bruises all over 'em. I think you'll agree, them bashes and bruises ain't no Crimbone's doin'. Fact, I think you'll see them wounds come from the same kinds of punches an' kicks you been trained to throw. Better yet, take a good look at them slices all over your daddy's carcass, an' see if they look like somethin' a beast's blade did. Then next time we meet up, tell me I'm lyin'. That's if you don't run into my beast or your sister first."

Before Cop-Boy gets done gapin' like an idiot, Puttergong's long gone.

FIVE

Jesse would rather have gone on foot, but suspected he'd return with cargo. As he drove, he cracked the window slightly to let in more of the area's sounds, smells and tastes on the air. Then he left the van, his body and the road to each other like three distant, synchronized mechanisms, and let the deeper sensations soak through his brain. He asked the spirit of Brattleboro to embrace his presence and purpose. A high gust pulled brittle straggling leaves from branches, pattering the van's windows. The skittering hitches in the debris's rhythm—which didn't match the low, steady whistle of the wind propelling it—reminded him how his kind and their enemies had disrupted this land's tranquility.

"Before I leave," he told it, "I'll do all I can to repair that disruption."

The wind made a strange downturn, pressing a moan from the roof. A few night birds flew too low and close, barely careening out of the windshield's way. Did he understand this burden, that of carrying away such potentially catastrophic sin on his back?

"Yes," he answered.

The wind picked up against the van, nudging him towards the turns he needed to take. These were always clear. Whenever he eyed what looked like a shortcut, traffic blocked it. At the end of Canal Street, he took the bridge across the Connecticut River. Halfway over the island, a skunk ran out in front of him. He swerved, barely missed the guardrail, and his wheels groaned through mud. He sighed and shifted into park. The mud was nothing the van couldn't handle, but it got his attention. He climbed out, stepped over the guardrail and looked out over the water. Splashes sounded. Through the trees, the surface rippled. Jesse followed a bare ditch between clumps of tall grass, hoping there weren't more skunks—Brattleboro's little way of letting him *carry away some sin.*

Ten yards out, someone kicked and thrashed against heavy undertow. Finally, the swimmer reached the bank. Two long arms shot up, fingers clawing through sand. Jesse almost reached to help. Then from beneath the waves came those same two knives he'd seen on the altar, now strapped to the kid's slender waist. Half the kid's head was a dark shimmer. For a second, it looked like a fair chunk of his face had been ripped clean off. Then the water streaming from his hair carried away some blood, revealing the wounds. Yeah, that looked like it hurt.

The kid fell on his side in the sand, gasping, snorting river water out of his nose. As Jesse knelt, the kid bolted upright and almost fell back in the water. When Jesse caught him, his hand went for one of those knives. Jesse punched him in the solar plexus, let him double up gagging again as the air left him, then hoisted him coughing and contorting over his shoulder. Then he hauled him up to the van and tossed him across the back. Jesse swiftly pulled both knives from the scabbards and set them out of the kid's reach.

"Give those back," the kid rasped, starting to sit up.

Jesse grabbed him by the throat and held him down. "I'm here to help you. If you make me punch you again, I'll knock the other half of your face off."

"How the fuck—*Ah!*" The kid's hand shot to his mangled cheek. His fingers winced back from the wounds, then lingered shaking over the spot. Watery blood pooled onto the floor next to his face, a fresh stain to mingle with older, faded ones.

Once he was sure the kid had stopped trying to fight, Jesse leaned into the front and turned the heater up. He'd heard quite a bit about Rob Coscan over the years. 'Til months ago, he'd been bracing himself for times like this, though not with Rob. Now the weirdness of the whole mess hit like a sack of bricks.

Rob shivered horridly but his head seemed more together. "How bad is it?" he mumbled through the right side of his mouth.

"Pretty nasty. Probably not as bad as you think."

"So half my face isn't dangling off?"

Jesse switched on the overhead light. "Move your hand." He caught Rob's wrist and guided it away. "Okay, yeah, you more or less do."

"Fuck."

"Might wanna talk less 'til we get that bleeding under control."

Jesse sniffed and realized that not all the blood was Rob's. The river had washed most of it away, but there were still smeared, clotted traces of someone else. Some of it was Spirelight blood, but not all of it. A little of it was Earth-line blood. Jesse reached for the medical kit. For the second time tonight, here he was patching up some wounded, incoherent kid who'd just tried to stab him. This was starting to feel like babysitting.

"Got a blanket in here or anything? I'm fuckin' freezing."

"Welcome to the Crimbone life." That shut the little bastard up, thank the Old Lords. "Don't worry, the van's warming up."

Jesse saturated a sterile cloth with disinfectant, started cleaning Rob's wounds. Rob winced, then gritted his teeth and held still. If the kid meant to impress Jesse, it worked, considering this disinfectant stung a lot worse than any Rob had likely felt. Jesse had chemically manufactured it personally to make over-the-counter rubbing alcohol seem like watery lotion. Not that it mattered. Obviously, Rob had done plenty of impressive things tonight…too many for his own good, in fact.

Soon the first cloth was deep red. As Jesse reached for

another, Rob said, "Then you're Crimbone too."

Jesse nodded.

"*Magur Sevi…*"

"Thanks, I think," Jesse chuckled, "but not quite." It was actually pretty strange that Rob knew the name, and more than a little unsettling. "I'm Jesse."

"So what happens now?"

"First off, I stitch your wounds. Before you ask, no, you don't get any painkillers."

Rob held still for the needle even better than he had for the disinfectant. Jesse sewed the stitches tight, then covered half the face in gauze bandages. The chest wounds weren't deep enough for stitches, by Crimbone standards. After that, Jesse drove the rest of the way over the river and parked in an empty lot across from a Wal-Mart. He'd cleaned off what was left of the spilt Spirelight blood, but still smelled it in Rob's hair. He'd have known it was heart's blood even if the smell hadn't told him so. How had the kid known to—

High Natural.

Hold on, don't jump to conclusions.

He made his First and Second Call within three nights of each other. The Second Call totaled a building. Then there are the blades he was sent—two blades. Any other theories?

Rob leaned against the side near the back. "What are we doing here?" He sounded almost mellow. The blood loss probably had something to do with it.

Jesse let the engine run and put some old blues tunes on the 8-track player. "We're gonna sit and talk a while. Then we'll go somewhere else."

"And do what?"

"Probably talk some more."

"Where?" Rob leaned forward. "With the rest of our kind?"

The question sounded loaded…because Rob *hadn't* thrown out the answer he was fishing for. Had he smelled Sally Wildfire on Jesse? "*Our kind*, huh? Well aren't you getting pretty enthusiastic pretty quick."

"Look, sorry I almost pulled my knives on you back there. I thought you were another one of them."

"Spirelights."

"I killed three of them…What? Isn't that what I'm supposed to do?"

Jesse had to answer carefully. "You're doing great. Congratulations. You've survived the easy part."

"How do you know who I am?"

"We keep track of our own."

"So you know about my dad. You know how he never told me about any of this. I've spent my whole fucking life 'til tonight just—"

"We'll talk about your dad later. First, tell me what you do know."

Rob told Jesse everything that had happened tonight, except about Sally. Listening, it was easy to figure where she fit into things. Even if Jesse hadn't known about her, he could have driven the van through the holes in the story. Rob still snarled out the tale with so much infectious energy that most listeners wouldn't pause to spot the gaps, at least 'til they reflected on it later. If he wasn't the High Natural— or hell, why not, maybe even if he was—he likely had a future as a Crimbone Poet. There hadn't been a proper one of those for a while, either.

That didn't explain the big question. Namely, why had

Rob fallen for Sally instead of killing her? It wasn't for lack of a Crimbone's predatory instincts, that was for damn sure. Jesse had a guess, which in itself still hadn't been explained. Sally's tainted glow, something different about her from other Spirelights…It sounded like Puttergong had used the whole mess to spur Rob up that mountain. Was the critter trying to get his fledgling killed? The kid had all the natural moxie and skill you could ask for in a fledgling, but half his victory tonight sounded like dumb fucking luck.

As Rob described the fight with the Spirelights, Jesse sniffed and his frown deepened. The kid never mentioned where those traces of Earth-line blood had come from. Jesse let it alone, reminding himself it was the least of their problems. Rob suppressed what little guilt he felt at killing, like another thing he assumed was expected of him. If *this* fledgling took that line of thought too far…

"What?" Rob asked, leaning forward.

"Nothing. So you got pissed and attacked your Familiar, huh?"

"Yeah, and the fucker—"

Jesse patted his own scarred neck. Rob stared, did the math, then laughed weakly. Then he winced again, and the humor bled out of his face.

"Mess with the Familiar, you get the talons," said Jesse. "Or something like that. You were right to be pissed at it, though. Your Crimbone nature is coming into its own at unheard of speed, and your Familiar's leading you into things too fast even for that."

"Yeah, and it's lied to me left and right."

"That's not the problem. Your Familiar's job is to lead you to the steps you need to reach. How it does that is its own business. But its job is also to make sure you're ready for those steps first. Do you even know about the Three Calls?"

"Puttergong mentioned something…Yeah, it said it came because I made my First Call."

"The First Call is when your blood's intent moves you forward, tells your natural surroundings that you're on your way into Crimbone adulthood. It's that natural world that brings you your Familiar, from some realm between the physical and the ephemeral." According to both science and lore, the natural world made no accidents in pairing fledglings with Familiars. "It happens late in the maturation process. Your instincts were triggered by the approach of our natural enemies."

"The Spirelights. They're the reason we had to leave the Old World."

"According to some versions. Did Puttergong tell you about the Second Call?"

"It told me I'd call my weapons to me when I needed them. You've seen my weapons." Rob pointed to the knives, his fingertip lingering lovingly.

"That's all Puttergong told you, though."

"What else was there to tell? The blades found me, and I used them."

"Yeah. Was that the first time you used a blade as a weapon?"

"I've done fencing and a lot of other martial arts. A couple of my old Senseis decided to train me some on Kendo. Does that count?"

There the kid went, leaving more out. "What else?"

"What, sports? I'm a pretty good little boxer, and I ain't

a bad grappler, if that—"

Jesse couldn't help smiling. "Last time I sat down to watch a match, they didn't let blades into the ring."

"Right. I grew up around thick woods. I cut a lot of trails with a machete."

"But you never used it as a weapon."

Maybe Rob started to say something. Then he squeezed his uncovered eye shut and rubbed at his forehead. When he opened his eye, something had changed. Trance-like, he picked up one of his new knives. Jesse almost moved to stop him, then sat back to watch. Rob held it close to his face. "Not in Virginia…not in my childhood there. I remember mountains…a temple…We slaughtered and feasted, and the mountain gave the Spirelights to us, guiding us to the gates." His eyes darted up, asking, *Don't you remember that glorious day, Jesse?*

Jesse didn't speak. The day Rob spoke of was in no living memory, except maybe the oldest Familiars. It was unlikely that any Familiar had witnessed the battle, unless the ways in the Old World had been even more different than the records suggested. Then again, that day had been the beginning of an end, a victory that had only seemed glorious 'til the celebrations were over. Much before it was unknown. Had a High Natural been there?

When Rob's strange gaze faded, he looked confused. He stared at the blade, then set it down as if scared of it. "Puttergong said…I should have grown up knowing about it, but still cut off."

"The custom of this world is for those born of the Crimbone line to grow to adolescence in the care of their birth families. They're taught the Schomite history—the art, the medicine, how these things have quietly affected that of the Earth-line cultures around the world, and what we've learned from them, despite themselves…everything but that of our own line, the Crimbone line. They know the basic nature of their purpose, but nothing of the trials they'll face. It's usually at age twelve or thirteen when they're taken from their parents' care and cast to this world until the First Call."

"Huh. Sweet treatment."

"A fledgling's trials must be by true fire. If there's one thing we've learned to count on about fledglings, you always find your way to the fire. Sometimes it's in the Earth-line military, sometimes urban street gangs. Hell, half the time these days, all it takes is the system they're put through as wards of the state. That or you end up as wanderers…let me guess, always just happening to stop for rest in the nastiest shithole imaginable, like you're seeking out spots where you'll have to learn what it is to fight for your life."

"What can I say?" said Rob. "I always found the best freaky pussy in those spots."

Once Jesse managed to stop laughing, he said, "It's also where you learn something else…that sense of where you're fighting, how to flow with its energies and signals, something you rely on other than your wits and physical skills, consciously or not. Anyway, yeah, that's how we know who's worthy. Who survives the trials they put themselves through."

Rob peered hard. "My dad didn't give me over to this world. I gave myself over to it."

"So, why'd you do that?"

"I just got sick of being raised like a caged rat, like a kid of this world—what did you call it? Earth-line? I got fed up being protected from the world, so I took off into it. What was I supposed to do?"

"That's your reason for abandoning your family, forcing yourself to grow up so fast?"

"Pretty much."

"There's nothing wrong in how you felt or what you did." *Except maybe whatever else you've left out.* "It's all to your credit, really. Here's the thing, though. You figured out your dad was hiding something from you, like he was protecting you from something you couldn't see…"

"Well obviously 'cause he pussied out of the game. I bet he used to be a badass like you, right? He squirmed out of it, that's his business, *but not to deny me my birthright.*"

"For a guy in your unique position, you're latching onto all that *birthright* bullshit pretty damn quick."

"It feels right, more than anything ever has. It feels true…*pure.*"

"It's simple, you mean. To fight and kill and conquer like a wild animal, to know absolutely that a friend is a friend and an enemy is an enemy, like knowing your hands from your feet, sure as a wolf in the wild spotting a deer and recognizing a tasty meal. That's pretty much all you've seen of all this so far. Earth-line culture—sometimes its most fundamental norms by which you're expected to abide—has never made sense to you deep down, so you spend your spare time thinking about everything you see, trying to make heads or tails of their ways, even though you've been handed all the same answers the rest of them get by with, from grade school civics class on. When you use those blades, when you taste the glow, all of that goes away."

"So you gonna try talking me out of it?"

"No, but think about this. You just got the ball dropped on you tonight. In the big scheme of things, you know dick. You're a blaze of newly woken instincts, but do you have any idea what they're really for? Whatever fire you've put yourself through, all it's accomplished for anyone is letting you know you can get through it, without stopping to think about whatever mess you've left along the way, so long as you don't get caught. You don't know what it is to fight your way through a fire for a true purpose. Do you have any idea what purpose is? Do you know anything about the ways of your people—not just the Crimbone line, but the rest of the Schomites? No. Other than your thirst for the glow, what could you possibly have against the Spirelights at this point? You do know of Deschemb, right?"

"The Old World…"

"Right. So think about this. Maybe your dad chose what he did because he saw two worlds: the one he was part of—the one he'd fought for all his life—and the one inhabited by the native people of this world. Maybe he'd seen the worst of one and the best of the other, and that's how he decided what kind of life he wanted for his family."

"You know, you're talking a lot like that Spirelight who tied me to a chair."

"How's that?"

"He told me to go back to living like another stooge, that I should—*Ah!*"

"Cool down, kid. You rip those stitches, you're gonna have to put 'em back yourself."

Rob nodded and settled down.

"So a Spirelight gave you a chance to live."

"I'm pretty sure he was just fucking with me."

"Probably, but why would he even bother with that? Why not just kill you outright?"

"I don't know."

"Sure you do. You're so eager to jump into this new life…except you're already planning your own agenda, assuming you can make it work with whatever comes next."

It took Rob a moment. Then he stared.

"No need to bullshit me. Think I ain't been watching the wheels turn in your head, waiting for the chance to slip away to find who you want? Don't say anything else now. Just climb up front."

"Where we going?"

"Back to the motel room I'm staying in. We're gonna find out how committed you are to this birthright and freedom and purity premise. Oh, and don't forget your knives."

SIX

Sally kept starting to fall asleep. Then she'd slip towards dreams of New Orleans, of Talino. So she kept herself awake, first trying to watch TV, then getting up and pacing. She was still dizzy, but she kept on her feet now. Maybe the Crimbone drugs were wearing off, or she might be adjusting to them.

When the lock turned and Rob stumbled in, she thought she was hallucinating. Half his face was covered in white gauze and medical tape. Bruises speckled the uncovered side. There were some smaller bandages on his chest. What had he gotten himself into? Why was he shirtless, and why did it look like he'd gone swimming in his jeans? She almost ran to him…then she spotted the knives hanging on his hips. A freezing chill spread through her. The other Crimbone watched from the doorway. Jesse, right?

Rob kept his hands clear of his knives, but she already saw what had always been in him. There was no more room for pretending. "Sally? Please, say something."

"Y'know, why don't you use those things on me?"

Rob looked back at Jesse. "What the hell did you do to her?"

"She was hurt when I found her. I patched her up and gave her some painkillers, plus some drugs for physical repair acceleration and brain stabilization."

"You said you didn't have any painkillers!"

"I said I wouldn't give you any."

Rob turned back to Sally. His hand went to his belt. "I'm…gonna take these off. Okay?"

She nodded, then stumbled left and right. When Rob unbuckled the belt, the heavy scabbards pulled it back through several loops. The knives thumped to the floor, and he walked towards her. Finally, her eyes softened.

"Don't be afraid of me, Sally." He touched her face. "It's still me."

She tensed, then broke down and threw her arms around him. *Everything can be okay.*

When she kissed him, he gave a hushed cry. "Ah, careful." He tapped his bandages, lightly as his shaking fingers let him. "There's like a gazillion stitches under here."

"What happened?" She stroked his good cheek.

"I had a disagreement with a little bird."

"What've you done?" She sounded so serious, you'd never guess how doped up she was.

Rob rested the good side of his face on her shoulder. "So much…too much. I'm fucking exhausted, Sally. Please, I can't talk about it anymore tonight. God, I'm so…"

"C'mere. Lie down." She glanced back at Jesse. "Could you excuse us?"

"Hey, take your time. I'll be in the van if you need anything."

Once Jesse left, Sally locked the door, even though he was still the one with the key. When she came back, Rob's uncovered eye had squeezed shut. Was the other eye still there under the bandages? His breathing came in soft shudders. She stroked his hair, found it stiff and grimy.

So where would she be in his book once he wasn't falling apart, once he looked clearly and decisively at this world he'd stepped into? She didn't think about it now, because she was almost as battered and exhausted as he was. It was the first thing that had felt right all night, just to feel him, to hold him close again. She stretched out, kissed his eyebrow and rested her head on his chest.

Once his breathing softened, she said, "Dear? Your pants are really nasty right now."

He muttered and nodded.

"So are you gonna take 'em off, or do I have to?"

"You can if you want…" He was practically asleep already. Great.

She shook her head, sat up and undid his jeans. There were more bruises all over him, along with a long cut above his right ankle. "Okay, let's get under these covers and pass out."

"Yeah…"

Drifting towards sleep, Sally let her consciousness melt in these strange Crimbone drugs, into this strange, wonderful man of hers.

SEVEN

One way or another, Jesse figured the girl would be dead before long. Oh, she'd recover from her injuries fine. She was tough, and he had confidence in his medical skills. When he thought of everything that lay ahead for Rob Coscan, though, he couldn't foresee it ending well for Sally. For one thing, Rob had yet to make his Third Call. That usually came much, much later, but Jesse had given up trying to gauge anything conventionally. While he bore Sally no ill will, it might be kinder if he went back in and sliced her head off right now.

No, the fledgling had to make the Third Call according to his personal nature, by whatever means presented itself. Sally seemed just a little too perfect, so far as potentially having something to do with those means. Jesse would give the lovers their time. He hoped they enjoyed it. As he neared the van, a high wheezing laugh echoed overhead. The Familiar bobbed in his face, upside down from a willow branch like an overgrown seedpod.

"This is all really something, Puttergong," said Jesse.

"Why you belly-achin', Ripper-Man?" Still bobbing, Puttergong's voice wavered like a bad electrical speaker. "Ain't you figured out what's goin' on?"

"What? You fucking over your fledgling a Call at a time?"

"Wha, you think we—me *or* you cocksuckers—could fuck that boy over if we tried? That's a High Natural in there, and you dumbasses has gotten so far from your old strength an' smarts, you don't even see the potential here." Puttergong's voice dropped. The bobbing quaver made the icy rasp worse. "Then again, now I think about it, how could any of you really know any better? Far as y'all can see, must look like all I'm doin' is tryin' to send the body count spikin' through the roof. Nah, that's only part of the fun.

"Or maybe ye do see it. Yeah, maybe y'all Crimbone have slumped so low, you actually *like* things so mellow and pussified, barely holdin' out against the Spirelights, keepin' it all on the lowdown from the Earth-liners, never gettin' nowhere. Oh, you can handle all the fightin' this world can throw at you, sure, but deep down, you're just scared you ain't got it in you no more, to take the wheel and run the show again. So here comes a sign like maybe it's time to knock everything back into gear, and here you go shittin' your pants!"

When Jesse's hand slipped into his duster, Puttergong flipped and scuttled up the branch like a beetle. Tiny leaves fluttered down in its wake. It still bobbed low enough that Jesse might skewer it with a jump.

"Careful there, Ripper-Man." The creature's little gold eyes twinkled, a grin spreading across pearly peg teeth like a wound splitting to show bone. "You gack me 'fore Biter-Boy makes the Third Call, you gack Biter-Boy. Or you might as well, 'cause a fledgling with a dead Familiar might as well be one more piece o' Earth-line shit."

Jesse slid out an inch of blade. "Maybe he should be, if he drew you for his Familiar."

Puttergong's front claws let go. The weight-shift pulled the branch lower, so the creature dangled in Jesse's face. "Go ahead then, Ripper-Man. Gack me, gack Biter-Boy."

As Jesse thought about it, laughter sounded to his left. Three good ol' boys walked by, each hauling a twelve pack of Budweiser back from the Price Chopper next door. Damn, those beers looked good right now…"Something funny?" Jesse felt like tugging back the duster, letting them see the knife.

"Nothin', skin. You just go right on talkin' to your pigeons."

First I'm a cowboy, now I'm a skinhead. What's next, a fucking pirate? Can't these Yankee hicks make up their minds? "You boys wanna come over, meet the pigeon?" Jesse's fingers curled towards fists.

The good ol' boys turned away. "Nah, that's jus' fine, ol' skin." With that, they hurried off.

Jesse turned back to Puttergong. "*Pigeons?*"

"Ye really gotta try the eats 'round here, Ripper-Man." Puttergong let go and spun into the air, nearly hitting Jesse in the face on its way up.

How the hell did a Familiar get that big and strong so fast, eating pigeons? At least the thing's glamours were still holding against Earth-line folks. Jesse would think clearer once he'd rested and eaten. With this in mind, he trudged towards the van.

PART TWO:

THE LESSONS

SHELDON

ONE

Somehow Janie found the guts to show her face at the teen center after yesterday. As it turned out, there weren't many folks to show it to. Parents might be keeping their kids at home, thanks to the murders. Had Mom even heard about all that? Likely it wouldn't make much difference. If your number was up, Mom always said, it was up wherever.

So how many numbers had been up in that earthquake up in Barre? Maybe the government would call it terrorism, try placing Vermont under martial law. Janie thought of Mom and Dad's old wilderness survivalist friends. She wondered how many of those crazy bastards were still lurking around, waiting and training for that day. From some of the news stories she'd read, it sounded like some weird group of people—like the Masons, or maybe an especially organized survivalist group—had used the building as an office. The police were investigating, or trying to. Not many folks were talking about all that in Brattleboro, though. Nothing focused you on your immediate surroundings like a few local corpses.

Right now, Janie was thinking of leaving before that weird new kid came back. At first, she'd figured he must be crazier than she'd thought, strolling in like he hadn't put three kids in the hospital yesterday. It was scarier to think he *wasn't* crazy. He'd zeroed right in on folks who gaped at him the most, had struck up conversations with them first. After a few words, they settled down like they'd just met him for the first time. It was like he'd *politely asked them* to see something other than what their eyes told them, and they just…obliged. He kept introducing himself as Stew, claimed he was fifteen and *just roaming around.*

Fifteen, Janie's ass. Hell, he had to be at least a year younger than her. Surely Lindsey wouldn't be fooled. Except she was, it turned out. She explained the rules, asked if he had shelter arrangements, offered him volunteer work, the whole bit. They had one more spare bed upstairs. If he wanted to sleep there, he'd need to talk with their volunteer nurse, who wouldn't be in 'til Monday. He'd smiled, nodded, and left. Janie had suspected that would be the last they'd see of him.

When he came back hours later, she hadn't recognized him at first…not 'cause he'd managed to play any tricks on *her* brain, but because he really looked different. For one thing, he'd gotten a haircut. He wore blue jeans and a sweatshirt, and a backpack was slung over his shoulder. Stuffed with more donation shelf clothes, she guessed. What about those weird clothes he'd worn before?

Finally, he'd approached Janie. So did he expect a *thank you* for yesterday? She had to admit, that wouldn't be unreasonable.

Except what if he turned out to be worse than Russ and them? Some kids were mean 'cause they were pissed at everything and wanted to dump it on anyone they thought would take it. It was something else with him, like he didn't feel anything for you, no matter how charming he acted. He'd still help you or hurt you if he thought he'd get something out of it. What had he hoped to get from Janie by beating up the kids who'd attacked her? She'd read a lot of psychology studies about those kinds of sociopaths. They were supposedly master manipulators, really good at lying.

By now, she couldn't even remember what they'd talked about, just the growing sense that he was sizing her up for…something. What if he'd realized she'd seen through him? Finally, he'd left, maybe to figure out what to do about that. She didn't feel like waiting around to find out, so she took off. Some of her friends were probably chilling in Harmony Parking Lot about now.

Two

On the other side of Main, Flat Street became a weed-choked alleyway, running down towards the river in a steep, rocky, curving ramp. Sheldon leaned against the alley wall, peering out. When that girl came out of the teen center, he almost followed her. No, not yet. Janie, yeah, that was her name. Those kids yesterday had shouted it at her.

Today he found she was the only person there who he liked much. She was also a problem. He thought of Spirelight girls he'd known at the homesteads—played with when he was little, hung out and trained with when he got older, had only recently started looking at with heavier interest. A Spirelight girl would hold onto your arm all day after seeing you fight like that, especially for her. A girl of the Secret Police bloodlines would drag you over to another group of kids and pick a fight to prove she was better. Sissy would have done that, probably would have bettered him.

Sheldon's whole body did a weird hitch-up, like halting sharply midstride, except he was standing still. That was the first time today he'd thought about Sissy, about any of them. It was the most he'd think of them 'til he took down Sally and the Crimbone. Rob Coscan was the name Sheldon would track. First, he had to find fresh shelter, so the Earth-line adults wouldn't try to *rescue the wandering homeless child*, and he wouldn't have to call one of the homesteads. That kids club was definitely out of the question.

Was that why he was thinking of this Janie girl? Sure, maybe. She'd also been the only one at the Boys & Girls Club whose mind wouldn't be swayed, at all. All he'd done was change his voice and posture just right, and the Earth-line folks let their ears tell them what to see.

This was one of the tricks he'd first learned in an old stack of papers from Grandpa's study, part of some old manual, one of the things Grandpa had never gotten around to teaching them. Plenty of information was missing, but Sheldon studied what was there, found he could apply such principles to other things he learned. Of course, he'd never known for sure, never had a chance to test it 'til today. The trick wasn't to convince anyone of anything, but rather to purge your own self-presentation of anything to dispute, despite meddlesome things like physical traits that ought to have made such deception impossible…to embody what you wanted to show with perfect casualness, to believe it a little yourself. It never would have worked with Sissy around.

Some kids had bought it more than others, but no one called him out as yesterday's troublemaker. It had been trial and error. Maybe his head injury was still throwing him off. Only the lady in charge really counted, and that's where he'd nailed it. None of it worked on Janie, though, not for a second. At least she was grateful enough not to blow his cover. She was still an *Earth-line* girl, though, so she'd be stupid with fear, no matter how smart she normally was. She was pretty smart, most of the time. Sheldon had figured that much out, watching her without seeming to, getting a few words in with her here and there. She liked reading books, which shouldn't be a big deal, but from most of the Earth-line kids he'd known, it sort of was.

Sheldon left the alley, crossed a short bridge near the end of Main Street, and found some weird *All Organic* grocery store nearby, called *The Brattleboro Food Co-Op*. He bought what he guessed was an all-organic cream soda, then sat on the stoop next to the sidewalk.

When Janie came back along, he said, "Hi."

She jolted less than he'd expected. "God, kid! You got some real balls, don't you?"

"What, for going back to that teen club today?"

"Well, yeah." She still looked ready to turn tail and run, but kept staring, pensively, studiously. "Stuff there doesn't get that bad most of the time. Mostly I feel safe there. There aren't usually crazy weirdos like you around."

"I'm a crazy weirdo? What, for beating up kids who tried to hurt you?"

"They wouldn't've even hurt me too bad, probably...not like you hurt them."

He shrugged. "You seemed cool, and they were assholes for messing with you like that. None of them are dead or anything, are they?"

"No, but you busted 'em up good enough that they had to go to the hospital. So ain't you worried someone'll recognize you and call the cops?"

"Not really. No one out there got a good look at me 'cept you and those three dumbasses. Oh, and that lady in charge—"

"Lindsey. Yeah, I heard you tell her you were fifteen."

"I am." His smile didn't match his eyes. "You didn't give 'em a good description of me, did you?"

"No."

"Cool, thanks. You're okay now, right?"

"Sure…Hey, you wanna go somewhere else and talk? I don't like it around here right now."

"You mean you…So you wanna hang out some more?"

"Just…around here…It usually feels comfortable for me. It's making me feel stir-crazy today, though. I need to relax somehow. You been to the graveyard?"

"Where's that?"

"Just up that hill, that way." She pointed up South Main Street.

"What's with that tower? The one you can see through the trees on the hill, back up that way?" He pointed the other way, up Main Street. "It looks all…medieval and shit."

Janie's face brightened. "You don't know the tower?"

"I don't really know anything in this town."

"Okay. I'll show you the path to it, then." She grabbed his hand and pulled him along, first up Main Street, then into a suburban area. As they walked, she asked, "So you really a runaway?"

"Yep."

"What, your parents beat you or something?"

"My parents are dead."

"Sorry." Her brow scrunched. "Didn't you…have a sister with you yesterday?"

"Nah, she was just some girl I'd met around here and was hanging out with."

"I guess she decided you were too crazy after seeing you in that fight."

"Yeah." He smiled. "I'm glad you didn't."

"Yeah, me too, I think." She kept peering at him. Yesterday, she'd have sworn him and that girl were twins. "So you don't have any other family you could go to?"

"I do, sort of, but I don't wanna be with them right now. There's some stuff I want to show I can do first. No, more like stuff I want to do my own way, and I don't want them to, like, step in and do it for me, only their way."

"Okay, I guess that's vague enough. How old are you, anyhow? I mean your real age. C'mon, it's not like I'll tell anyone."

"I'm eleven. I'll be twelve in May."

"You're eleven years old and you just wanna *do stuff on your own* without whatever family you got left? And you're just fine with living on the streets to do that?"

"Well, yeah."

That wasn't exactly normal among Spirelights, but it was more reasonable than it must sound to her. If things got out of control in the field, you were expected to call the nearest homestead. If you couldn't make contact for whatever reason, you were expected to handle yourself until you could. Yeah, things had gone unspeakably bad, but they weren't out of control, not while Sheldon could still think and fight. He'd never been good at playing down to Earth-line people, but Janie hadn't let go of his hand since they'd started walking. So he guessed he hadn't done so bad with her, so far.

"So, what's your real name?" she asked.

"How'd you know I lied about that?"

"Just the way you said it. For some reason it, y'know, didn't sound like it usually does when someone tells you their own name."

Wow. Yeah, she was smart, but even smart Earth-line people didn't usually pick up on things like that. "You won't tell anyone that, either?"

"Of course not."

"Okay. I'm Sheldon. And you're Janie."

"Yeah, I know. That second part, I mean."

They cut down a path that ran alongside someone's house, then onto a smoothly beaten forest trail. The fog held thicker here, amidst the trees. No brush cluttered the way 'til the trail wound and rose, and then it was mostly dead brambles that broke away easily.

"You okay?" asked Janie.

Sheldon stared at the trees. Where had this sudden weird feeling come from? He didn't worry about what he might see through the branches, but what he might spot about those branches themselves. If there'd been certain mutations and deformities—an abnormal seedpod drying in the brush, maybe—he'd be the one dragging her, away from here, quickly as possible.

"You come in these woods a lot?" he asked.

"Sure. Mostly when it's warmer, but it ain't so bad out today for this time of year."

"What's gone on here? I mean, any history back here people talk about? Like Civil War battles and stuff?"

She rolled her eyes. "I don't think they had Civil War battles in Vermont."

"Right. But you know what I mean." Actually, he only expected her to *think* she knew.

"This tower we're going to? It's called the Bloody Tower. You know that big building down by the road? That's the Brattleboro Retreat. It's the oldest mental institution in New England. Back in like the nineteenth century, the doctors thought it'd be healthy for the crazy people to have physical work to do, like they'd feel more normal or something, like they had a real job. So they had them go out during the day and build this big medieval tower up here. Except some patients snuck out at night, climbed up and threw themselves off the top. So the doctors locked the place up. Then during prohibition, bootleggers would use it as a meetup point. They'd break in and have someone sit up top, on the lookout for cops."

Sheldon was sorry to hear the place was always locked. When he'd spotted it from the road, he'd imagined climbing to the top and being able to see out all over town.

Janie continued, "Then the bootleggers started seeing the ghosts around here, like of all the crazy people who'd jumped off, so they stopped coming."

"What, did the ghosts kill any of them, like scare the guy up top into jumping off too?"

"I don't think so. I don't think people were seeing

ghosts actually *in* the tower. More like around it, on the paths leading to it and stuff."

"Like this path we're taking now. So why'd they get scared if the ghosts weren't doing anything to them?"

"I don't know," said Janie. "Do you feel ghosts or something?"

Wow, he'd completely forgotten about his suspicions. That never happened to him! He hadn't spotted anything, so he guessed it was all right. Janie had narrated her ghost story with perfect relish, and Sheldon had been absorbed. No, there was nothing wrong with these woods. Even when the enemy had long since released a place, when it had filtered the Schomites from itself, you still had to watch out for pockets of their unnatural energy. North America was still particularly bad about it. Once, such powers had almost managed to derail Spirelight-puppeted Earth-line enterprises from carving out and staking their claim on the continent.

"Ghosts?" said Sheldon. "Yeah, sometimes. Don't worry, though. Everything here's fine about this place."

"Uh, okay, cool. My mom says she sees ghosts. You believe in that stuff?"

"Sure." That was another thing Sheldon didn't get about Earth-line people. So much revolved around belief, about what was real beyond things you could see, touch, taste, hear, feel. He'd always wondered, just how weak were their five basic physical senses?

"I don't know." Janie's eyes drifted. "My mom tells me I could see ghosts too if I wanted, but I listen to too much of this world's loud noise. Like I'm supposed to somehow zone it all out and then be able to see all the spirits or something."

"Maybe she's right."

"So…what was your family like?"

"I don't know. They were just…my family, you know? I mean, what's your mom like?"

"I…well…Hey, you can tell me at the top. C'mon, we're almost there."

The path narrowed, all knotted roots and gravel-strewn lumps. The bank was steep on either side, high and muddy on the right, dropping off sharply to the left. Through the branches, Sheldon spotted the big curving stone wall, parapets lining the top. Yards from the trail's end, he turned and scrambled up the steep embankment, then stood in what he guessed you'd call the front yard. Gravel spread out from the door like someone had tried to build a driveway once. Larger rocks were clustered around the base. Janie was still on the trail, so Sheldon offered his hand.

"Ah, that's okay." She chuckled. "I don't wanna get muddy."

"You wouldn't get muddy. Look at me, I didn't."

She looked his jeans and shirt over. The bank between them was all damp earth, not quite mud. A few rocks poked out, nothing that would make good footholds. She hurried up the rest of the path, made to walk up beside him, but something sickly flooded her face as though rising from her gut.

"Now you look like something's bothering you," he said.

"I'm fine. Well, here's the Bloody Tower. What do you think?"

He walked towards it, peering at the iron padlock. The archway receded so far into shadow that it was almost a short tunnel. "Too bad we can't go inside."

"I hear people sometimes go down to the Retreat and ask for the key. Like if they wanna go up there and look out over the town. 'Cept you probably gotta be eighteen for them to give you the keys. Or have an adult with you." She looked around. "Wow, this fog's thicker up here. It must be thinking about raining."

"What?" he said sharply.

"I said it's…I mean, I think it's probably gonna rain. Sorry, sometimes I talk like Mom without realizing it."

"It's cool. I'd like to meet your mom. Let's sit here." A wave of dizziness hit Sheldon as he sat down beneath the archway. It must be his injured head, he told himself.

Janie scooted into the narrow space. Her shoulder pressed up against his. Had she brought it on with what she'd said? She obviously wasn't a Schomite. Somehow, though, she was closer to the Old World than most Earth-line folks, or at least how Sheldon had always imagined the people of the Old World. Then again, if you believed some legends, these so-called Earth-liners were the full-grown evolution of the Lepods, the first Deschembine refugees to cross the shrouded sea, long before the final wars. That's right, and when the Spirelights and Schomites showed up, they found those Lepods had evolved into people like Janie. Except they no longer remembered that they'd been Lepods, or that they'd come from the Old World. There were still a few Lepods who hadn't turned into Earth-line people, but they kept hidden from their taller, duller-witted cousins, far more so than the Spirelights or Schomites.

Sheldon had always liked those old stories, but he'd never really wondered if they were true or not. A good story was true while he heard it, swept up in it. The rest of the time, the truth was made of the goings on of your immediate surroundings. He knew the most important stories were true, about the kingdom of Spiralla where his people originated, of the gifts from the gods of the Spirah Pantheon. That was why he fought, why the Secret Police were obligated to eventually claim this world for the Spirelight people. It was still weird, drawing possible *direct connections* between right here and those old stories, especially at a time like this.

Maybe the disorientation made him too sensitive. He deciding to test his coordination and plucked up a pebble. Out across the gravel, he spotted a bare dusty spot and flicked the stone towards it. It skipped twice then bounced, inches off the mark. Sheldon sighed, smiled when he heard Janie laugh. When he shot another pebble, she picked one up and tossed it in the same direction, mimicking him. Deciding to try something else, he plucked up another pebble, tightened certain hand muscles, relaxing others. As before, he tossed it in a straight line. This time, he watched where it struck, closer to the earthen spot or the direction Janie's stone had gone.

THREE

As they hiked up South Main through the light drizzle, that weird agitation crept back through Sheldon. Again, there was no immediate threat, but something lingered in the air that wouldn't let him relax. It ran in a line up the street, floating off to smaller, shorter trails here and there. A sprawling cemetery stretched out to their left, running down the hillside further than he could see. Janie's house was second down the right side of Washington Street, a small, peeling, sharp-roofed dwelling with a weed-choked yard. It looked almost like an old-time cottage, hardly at home among larger, better-kept homes.

Janie tried the front door. "Shit. She went out and locked it." Just to make sure, though, she knocked and waited a moment.

"You don't have your own key?"

She dug through her pockets and shook her head. "C'mon. The back door's probably unlocked."

A high, rusty wire fence flanked the house. They scrunched alongside the outer wall, against woven clumps of vines that splashed gobs of water on them. Janie shoved some battered lawn equipment out of the way to reach the back door.

"Shit, that's locked too," she said. "Okay, let me try the window."

While she worked at that, he ambled around in the yard. Trees grew at both outer corners. Giant clumps of vines and weeds covered much of the wire mesh. Close to one corner sat a large metal barrel. Sheldon looked inside and found the bottom hidden beneath murky old rainwater. Some long instrument festered inside, the end wedged at the bottom, the handle resting against the side halfway to the top. He reached in, peering close in case spiders or anything guarded it. He gripped the handle and drew out a long machete. In the fading, foggy light, he passed it back and forth between hands, getting a feel for the weight. The grip felt perfect, as though crafted specially for his palm and fingers.

He extended his arm to the side and spun his wrist downward, the flat facing forward so the blade gave a heavy whoosh. Frowning, he held it sidelong and took slow, deep breaths, aligning the energies in his body. When he swept the blade forward this time, he led with the edge, so it cut a perfect whistle through the air. He brought it to a stop, arm crooked, the butt of the handle pointing squarely at his chest. After one perfect iron thrust out above the barrel, he rotated so the blade faced downward. His shoulder, arm and wrist moved in a figure eight, spinning the blade in a blurred pattern. He passed it to his other hand and repeated the process. The blade was slimy and mud-colored, the edges chipped, but there was good metal under all that rust. With the right tools and time, he could make it shine like never before, as only a Spirelight Secret Policeman could. *He'd make it so sharp…*

"All right, Lancelot, I got it open. Wanna come on in?"

Janie already had one leg through the window. Her eyes sparkled and teased. He smiled back with the embarrassment of a little boy caught at folly. He didn't actually feel embarrassed, but it was what she expected, and he was trying to get the hang of humoring her. *Except it wasn't* all *an act…*Wow, she was pretty, poised like that over the windowsill…

He turned away before she saw him gulp, leaned the machete against the fence, then hurried up onto the porch and followed her through the window.

"You mind taking your shoes, er, sandals off?"

He obeyed, then looked around at her bedroom. One

side held only a small wire-framed bed. The other sported a bookshelf and a blue beanbag chair. Posters covered the wall, mostly of rock and rap performers, some of whom he recognized. Back in school, Dad had encouraged him to listen to the modern Earth-line music, especially the *hard stuff.*

Mom had always been leery about exposing the kids to too much Earth-line culture, at least the modern stuff. They needed to learn some of it, but only enough to blend in with the Earth-line people when they had to. Civilian kids—whole civilian families, in fact—absorbed all the Earth-line ways, all but took it on as a second way of life, just to *have* a way of life that could be lived in the open, like learning multiple languages…but none of that for a child of the Secret Police. Still, Dad had insisted the hard stuff was perfect music by which to train a child for police work: the pounding beats, the raw fury of the vocals…

Listen to it, find the bands or artists you like and get used to those sounds. Let it play in the background while you listen to Grandpa's teachings. Don't let it distract you. Just learn to hear it, to really listen to it and still not miss a thing he says.

Learn to center and hold your focus, your convictions, but absorb the rhythms of the chaos you face, the chaos around you. Know how to move in tune to it, but always on the terms you've been taught to uphold.

Except this world wasn't their enemy, was it? Wasn't it the Schomites they were supposed to hold back, from tearing this whole world to shreds or something? Yes, it was because of the Schomites that the Spirelights had to keep to the hidden fringes. When their ancestors had landed here, according to some stories, the Schomites had been all but ruling the Earth-line people openly. This world would one day belong to the Spirelights by right, but only after they'd purged it of the horror from their own land. Sure, sometimes individual Earth-line folks got in the way, had to be treated without mercy, but that was just one of those things that couldn't be helped.

Then came the day Sheldon watched Dad fight a Crimbone—the first one he ever saw—and he understood, about the need to absorb and flow through the harsher rhythms, even that of the enemy. Since he and Sissy had been taken into the field, he hadn't had much chance to follow Earth-line music. Now, without thinking about it, he threw himself onto the beanbag chair. As it sank and crunched and billowed, his head lolled.

"You ain't fallin' asleep on me, are you?" Janie set a small CD player on the bookshelf, then rifled through a short stack of CDs. "Mind if I put on some music?"

"That's fine."

"You like Pink Floyd?"

He lifted his head, recognized the name but couldn't think of any songs. "Sure."

Soon a smooth keyboard flooded from the speakers, followed by a drunken, stewing guitar riff. Vocals came, hoarse yet melodic, desperate and confused yet so strong, imploring, "*What do you want from me?*"

"Perfect," Sheldon sighed, head falling back again.

"You want anything to eat?"

"Sure, what do you got?"

"You mind microwave popcorn?"

"Sounds great." Truthfully, he'd never tasted popcorn, microwaved or otherwise.

What do you want from me? There was no one left for him to ask.

FOUR

Out in the kitchen, Janie started the popcorn. What was up with that kid in there? The longer she was around him, the more confusing he got. His eyes and voice were full of a concern you couldn't fake, not the gushy, overly fawning kind Lindsey always showed. No, more like the way Larry would get when he spotted someone needing a shoulder to cry on or an ear to listen, not pushy, but letting you know the offer stood, because why the hell shouldn't it?

Now that the kid had cleaned up some, he was sort of cute. Did he even have anywhere to stay? Maybe Mom would let him sleep in Larry's bed, for a night or so. Maybe it felt wrong, thinking of putting some strange kid where her dead brother used to sleep. It might still be a bad idea, to let a guy like him sleep under the same roof as her.

Something about him wasn't kid-like at all. In some ways he acted older than eleven, in other ways younger; so naïve, but at the same time, he knew about things no one around here had heard of. Did he know the same secrets Mom did, or something even weirder? Then there was the way he fought. She guessed she wasn't scared anymore, except…Where did an eleven-year-old learn to hit like that, *to move like that?* Seeing him with that old machete, she'd thought at first of a younger kid playing with a toy sword. Then it was like watching him fist fight, only worse, like he imagined real people in front of that blade, rushing in to kill him, and he was cutting them to pieces…*like he already knew how that experience felt.*

The front door bolt turned, and in came Mom. She was shorter than her daughter, with the same lean features and a more athletic build. The rough weather-beaten features weren't what you noticed when you saw her face, because her eyes and mouth still held more girlish mirth and mischief than her daughter's ever had. Janie glanced at her watch. It would be about four hours before Mom went to work, as a nighttime cleaning lady at the Marlboro Graduate Center.

"Kiddo!" Mom's voice was thick and slow as mud, sweet and smooth like spring nectar, musical in its rhythm. She peeled off her long, damp coat and ratty slouch hat. "Didn't think you'd be home for a while. Looks like you got in okay."

"We came in through the window."

"*We?*"

"I brought a friend home. How was your day?"

"Ugh. The damn woolly worms are too thick with fur and too bright with stripes. That means winter's gonna be a bitch, you know." The microwave's buzzing croon now mingled with thickening pops. "Microwave popcorn, no less. Ain't that hospitable."

"He's just a new kid in town." Janie didn't feel comfortable bringing up Sheldon's situation right off the bat.

"Oh, it's a boy! See? I guessed right. This is an occasion."

"He's just a friend, Mom." Janie dropped her eyes, trying not to smile. What few boys she'd gone with, she'd never brought to the house. She'd only brought guy friends over in groups, with at least one other girl. She often felt weird letting friends meet Mom, even though Mom won them over quickly more often than not. Though Janie would never admit it, she sometimes chose who she kept hanging out with based on how well they accepted her mom.

"That's good, that's fine. Friends are good. You need more real, true friends, Janikens." This startled Janie. Mom never commented on her choice of friends, had always seemed unconditionally outgoing and accepting of kids from town. "So, let's go meet this young *Ubermensch*."

They found Sheldon stretched out, legs across the floor, back across the beanbag chair's flattened center, arms folded over his chest, his breathing that of a deep sleeper.

"Robbing the cradle a little here, huh, Janikens?"

"Mom! I told you, no, he's just—"

"Shhh. He's a tough, busy little brave. Let him sleep."

Janie let that one slide. If she tried to figure out everything Mom said, she'd never have time for anything else. She hadn't even told Mom about the fight yesterday.

When the microwave dinged, Sheldon sat up fresh and alert, like he'd just had a full night's rest plus a cup of coffee or two. "Oh. Hi, ma'am."

"*Ma'am!* Would you listen to this kid? Please, little brave, call me Annie."

"Uh, sure, Annie. I'm Sheldon."

"Good for you. So how'd you end up in Brattleboro, Sheldon?"

"Well, I—Sorry, I don't really know."

"Sure you do. That's fine, though, honey. You can tell us when you feel like it. 'Less you've already told Janie here.

Then I'll have to just tickle it out of her later."

Janie rolled her eyes. "He hasn't told me much, Mom."

"Oh, bull. You spent all day with this nice young man and you didn't get him to spill the goods? Janikens, you and me gotta have us a woman-to-woman talk on how to handle the menfolk. Oh, never mind. Janie, go get that popcorn. I'm smellin' it and it's driving me nuts."

* * * *

Once Janie left the room, something more serious crept into Annie's eyes. "Sheldon, you're not in town with your parents, are you."

"How'd you—No. My parents are dead."

"Oh…Y'know, maybe I should've guessed that. Could be I got those signals confused with my own life's crap lately." Her voice quavered, tears kissing the corners of her eyes. "I guess Janie's told you, we've had our own time of loss lately."

"Yeah. I'm real sorry to hear that, ma'am, er, Annie. How'd you guess the other stuff?"

Annie knelt. "Sheldon, I like to spend my free time off in the forest around here. It's a good place to go think, only not think at the same time. Some folks call that meditation. Me, I just call it getting to where the noise goes away—the noise you hear all the time, I mean—so you can listen for the sort of noises that are always talkin' to you, but you don't always hear. Am I making sense so far?"

"Yeah, actually."

"Good, 'cause those are the ones with the most useful things to say. It helps me understand better what's happening in my life and the lives of those I love. Or for times when there's just no understanding, it at least lets me see a little more of the big picture, be more comfortable with things so I can accept 'em and deal with 'em better. Sometimes it lets me in on what's coming, things I gotta be ready for. No, it don't let me see the future or anything solid like that. Just…I get feelings, you know? Like I can feel what's headed my way and how I gotta be ready for it. So I ain't exactly surprised too often by anything, except I don't know what form it'll take."

"What, so you felt that you were gonna meet me today?"

"Well, something like that. I never exactly know the details, just impressions of the kinds of times and people on their way into my life…the *shape* of it all, you might say. Then when I do see someone or something come along that fits into the empty space, I already have an idea what I'm lookin' at, so that helps me get a better idea what'll happen next. To put it another way, around when my husband and son were taken from us, things were pretty tough for everyone, for lots of messy reasons I'm not gonna dump on your dear head. But my time off to myself, when I could still get it, was what helped me know how to get through it, how to keep makin' the right choices even when no one else did. Right before our loved ones were taken, I knew things were about to get a lot harder and I'd have to be a lot stronger, had to be ready for big changes, would have to make a lot of big changes myself to stay afloat. Nothing prepares you for a thing like that, but it gave me time to gather my strength so I could hold things together for me and Janie when it did happen."

"So what kinds of…general things did you know about me in advance?"

"Well, little brave, now that you're right here in front of me, there's a lot I can see that I could tell you, if you're not afraid to hear."

Such warmth and joy surrounded Annie that Sheldon wanted to trust her. He felt overwhelmed, though. She wasn't just someone with a lot of personality, more like an inexhaustible well of it that just flowed faster and thicker 'til it knocked you over. Damn right he was afraid to hear. "You can tell me," he said. "Yeah, please do."

"Well first off, you're a good, true-hearted young man. Maybe you always assumed that, but lately I'll bet you've been confused, all of a sudden not so sure about stuff you took for granted, for as long as you can remember."

"Yes," he said quietly.

"Well, as far as I'm concerned, there's nothing to be confused about there. You're in my house, so right now the important thing is that I like you. So as long as you're in my house, you're one fine young man. Understand?"

He chuckled. "Sure."

"You've got all the potential in the world. If you ever hope to realize it, you gotta work past all that confusion you got upstairs." She leaned close and tapped his forehead. "You know what's really causing that confusion?"

"It's…the noise I need to learn to stop hearing?"

"Exactly. It's the noise you hear all the time, fightin' with the sounds underneath, the sounds of truth. Those truths have decided it's high time you figured 'em out, and you'll have to learn to hear 'em sooner than you think. See, Sheldon, I'll bet you're here in town after something. I'll bet you'd swear up an' down you know exactly what that is. In a way, you do. Yeah, you know what you're supposed to look for, and you'll find it, if that's what you keep your mind on. I don't think that's what you're really lookin' for, though. Or not for the reasons you assume. You understand?"

"Not really."

"Good answer." She laughed and clapped his shoulder. "You said yes, I'd've said you're sillier than I guessed, which is sayin' somethin'. But will you do me one favor, little brave?"

Why did she keep calling him that? "Sure, Annie."

"When you figure it out, let me know. If it ain't too personal to tell the crazy old mom of one of your little friends, that is." She winked. "Anyway, enough of this serious talk. Time to relax, I say. Janikens? Where'd you go with that popcorn? Ain't hoggin' it all, are you?"

Janie came in with the popcorn. "I got it, Mom. I just went to the bathroom first."

As the beanbag chair had made Sheldon realize how worn out he'd been, the hot, salty-cheesy aroma made him realize how hungry he was. He thought of what Annie had said. Of course he knew why he was here! He meant to find Sally, find the beast for which she'd betrayed him and the family, her whole coterie. What could be simpler?

Sheldon would kill the Crimbone without special passion. Oh, he hated the beast, but it was just another enemy. Mom, Dad, and Sissy may as well have died by the hand of Rob Coscan as any other Crimbone. Sally was the betrayer, the one to whom he'd show true vengeance.

PRECAUTIONS

ONE

Pain ran like a fishhook through his face, yanking him up towards consciousness. He held Sally tighter, as if she could hold him down here in dreamland. She stroked his unbandaged cheek and ran a hand through his hair, sending a sweet tingle through his scalp. When he opened his good eye, he saw her gazing at him.

"What am I gonna do with you, little Robbie Coscan?"

"Probably not gonna be able to look at me once these bandages come off."

"What, you used to girls who'd ditch you if you lost some of the looks?" She shook her head. "What the hell did you get yourself into, anyway?"

"I thought you'd left me." When she didn't say anything, he went on, "But…I had to know, at least that you were okay. I went looking for you. Then shit went crazy."

"Shit's been crazy a lot longer than that. How much do you know?"

"About the Spirelights and the Schomites?"

"Okay, then. What about what that guy said? About you being Crimbone?"

"I don't know."

She huffed and pushed herself up. *"Will you quit that shit?"*

"What shit?"

"You keep saying you don't know this, you can't remember that. It's like you keep one big drunken blackout excuse handy for whatever you don't wanna deal with. Come on, you're not senile. And let's not forget those two giant fucking knives lying in the corner over there. Now please, if you care about me, try to come up with a few straight answers."

Oh great, the old *if you really care about me* card. This relationship was moving even quicker than he'd thought. "Sally…I'm not gonna hurt you, if that's what you're scared of."

"That's not an answer."

"What else is there? Okay, fine. Yeah, I'm Crimbone. I'm a different race—hell, maybe a whole different *species*—than I thought. For whatever damn reason, we look enough like the species I thought I was that we can pass ourselves off as the same thing, and it sort of sounds like both sides have been pulling the strings behind the scenes, since, I don't know, forever, like some crackpot conspiracy theory about lizard men or some shit."

Her face wrinkled in confusion. *"Lizard men?"*

Oh, right. It hadn't escaped him how she seemed baffled by so many little things about day-to-day modern culture. That made more sense, in light of recent revelations. Now she was the one leading him around by the hand, through an unknown world in which he was the stranger. "I'll explain later," he said. "My point is, that's just the start of everything I have to wrap my brain around now. So you're a Spirelight, from one of their most badass fighter families, no less. Meaning we should've been spending all this time trying to kill each other instead of fucking each other senseless."

"Well, y'know, now that you put it that way…"

"Okay, fine. You know what? To hell with that! We were crazy about each other without knowing—"

"I knew right away," she said. "I just tried to tell myself it wasn't true."

"Right, because of how we feel about each other."

Before she could answer, a click sounded as someone unlocked the door from outside. Jesse Karn stepped in with a bundle of clothes under one arm. Sally jumped and yelled, pulling the sheet up over herself.

The way Jesse looked at them, they might as well be babies with diapers that needed changing. "Oh good, you're both up," he said. "Looks like you're getting your strength back, too."

Sally huffed, dropped back onto her side and looked at Rob's bruises and scrapes.

"Man, could you give us a few?" Rob grunted.

"Sure, but only a few. We've got a lot to talk about. All three of us. Here's some clean clothes. I guessed about your sizes. Hope you don't mind thrift shop rags." Jesse tossed the bundle onto the floor and shut the door.

Rob watched Sally go over to the clothes pile. God, even with her own bandages and bruises, the sight of her naked body made him feel stronger already. He inhaled, caught her scent, and it drove him crazier than ever. Her smell—all smells—seemed almost solid now, textured like the smoothness of her skin. Now, though, it wasn't just love and lust she stirred up within him. The thought of hurting her still made him sick, but he recognized that other thing, what had already caused him to harm others…*the Spirelight glow*. Except where those other Spirelights had been like blazing, maddening suns he thirsted to extinguish, she shimmered like a soothing moonbeam.

For a moment, he had to look away. "This is so fucked…"

"Yep." She sorted a blouse and khaki pants from a dark brown shirt and men's jeans.

He climbed out of bed, hurried over and embraced her.

"Look at me," he whispered, lifting her hand and kissing her palm.

"We need to get dressed," she said. "You heard the man, there's shit to talk about."

Oh Christ, did she already know about her family somehow? "Please." He rubbed her shoulders and whispered, "Don't tell me your feelings just changed like that. I mean, you say you already knew. Now that I know too, I still feel the same way, and—"

"It's not that simple."

"Sure it is. We want to be together, but there are other people who say we shouldn't. I say fuck 'em. It looks like we're gonna have people trying to kill us either way."

She settled back against him and and let him hold her. "Your logic sure is tempting."

"So why be tempted?"

"Look," she said, "you're obviously good at deciding what you want, running with it, telling anyone who doesn't like it to go fuck themselves. This is a playing field you don't know. You try to pull that cocky attitude now, it'll get you killed.”

“So I’ll learn it. I’m learning with you. What exactly do you think I haven’t wrapped my head around?”

“You know about my family, right?”

“Yeah,” he said uncomfortably.

“And you had a run-in with them, didn’t you?”

“Yeah. But no, that’s not how I got this…” He tapped his bandaged face. “What is it between you and them, anyway?”

“Absolutely nothing, that’s what, long as I can help it. I’ve been running from them for years. They want to force me to go back with them. I thought you knew that.”

“I did. But…”

She pulled away. “Let’s dress while we talk, okay?”

With a nod, he plucked up the jeans. They fit snugly, not uncomfortable, but tight enough that he wouldn’t need a belt. That was good, because he’d lost his old one somewhere. There was his new one near the door, with the Crimbone knives strapped to it in their scabbards. Such beautiful pieces of work…*Motherfucker, I can’t wait to use them again!* He wanted to strap them on, but he curbed the urge for Sally’s sake. Instead, he watched her button her shirt, wondering when he’d get to unbutton it for her again.

“So what about your family?” he asked.

“Let’s just hope we never run into them again.”

“You do. Really.”

“Why do you keep jumping on that? Yes! You have no idea what they’re like, Rob. They’re horrible, sick, fucking monsters. I mean no one has their hands clean in the world we live in, at least not the fighters, and I mean Schomites and Spirelights both. But my family…” Her next words came out in a sob. "Did you know Clover's dead?"

"Huh?"

"Clover Waits. A girl from the Common Ground. She mentioned you two were friends. Well, now she's dead. So's her boyfriend. My family tortured him to death, so he told them where I was. I was hanging out with Clover, just…watching some stupid, silly old movie. Then *they* showed up. They threatened her so I'd go with them. Then they killed her anyway." She squeezed his shoulders, pressing her face to his chest. "See? That's my family. That's what I've been running from. That's what all this is like, this whole world you don't know about yet. If you think any of all that big Earth-line military and law enforcement technology like guns and radars is anything we can hide behind, anywhere…Well, there are reasons it just never works out like that. With them, though, the Wildfires…"

His one uncovered eye blazed at her, boring relentlessly, so she recoiled a little.

"Rob, what's going on?" she said.

Before he could answer, someone knocked on the door. Rob started towards it. Sally caught his hand.

"What do you have to say?" she hissed.

"I'll tell you later," he said. "There's other shit to talk about, like you said." He called out, "Be right there."

TWO

Shit, Dad, there you are!

That was weird. How did five words, blurted through a

phone three years ago, sound like they'd just gone right into Jesse's ear?

Louis's voice had sounded like that on all those recent answering machine messages…more enthusiastic, more like an excited kid than ever…even more than he'd been as a kid.

Jesse hadn't had Louis's college phone number. Those were the rules, which also excluded the caller ID boxes, or even—later—cell phone recognition. How had the kid even known Jesse was in Vermont? Had the state—as in the lands—told him?

Either way, after those first few messages, Jesse waited around for the next phone call. "You sound good," he'd said, when he finally found himself speaking with his son on the phone. "How's college going?"

"Uh, yeah. The place is great. I already hooked up with a girlfriend."

"That's great, Lou. What's she like?"

"Amazing! Her name's Ellie. Listen, Dad. You won't believe this, but there's another fledgling here."

"Your girlfriend?"

"No, this other kid, a friend of mine."

"What's the name?" Jesse would have to check with the Cabinet about this. The custom was to not let fledglings wind up so close together. Apparently, the lands had other ideas.

From what Jesse understood, his son attended a small school, around two hundred and fifty students. It was a pretty expensive place, too, at least for a full-time student. Louis had joined the Vermont National Guard so he could pay for college. Then he'd been called up for a tour in

Afghanistan before he could enroll. Go figure. He'd been sent home and taken off active duty after being wounded. The military had of course planned to fuck him out of his benefits, on trumped-up technicalities like *preexisting conditions* etcetera, but unlike an Earth-line soldier in his position, he never found this out, because Cabinet operatives found out first, and they quietly pulled the appropriate strings.

"His name's Rob. Rob…Coscan."

Jesse didn't mention how that rang a bell.

"Here's the thing, though, Dad. I don't think he knows what he is."

"What do you mean?"

"I mean I can recognize my own, and he's a pack brother if there ever was one. But when I talk to him, I sort of dance around it—"

"Exactly as you're supposed to." The boy had said *pack brother*. Louis always had a way of knowing more than fledglings were supposed to learn before their First Calls.

"Yeah, but he doesn't even seem aware of it, like he's been raised to think he's Earth-line or something."

Good ol' crazy Metaiew…Figured. For the next hour, Jesse listened to his son go on and on about Rob Coscan. Part of it was the connection of a shared nature, even if Coscan didn't know it. That hadn't been the point. The important thing was that Jesse's son found one of his best friends ever.

All of this reaffirmed to Jesse what none of his contemporaries admitted, even if their children took it as a given on some level. This world was absorbing them, just like—some said—it had absorbed the Lepod refugees.

So why hadn't the lands led them openly down that

trail? Maybe they had, and only the young ones noticed. Jesse's fellow veterans already thought he was crazy. They wouldn't care as long as he kept killing Spirelights. It was happening among the other side, too, though it manifested differently. That was good, because otherwise the Schomites would have been wiped out by now.

Eventually, Jesse predicted, the wars would come down to a relative few fighters in either camp, the only ones who still gave a shit about the old grudges, about anything remembered from the Old World. They'd kill each other off while everyone else got on with something else. It might take a few centuries, or just one. Assuming the Earth-liners didn't make this world unlivable first, forcing the Old World races to go somewhere else, if they even still had that option.

For now, Jesse went on fighting, because that's what there was for an old dog like him to do. He'd been born with an insatiable taste for the life essence of his people's natural enemies, and he'd learned how to put it to use. If there was such a thing as reincarnation, he looked forward to a life where he could relax. Maybe like Rob Coscan's life had been, until recently.

For now, Jesse paced the parking lot, waiting for Rob and Sally. Screwed up as it was, those two kids were falling in love, which somehow drove all Jesse's points deeper. The whole idea of sex with a Spirelight was weird enough. Jesse might not have seen it as a bad thing, if he'd been a more sentimental man.

Then there was Sally's inexplicable uniqueness. Mixed descent, maybe? No, even if that were genetically possible, Sally's difference had started well into life. It had given her what Earth-line people called an identity crisis. Maybe the hatred was leaking out of the bloodlines, had outlived its usefulness. The Spirelight's end of the evolutionary deal was to alter its metaphysical energy as Sally grew into herself. The Crimbone's was for Rob to respond as he had, by not raping and murdering her, then keeping her skin around as a trophy.

Jesse rounded the corner and found Zane leaning against the side of the van. Zane eyed Jesse severely.

"Where the hell did you come from?" said Jesse.,,

"Barre, same as you," said Zane.

They clasped hands, then roughly jerked each other close and clapped backs.

"What the hell's going on back up there, anyway?" Jesse asked.

"You mean other than trying to figure out what's going on down here?"

"That why they sent you?"

"No one sent me. When the cave-in woke everyone up, I crept out of my sleep-rig and stayed out of sight. After listening in here and there, it sounded to me like you were gonna need my help."

"Why?"

"Rumors go, the Spirelight Secret Police are about to swarm this town. Matter of fact, they've already started creeping in. That fledgling— Metaiew's son—is the magnet."

"You don't say."

"I don't, but it's a safe bet. Been catching the frequencies? There was a little car accident on Putney Road last night."

"I know. And yeah, it was Spirelight Secret Police.

Don't worry, they're dead."

"You got 'em already?"

"Nope. The fledgling did."

Zane arched an eyebrow and whistled.

"Yeah, I know," said Jesse. "Look, let's—"

"There's more. That wreck? Turns out, when they were prying people out of it, they missed a few the first time. Specifically, the ones in the trunk."

"Fuck. Who?"

"My money says those missing townies."

Jesse remembered the smells he'd picked up in Harmony Lot. "Motherfucker. They're gonna pull together a pack from all over, about this shit."

"Yeah," said Zane. "Depending how they like that Coscan kid, I'm not sure Spirelights are all they plan to kill."

"That's insane. He's a High Natural, I know it. Shit, you should meet him! He's—"

"A fledgling who damn near leveled a town with his Second Call, days after making his first. Yeah, I noticed. That and…well, like you said, look who his Familiar is."

"Don't fucking remind me. Why'd you hide from everyone?"

"After the way you took off, you think I was gonna wait around, let it come out that I covered your ass?"

"Right. So what do we do now?"

"Well, what else we got to work with?"

Jesse explained it as briefly as possible, for now avoiding certain cans of worms, like Rob's mentioning *Magur Sevi*.

"Old Lords," said Zane. "You know, you could've just made the Spirelight girl spill the info you needed, then killed her and gotten rid of the body before finding the boy."

"Then what? Wait to mention it 'til he seemed ready to hear it, get over it, and move on?"

"Well, yeah."

"I don't know. There's something weird about her, too. She's too much of a rarity, a mystery, to just snuff out."

"Sounds like you're the one who's in love with her."

"You know," said Jesse, "sometimes I wonder if it'd really brighten my day if I kicked you in the nuts. Just randomly, whenever, you know? Anyway, come have a look at the kids."

THREE

When the door opened, Rob stared at Zane…and not just as a fresh face. Sally tensed up at the sight of a third Crimbone.

"Don't shit yourselves quite yet, kids," said Jesse. "This is my pal Zane. He's come to help us all out. Right, Zane?"

Zane stepped past Jesse. "Hey, Rob. I hear you've been having an interesting time lately."

Rob almost said a million things. Finally, he just nodded.

"You guys ready to figure some shit out?" Jesse said.

"Ready as we'll ever be, I guess," Sally breathed bitterly.

Jesse whispered to Zane, "See what I mean? About her?"

"I see something, all right," said Zane. "No clue what it means, though."

At this exchange, Rob and Sally shared their own looks.

Zane spotted the knives on the floor. "You shouldn't leave those lying around like that, Rob."

Rob nodded and picked up the knives. He carried them to the nightstand.

"I mean you should wear them," said Zane. "Get used to their weight on your hips. If you really want them, and take them seriously, that is."

Rob stared at the knives on the floor. Then he stared at Sally, as if asking permission. Her face stayed blank. Jesse was no easier to read, but less cold. Finally, Rob gulped and started threading on the belt. He took another look at Zane, trying to decide if his eyes were playing tricks.

Yes, he realized, here stood the first Crimbone he'd ever seen besides himself and Dad. The man hadn't aged a day, and he was encouraging Rob to wear his blades, to do what everyone else seemed hellbent on talking him out of, for one reason or another.

"So I guess you two have done some talking of your own?" Jesse said.

Rob and Sally nodded. Rob walked to Sally's side and slipped his hand into hers.

"Good," said Jesse. "I don't have to spill a bunch of reiterative bullshit to make sure we're all on the same page."

"Wait a second," said Rob. "You're saying there are Crimbone coming, and they might butcher Sally on sight just for being a Spirelight, even if she hasn't done anything wrong?"

Zane glanced at Jesse. "Kid's quick. You say he's supposed to be a High Natural or some shit?"

"Right," Rob grumbled. "And now you tell me these

other Crimbone might decide to kill me?"

"They might," Zane said. "Probably not, long as you don't give 'em a reason to."

"Yeah, like I'm gonna go out there like a maniac and do something that stupid," said Rob.

At this, even Sally couldn't help exchanging looks with Jesse and Zane. Then Jesse brought up his hands. "Okay folks, here's what's what. Zane, where's the nearest reserve space?"

"Oh, a little over thirty miles from here, other side of Marlboro Mountain."

"Okay. Yeah, that place. I remember now. Perfect. Zane, what vehicle did you steal to get here?"

"The old Jeep."

"*The* old Jeep, at a time like this? Man, have you been beating yourself on the head with that hammer of yours?"

"The Jeep runs fine," said Zane. "And yeah, it'll keep up with the Big Red Beast."

"Good," said Jesse. "Everybody pack up. You kids wash up first. Be quick about it, no distracting each other. You both need it, you especially, Rob. We're going for a drive. Rob, you ride with Zane. There's things I need to talk to Sally about."

Rob felt Sally tense up. His hand tightened on hers. "She goes with you, we'd better all pull up at the same spot and I'd better see her jump out, just—"

"Rob. I'm on your side. So is Zane, probably, maybe, if you don't piss him off. And trust me, right now, that's it, buddy. So please, let the masters work."

A LIL HEART TO HEART

ONE

Zane lit a cigarette and drove with the Jeep's top down. It looked even more beat up than it had years ago, but it ran just as smoothly. Could this really be the same Jeep? Of course it was. Rob tried to concentrate on the wind in his face and hair, not all the gnawing injuries all over his body, or his itchy face beneath the bandages. It was colder up Marlboro Mountain, which helped. Still, he kept running his fingers over the gauze, sometimes plucking at the medical tape.

Well, here you are, off to unknown adventure with the bald black giant in his Jeep, and all you can think to do is pick at your bandages like a kid with a scraped knee.

Yeah, and stare with your good eye at the van ahead, wishing you were in there.

Still, for a second, he almost felt that wild, free elation he'd thirsted for as a child. Then he remembered that he couldn't dream like that anymore, because here he was in the middle of it, out the other end of that alley in Richmond. Life had sure gone off the rails, and the grand adventure felt less and less like freedom with every fresh turn.

"So, uh, Zane, I guess…How've you been? Since that

day?”

“Thought you'd never ask, like maybe you didn't recognize me or some shit.”

“No, I recognized you fine. You're…kind's hard to miss.”

“That's a little racist, don't you think? What, you think I'm the only black bald Crimbone giant?” When Rob drew up sharply, Zane slapped his shoulder and bellowed laughter. “I'm just fuckin' with you, you little punk.”

“Heh. Cool. Guess you've been…same as always, pretty much?”

“There's no *same as always* in Crimbone life. Been a bit of a dull stretch lately, but you've sure fucked that to death, so thanks.”

“Hey, always glad to help. I guess what I wanna ask is…About that day…”

“Was I there to cajole your dad back onto the trail? Yes and no. Much as I'd have liked for it to go back to being like old times, I didn't expect it to. It never does. But some of the local Spirelights and Schomites had broken local truce. No, the Schomites weren't Crimbone, just punk kids who'd fallen in with Earth-line gang-banging bullshit, thought they'd impress the Cabinets by taking that Spirelight bait. Neutral territories are important. Both sides need some space for quieter politics, or neither would sustain themselves, let alone keep all this under the table, so those are the zones where a sort of truce is held, and by truce, I really mean *agree to disagree with each other's existence*. But the youngsters on both sides had threatened to fuck that up. In the end, the agreement was for the Crimbone to take out both bunches.”

Rob glowered. "Crimbone killing civilian Schomites… under agreement with *them*…"

"Yeah. I know. Nothing's simple…'cept when it comes down to our kind doing what we do best, which is hunting and feeding. But this wasn't so simple, 'cause *civilian* doesn't mean *pussy*, and I remembered how your dad did his thing. I'd also learned about you, how he was trying to raise you."

"So you went to talk him into your sweep an' clear, by threatening to reveal to me what he'd been hiding."

"No. I hoped seeing me, being reminded of the bigger picture, would knock some sense into him so he'd tell you himself, so you could make your own choices. I never threatened to deny him his."

"Yeah, well, you should've."

"He was your father, not me. You're still where you're at, making your Calls…making your choices, just like he made his. His reasons might not be so different from yours as you think. Either way, that's not why he decided to make that one last run." Some of Zane's smoke blew into Rob's face.

"Mind if I bum one of those?"

Zane held out the pack of Camels, flicked the bottom so a single filtered tip slid up. Rob took it and lit it with the Jeep's lighter. It got his mind off the bandages, but not the van ahead. *Jesse probably assumes I've told her about her dead family. What if he mentions it offhand? Will she decide I've betrayed her by lying? Have I betrayed her?* The anxiety congealed in his gut, so he sucked harder on the cigarette.

"Don't worry so much, kid."

"I'm not worrying. These just itch." He scratched at the edges of the bandages.

"You can probably peel those off by now. The stitches would hold. So you met the Spirelight girl before you knew?"

"That I'm Crimbone?" Rob's eyes stayed forward. "Yeah."

"So, how do you stand looking at her now?"

Rob shrugged. "I guess love cancels out all this blood-hate bullshit, huh?"

"With a woman? Kid, you're young. Trust me, they'll all figure some way to stir up your murderous psychotic urges sometimes, without throwing a Spirelight glow on top of it. Seriously, though, Jesse thinks there's more to it. As in something unusual about her, biophysically."

"You disagree?"

"You're the one fucking her. What do you think?"

"I don't care. To me, she's just Sally." Rob decided to shift subjects. "How's a war like this lasted so long, anyway? I mean, it was going on back in the Old World, it followed us here, which is where we've been for, what, three thousand years or something?"

"It'll go on 'til either the Spirelights back off, or 'til one side or the other is extinct."

"So, why put so much work into keeping it secret?"

"We—the Deschembine refugees—are here on these lands' good graces, and that's a tenuous thing. We—the Crimbone—are here to preserve the rest of our kind. None of us would last long on this land if its protectors made spectacles of themselves to the Earth-liners. Think about it."

Oh, Rob thought about it, alright. Last night, he'd brought knives to a gunfight…his new Crimbone knives, against a gun pulled on him at thirty feet at least. He'd won, and he was just starting out.

He could only imagine what Jesse and Zane must be able to do, what a badass Dad must have been in his day…and Dad had gone with Zane to kill Schomites and Spirelights alike, to preserve *neutral territory*, for the sake of *quiet politics*. Imagine a land whose dominant beings ruled in true communion with their earth, through *true imparted wisdom*…

Why should the Crimbone compromise? Why shouldn't they flare to full strength, ending the threat and showing the Earth-liners who really belonged in charge? After that, they might actually get something done other than more killing.

Instead of saying so, he asked, "So now you plan to hide Sally and me somewhere?"

"That's right. You'll have provisions for a little over a week."

"So this *voice of the land*…I hear it because I'm Crimbone, right?"

"Civilian Schomites have a little of the sense, but only the Crimbone fully harness it. It's not exactly a sixth sense the way you think, more an…amalgamation of the other five, something more than the sum of its parts."

Exactly. So what are we doing, tip-toeing through this world, around those who don't get it? "I think I knew that, but…since waking up to it all—since making the *First Call*—my life before feels…blurrier. I mean, I remember facts well enough to tell 'em, but—"

"But try thinking of some mundane bullshit from your life you thought was so important, except you haven't told it to a million people so it hasn't been branded so strong as all your favorite little anecdotes. Think of your Earth-line friends in Brattleboro, the things you've been through with 'em most recently. See what's stuck around, what hasn't. They say the things that stick around—as more than just catalogued facts you don't even know firsthand anymore—are the things in which you find your true self. Think of it like the basis on which you can refill yourself, once you've been drained of all the mess of the cast-off life."

"What the fuck? Now that I'm *awake*, my whole identity is gonna fade?"

"Your false identity, the idea of who you are, according to Earth-line civilization. You don't need it anymore, so your soul sheds it like baby fat as you get comfortable with your real instincts."

"I'm not gonna be drained of Sally, if that's what you're thinking."

"Talk to me in a week. The choices are always yours to make. Now you know what you are, and it doesn't have a damn thing to do with ideology or principal or any kind of opinion. As you figure out what it does have to do with, you'll find yourself consciously making those decisions as a Crimbone. But the Cabinet's a political construct, not an invention of nature. It doesn't own you, any more than it owned your dad. But then, what's a choice but the final confirmation of *who* you really are?"

"What was he like, as a Crimbone? My dad, I mean."

"He…Well, he was an odd case. Even at the height of bloodlust for the Spirelight glow, he never took joy in it, I don't think. At the same time, he was absolutely devoted to his pack brothers, to keeping those around him alive and safe. So when it came to any of us being threatened, to standing by us, you'd never meet a man more vicious and ruthless when the chips were down. That last run…To be honest, not many Crimbone would be up for something like that. So it's the sort of shit job I always get. Same with Jesse, same with your dad. Part of why we always got along so well. But he didn't decide to go because of me…See, by then, you were the one he was that devoted to…because he'd have killed *anyone* to keep you safe, in that world he'd thought to make for you. You had a point, I believe, about sensing the land's wishes?"

"Right. So…if this Cabinet has other Crimbone out looking for me, couldn't they just ask directions from the spirit of Brattleboro, or the spirit of Marlboro Mountain, or something?"

"They'll try, and if the land wants them to find you, it'll lead them to you. Or it might guide them part of the way, leave the rest to them, then if you run into each other, let you sort it out between yourselves."

"Isn't Marlboro Mountain cutting it a little close, then?"

"I think that's Jesse's idea. They'd expect you to hide either right in town or much further away. Like I said, whatever land you're on, if it embraces you, it'll aid you. Even if it sometimes seems to just make things tougher."

"Right. But I thought, you know, they've mastered it all, know how to—"

"The land is the master, not the puppet. Never forget that, because it doesn't change, no matter how good you get, no matter how many rules you think you rewrite for yourself."

"Fair enough. So what do you and Jesse have

planned?"

"To find out how bad the Cabinet has it out for your ass, then try to get you off the hook. If he does, you'll be allowed to begin life properly as a fledgling."

Two

"Where do you come off asking that?"

"Trying to buy you a shot at survival. You don't tell me, I might as well cut your head off right now."

Sally kept her eyes forward and only flinched a little. "Rob would kill you."

"He'd try. That'd be more his problem than mine, whether he managed to or not. Right now, your problem is that you're in Crimbone custody, and I have to convince a whole lot of other Crimbone that you're interesting and maybe even important enough to keep in one piece before they figure out where you're stashed. The better I understand you, the better chance I'll have convincing 'em."

Sally gulped. "So you wanna know how I don't know whether or not I'm really a Spirelight."

"Start talking whenever you're ready," said Jesse.

Three

"Why you leaving, Sally?"

She halted three steps from the front door. Damn,

Sheldon was quiet for a seven-year-old. Sally had lain in bed for hours, regulating her breathing to sound like she was asleep. Yeah, she'd recognized his nimble tread, padding in time with Sissy's down the hall towards their room. Then she'd slid her backpack from under the bed, the one she'd packed earlier that day. Now here sat Sheldon at the kitchen table, asking why, like he'd known all along.

"I'm just going for a walk," she said.

He didn't answer, but she noticed him eyeing the backpack. Gods, it was creepy how he picked up on shit sometimes. Except no, not creepy…He was a child of the Secret Police. Except so was she, and older. She'd paid too much attention to Earth-line ways, though, hanging out with too many slow, soft, bestial Earth-line kids. You were supposed to hang with them some, learn their rhythms so you could mingle when you needed to. Except had she been as quiet as Sheldon when she was seven? She didn't know what was what in this family anymore, with anything, least of all herself.

"Why so late?" he asked.

"I need to clear my head, think some things through."

That was true. In her life, there'd been so much education about the Old World, the old ways, the old reasons for the feuds. What about right here and now, in this world they were supposed to save from the Schomites?

"Well," Sheldon said, "I'll probably be asleep when you get back."

When Sally's little brother put out his arms, she went and hugged him tight.

The first few days and nights on the road were a nightmare. Her Secret Police fighting-girl instincts were still sharp, so no one could fuck with her too much, but that didn't make it easier to get food or shelter. If she hadn't hooked up with Kim on the third day, she might have turned back. Kim had been at this for a while. She didn't so much teach Sally as pull her along, letting her watch and figure things out as they went. Maybe Kim hadn't thought to care how much Sally watched and learned. Either way, it was Kim who suggested they hit Louisiana.

"So, what're you runnin' from, anyway?" Kim asked from the next cot over, at the shelter she'd found them in Baton Rouge. This girl had run off because she'd been sick of getting molested by her mother's various druggie boyfriends.

Hearing stories like that, Sally found it harder than ever to answer. *No, it's not that my family molested me or anything. They just want me to torture and kill people. I know they're not my people and all, but as I get older, I'm still not sure I'm cool with that anymore.* Instead, she said, "I don't really know."

"Don't like to remember, you mean? Hey, cool, whatever."

Sally shrugged and drifted to sleep. Tomorrow, Kim said, they'd head for New Orleans. She knew people there, and the place sounded interesting. When they got there, though, she didn't go looking for those folks she knew. She wanted to see the French Quarter first.

"Yeah, but that's, like, mostly bars and shit, right?" said Sally. "We don't even look twenty-one." Well, Kim could probably pass for it, now that Sally looked her over. When she looked down at her own body, though, glimpsed her face in the mirror, she still might pass for twelve. "What, you know how to get fake IDs, too?"

Kim sputtered laughter. "No one's gonna card us there, not if there's a squirt of piss worth of truth in the stories I've heard of this town. C'mon, we'll find some hot guys, get 'em to buy us drinks an' shit all night."

This jiggled Sally's stomach. She'd seen Kim's idea of *hot guys*, and she didn't like the thought of getting drunk with them. Soon, though, the beer-heady swelter of the Quarter sucked them in, and she almost felt drunk before touching a drop. Everyone seemed lost and loving it, and for a while Sally thought she might love it too. Then she and Kim found their way to an ornate, smoky alcove of a pub, down the alley from Jackson Square. They only had twenty bucks between them, so they ordered tea. The walls were covered in paintings of a swirling, ancient romance that reminded Sally of her own people—not just the Secret Police, or even the Spirelights, but all things Deschembine. Then she had to use the bathroom, came back and saw the three guys Kim was talking to.

One was medium height and stocky, another tall and skinny, the third tall and fat. The fat one and the skinny one wore heavy duster coats. The stocky one wore a trim leather trench coat. They were all sharp-featured except the fat one. Sally still saw hard, angled bone structure beneath his puffy face flesh. He might have been mistaken for merely lazy and out of shape, unless you spotted him moving, like a big carnivorous jungle reptile you think is sleeping, 'til it suddenly stretches its long neck and starts staring at you. Every motion was economical, savagely deliberate and graceful, down to the tiniest finger twitch.

Kim sat between the fat one and the skinny one, gulping a cloudy green drink. "Hey, there's my girl. Sally, check these guys out, they're loaded!"

Sally already knew what these guys were. They seemed made of scars, especially the kind you couldn't see. That's what the Schomites made their monsters from, scars. These three looked like they were in their late teens. Being Crimbone, from what she'd read, they might be in their forties, or older. No one else here moved quite like them, because only the Crimbone were anatomically built to move just so.

Goddamn, she'd been an idiot. She'd readied herself for all the Earth-line dangers, but somehow this—running into her race's ancient enemies—had never crossed her mind. Maybe she'd always figured, in the back of her mind, that only her family would bring her into contact with them. Except she wasn't here to bother them. She was dressed like a civilian and everything. If she didn't suggest a threat, they wouldn't present one.

"That's cool." She walked towards Kim. "Hey, you wanna go explore some more?"

"Shit no, girl. Now wha' you wanna drink?"

"I don't—"

The stocky one's hand settled heavily on Sally's shoulder. "Hey, glow-girl." He winked when he saw that she understood. "Where you wanna explore, you ain't already? Fuckin' moron-tourist Bourbon Street? Have a few drinks, then me and the boys'll show you some real sights."

It was a test, she told herself. Maybe they were debating whether to do anything to her, but if she broke now, they surely would. At least this way, she might figure a way out. The bar girl served her a tall, strong, bright red drink. She took it slow while Kim drained three tall glasses of that cloudy green stuff. The fat one and the skinny one kept buying, kept downing shots of some spicy-smelling, darker green liquor.

"You're gonna make me look bad, glow-girl, you don't keep up with your friend." The stocky Crimbone's smile looked innocently flirty, but she heard every icy drop in his voice.

"Don't take it personally," she said. "I ain't used to drinking."

"Well, you've come to the right town to learn," interjected the bar girl, a caustic-eyed waif who wore as little as local regulations allowed. Sally would later wonder if she'd actually been stupid enough to try living up to the pressure, like any dumbass pissing match. Either way, she gulped her drink quicker.

The stocky Crimbone clapped her back. "Now that's how it's done around here! Tess, get her another."

Tess shrugged and fixed another tall red drink. This one tasted stronger. After her third, Sally flatly refused to drink anymore.

"Aw…" Kim had an arm around either of her Crimbone suitors, grinning sloppily with them. "You gotta be more of a party-girl than that, you gonna make it in this town."

Sally thought of ditching the bitch, but the thought of being stranded alone in this weird, wild town scared her almost as much as the three Crimbone guys. "Guess I gotta learn to crawl before I learn to walk." She forced a smile.

"Oh, you'll learn to crawl in this town alright," cheered the fat one. His teeth were small and sharp, so when his cheeks puffed in a grin, his face looked like a mangled clown mask, something someone had glued back together after a dog chewed it up. "Proud to Crawl Home, that's the Quarter motto."

When Sally stood, her head swam. She'd never had more than two beers at a time, so she didn't know if this qualified as drunk. The fat Crimbone was paying up from a big wad of cash. When she looked back, the stocky one stood close behind her.

The fat one and the skinny one hauled Kim up between them. "So, Nergal," said the fat one to the stocky one as they walked out, "you wanna check in soon or what?"

Kim nuzzled her face in the skinny Crimbone's neck. "*Check in*, huh? You guys ain't cops, are you?"

"We ain't cops," said the skinny Crimbone, hand sliding to Kim's thigh, pressing her against him, maybe trying to tug her away from the fat one. "You girls want us to be cops? Actually, you might say we sorta work for a security company."

Kim let out a wild, idiot laugh.

"Shut up, Hobs," growled Nergal.

"So, glow-girl," Hobs went on, ignoring him, "*you* ain't a cop, are you? Not *secretly* the *police?*" A sharp finger jabbed Sally's back.

"Whatever," she muttered like some air-headed Earth-line girl.

Nergal draped an arm around her and her body cooled beneath a layer of sweat. "Yeah, well…you're *definitely* not supposed to be in a place like this, are you, glow-girl?"

"Why's he keep calling her that?" Kim asked.

"Nah, we ain't cops." Nergal looked back at the others. "And no, we ain't gonna go check in yet. Didn't you hear?

This little glow-girl wants to explore. So let's show her around. Then we go check in."

At the homesteads, Sally had had a million ways drilled into her, how to fight her way out of something like this. 'Til today, she'd guessed she'd be ready for the real thing. It was all she could do to stay alert, so she could slip free and vanish into the crowd at the first opportunity. The homesteads didn't train you for the shakes, though.

Soon after they left the bar, the tourist-choked thick of the Quarter dropped away, giving way to pastel multicolored townhouse fronts, half of them boarded up, the other half looking like they should be. Nergal halted outside a padlocked iron gate. Everyone else pulled to a stop next to him.

As he held Sally fast, she thought, *This is where I should jerk free and make a break for it. I'll get some money somehow and be on the first bus out of this city. Maybe I'll go home, maybe somewhere else, I don't care right now. I should help Kim, but I can't. She looks happy anyway. They won't do to her like they'll do to me. They'll just—*

Except Nergal's arm felt like half a ton of chain draped on her shoulders. He gave the gate a harsh kick. It groaned on its hinges, but the padlock held, so he brushed his coat back. Sally saw the flash of a black blade, heard the singing shiver as two halves of padlock clattered on the flagstones. Then the knife was gone, back into the trench coat. Sally's brain wanted to register the blade as a flare of red, but no…The metal had been solid black.

"What the fuck is this place?" the fat one growled, annoyed that Kim was giving more attention to Hobs, though she was still groping them both.

"Old-fashioned French Quarter courtyard, Sam ol' boy," proclaimed Nergal. "Ain't you guys ever seen one of these before? Well this is these two little girls' first time in New Orleans and I think we should show 'em."

The Crimbone exchanged grins. Kim looked worried for a moment, then she grinned too, trying to look crazy and badass like them. Nergal's fingers dug into Sally's shoulder through her t-shirt, almost hard enough to break skin, as he guided her down the alley towards the courtyard. Kim grabbed Hobs's ass and licked Sam's ear. Damnit, this was Kim's fault, or maybe Sally's for following the drunkass, fucked-in-the-head bitch.

In the center of the courtyard, there stood the crumbling remnants of a fountain. Spindly overgrown ferns lined the walls, getting steadily choked off by weeds. Kim was getting smothered between Hobs and Sam, so it was hard to tell if she was still willing. Then Sally couldn't see anything because Nergal shoved her against the wall. Her legs got tangled in overgrown weeds and thorns. His acrid mouth worked her lips, and even his jaw muscles were too rock-tough to fight, and her skull felt ready to split like a pumpkin against the stone. She heard the black blade hiss back out, felt the cold edge hovering on her windpipe. Then he was ripping at her jeans.

"Hey, Nergal!"

He drew back irritated, hand squeezing Sally's jaw. "*What?*"

"Don't use her all up, man."

Sally felt air against her naked thighs, felt the heat of Nergal's crotch. She squirmed and whimpered, trying to squeeze her legs shut.

"Shut the fuck up, Hobs. You guys got that other bitch."

"Yeah," came Sam's voice, "but this one's Earth-line. Just make sure you toss the glow-girl our way before her glow's all used up."

"No, 'cause then *you* guys'll use her up."

"Well, yeah. Ain't that what Spirelights are for?"

Kim groaned, "What're you guys—" Sam crushed her against him, drowning her out.

"We ain't using this one up." The edge pressed harder to Sally's throat. "Nah, I think Talino needs to see this one…"

Then Nergal bucked his hips, and pain hammered through her while the knife's edge pressed her throat. Her glow…that's right, that's what they called it, the light of the Spirah gods as it shown only upon her people.

The higher he drove her pain and fear, the more she'd glow, the more of the light of her gods would spill out for him to drink up like cheap beer. Now he was soaking it up, bathing in it, getting stronger, crueler…Before long, it felt like everything but the pain had been sucked out of her.

Afterwards, Nergal buttoned her pants for her, while he led her out of the courtyard. Later, on the streetcar, he said, "It's okay, baby. Just don't puke 'til we're back on the sidewalk." Then to some concerned fellow passenger, "What can I say? They usually hold their liquor better than this."

Sally wasn't sure how long it was before they reached the big Garden District house. It must have looked normal enough from the outside. Within, music played somewhere, and the thick endoskeleton of vines might have been the only thing holding the structure together. The halls and rooms were lit, not by glass bulbs or even candles, but by big pods that dangled from the ceiling, glowing incandescently like firefly tails.

Guests gathered in the middle of a great dining room. They were all Schomites, but Nergal was the only Crimbone. Except where were his buddies, and where was Kim? Sally felt everyone eyeing her curiously, but only one came forward; a tall, proud-standing, hatchet-faced man with slicked back hair and a dark green pinstripe suit. This one wasn't Crimbone either, but he was somehow spiritually and physiologically different from the others in his own way. He spoke in a high, sharply enunciated voice, though Sally caught only a few words. Nergal held her close, but all she caught from him was that the hatchet-faced Schomite was named Talino.

Then Sally was handed over to Talino, and he led her to a darkened room. She was sure she was about to be raped again, especially with the way he held her limp form against him, whispering things in her ear she didn't understand. Later she'd realize he'd been chanting. That hadn't started the changes, but it paved the way for it. He laid her down across vines so tightly woven that it was hard to tell them from the boards. She didn't know when he left, or how long he was gone. When he returned, he'd exchanged his pinstripe jacket for a long, flowing, silky emerald housecoat. He hauled her back to the dining room. There they all were, seated around the long table. At the opposite end stood Nergal, like a proud maitre'd. His chefs—Hobs and Sam— flanked him, smeared in gore and grease. On the center of the table lay dinner, splayed open, sections already carved and divided off onto plates. Only the face was still Kim's.

Talino sat Sally by the head of the table. The head seat must be his, but he stayed behind her. "Ah, but we almost forgot. We have a recovering Spirelight's daughter in our midst, and she didn't even get to eat before she sat down. Let's get her something, shall we?"

For the second time, she felt a blade's edge on her neck. Except it wasn't a Crimbone battle knife now, but her own pocketknife, the one she hadn't tried to use on Nergal because she'd panicked like a little idiot. Then the handle pressed her palm. At first, she thought Talino was fucking with her, daring her to try to fight her way out.

"Go ahead, little Spirelight girl. Cut off a piece to eat. It'll help you recover, yeah that's right." Then softer, "You start cutting, or I do."

Clearer and clearer, the other Schomites chanted. They weren't getting louder, but their sound resonated stronger and stronger, invading her brain. Not 'til that first taste did she really feel the invasion of the chant. It no longer came from the Schomites, but pounded from within her, in time with her heartbeat, flowing out through her blood from the vile meat she'd just chewed and swallowed...

That's how the change started.

FOUR

Jesse's eyes stayed on the road. "What changed?"

"You know what they were doing, with that chanting shit?"

"There are a few possibilities."

Sally trembled, then tightened up her face and shoulders. "I still don't quite know. But it's never stopped…and I mean, nothing's really changed in me that most people could see. But…it's like the chanting, those old Schomite words I didn't understand… While they made me eat, it felt—not just tasted, *felt*, all through me—like they'd done something to the meat, so it changed my blood somehow, made me susceptible to their…spell, I guess you'd call it. Like my heartbeat synchronized to it, and even after they stopped, the new rhythm never went away, so I could never stop hearing them. I never have, either…I still feel it now."

"What they did, both to you and your friend…it never should have happened."

"Wow, really! What a relief."

"I mean it was way out of line, by our laws. Partly for what they did to the other girl, since she wasn't even a Spirelight. A ritual like that, though…Old Lords…"

"Well, I don't know what they wanted to accomplish. All it did was taint me, left me feeling like some freak. Other Spirelights sense it too, so they don't…*Damnit, those fuckers turned me into a pariah.*"

Jesse sighed. The saddest part was, he couldn't argue. Except now her pariah status increased her survival chances. If there were anything with which he could plead her case to the Cabinet, this was it. Plus, this Talino guy might still be around to hold accountable. Officially, Louisiana was still Schomite territory, but the Cabinets avoided involving it in political traffic as much as possible. The problem was, it grew more and more unchecked that way. Those swamp spirits were strange and serpentine, warmly embracing young

Schomites—Crimbone especially—caressing their brains, stroking strange things awake. The ritual Sally described should never have been performed by anyone but those of the Crimbone line, and then only on captured combatants. Properly performed, it would turn a member of the Secret Police into a living weapon against their fellows, undetectable 'til it was too late. Botched or not, it wasn't the sort of thing you could just throw together any old evening out of the blue because you had a Spirelight prisoner handy. Talino had obviously prepared and waited for just the right opportunity, so he'd put his thugs on the lookout. Jesse would have to argue against the question, *what new threat might this unclassifiable girl be?*

"I think that was their intention," he said. "To stain you before your own kind. There's no other logic in letting you live."

She squeezed the armrest and dug her feet into the floor. "I guess it worked."

"How'd you escape?"

"I didn't. After the dinner, I was locked in a dark room for days. I hurt so bad, I couldn't move, sure I had broken bones all through me."

"Did you?"

"Huh? No…Not a thing…That always seemed weird to me."

Unless they healed faster than you'd think possible…faster than you'd have healed before that ritual. Sort of like a Crimbone's injuries heal. He waited for her to continue.

"The place was deserted when my family found me. I remember my dad carrying me out, me clinging to him like a little kid again…Y'know, I remember watching Earth-line girls with their fathers, hell, even civilian Spirelights. What's the saying? *Daddy's little girl?* Well, Secret Police girls don't get that. We're not allowed to be little girls that long. But Dad…Somehow he noticed that too, and he always had a way of letting me know. Somehow, he knew how I felt, and he wished it didn't have to be that way. Like maybe part of him doubted the whole structure, everything we were all supposed to be. That's kinda funny…Y'know, thinking back, maybe seeing that in him was what got me questioning everything I looked at, so I ended up running off in the first place. Sorry, I got way off track there."

Jesse whispered, "It's okay."

"While he carried me out, I noticed the smell for the first time. I knew while I was lying there that everything stank, but I guess I figured it was my own piss and shit." She looked embarrassed. "Understand, I couldn't move while I was lying in there. It was like—"

"I know. Go on."

"While I was being carried out, I saw the light flooding in from outside. All the vines were rotting and the house was falling apart, I guess like it should've done a long time ago."

"Talino must've figured out you were a runaway."

"Kim must have mentioned it before they roasted and served her up."

"Either way, he'd realize you'd have the Secret Police— your family or another—looking for you. Did your folks have any trouble getting in and out of the city?"

"I—" Wow, she'd never thought about that before. "No. Not that I ever heard about. Then again, I was pretty out of it for a while."

"Didn't think so. I'll bet my left nut, Talino watched that house from somewhere when you were found. Obviously, your family saw the change in you."

"Oh yeah. That's how I found out how much Daddy's Little Killer Girl really ever meant to him." She spoke fast, before she could lose her nerve.

FIVE

Every time she awoke, the steel table felt a little colder, as if she hadn't had days to get used to it. When her head fell to the side, the color of the liquid in the IV bag told her something new had been added. That must be why she was waking up now. The drugs were taking effect. Soon she'd bolt against the restraints, teeth chattering to the breaking point, guts boiling 'til it felt like they must have liquefied, running out in hot waste, collecting in a pan beneath the table.

Mom would come collect a sample, after which Sheldon and Sissy would come to clean Sally up. Sometimes she still heard herself calling, begging them to at least loosen the straps. Couldn't one of them stay and talk to her, pretend she was still their sister instead of another of Mom's experiments, no better than the excrement they wiped away?

"Just tell me what the hell's going on. Please…Sheldon!"

He paused and stood in the doorway, like he might look back.

Sissy tugged his sleeve. "We should go."

"Sheldon…Sissy…I'm your sister…still your sister… Don't you still know it's me?"

"Are you really Sally?" That was Sheldon. "You at least still look like her, most of the time, but…"

"Didn't you listen to Mom and Dad? She's sort of still Sally, but the Schomites started turning her into something else. We don't know yet how far they got. Mom's trying to turn her all the way back to Sally."

"No," Sally moaned, probably too weak for either of them to hear. "Sissy…Sheldon…I wanna be just Sally again. Really. Please. Don't leave me alone like this."

"We should leave," Sissy said. "The new formula will start to work soon."

"Formula?" Sally said.

"Mom doesn't think this one will cure you, but it'll alter the infection in a way that'll make it easier to analyze, easier to figure out *how* to cure you."

The idiots were looking for a *biological* source. Of course it could be seen there, along with everywhere else in her being. It ran deeper, though, beyond anything that could be physically cured. The most profound effects were dormant, yet to be triggered. Even if Mom isolated all apparent taint, those more deeply planted seeds would lie in wait.

Sally was afraid to tell them that…but *more afraid that Mom already knew*. Because if Mom really wanted to find a cure, she would have by now. Sissy put it best…*Mom wanted to analyze the infection*. After all, it had been a while since she'd found a challenge in the lab.

"*Then at least stay and talk to me.*" How'd she found the breath for that shriek? *No, don't let them leave…not alone when I just realized*— "If I've gone somewhere else, I need help finding my way back." Then the first new stab of pain hit, so she lurched and champed.

"It's starting now." Sissy was prying Sheldon from the room. "We'd better go."

Soon Sally was lost in Mom's latest chemical hell. In the days that followed, her body froze with sweat, went dry and raw, withering like a husk. She tried to cough up saliva onto her scratchy tongue. Finally, her windpipe felt damp, probably with blood. Mom didn't seem aware of any of this, not when she came to check or add the chemicals, not when she took Sally's blood pressure, not when she stood with the rest of the family, explaining her progress. They didn't see a daughter or sister strapped there. How could they, and still watch this happen?

"Sally?"

When she blinked, the lamp spilled razors into her eyes. Once she'd squeezed them as tight as they'd go into darkness, some broken thing croaked, "*Sheldon?*"

"Shhh…They don't know I'm here."

"Please, Sheldon. Just loosen the binds."

"I can't."

"If I don't get up soon, I'll die."

"But Mom says, if we let you up before you're cured, you'd be dangerous to us."

"*She doesn't know what she's talking about.* I wouldn't hurt any of you. Okay, so maybe I'd just be a danger to myself. You can't cure me, 'cause I'm not Sally anymore. I mean I am, but not like you used to know me. I feel like I'm still myself, but different too. I don't understand it either…"

"But if you don't understand it, how do you know

you—"

"I'll go away. If you let me up, I promise I'll go. I'll sneak out, fend for myself, and they'll never know it was you that helped me."

"But…what if something even worse happens to you this time?"

"That'll be my problem. If I stay here, I'll definitely die."

"I'd better go." He squeezed her hand, like he always did before slipping out. Only this time, there was something harder about his grip, something that lingered when he drew away.

Sally's nerves must really have been shot, because she didn't realize 'til the door closed that she was holding her pocketknife. At full concentration, she pried the blade open, maneuvered it around, and sawed at the wrist strap.

SIX

A *punch-click-flip* sounded, and a small cassette popped from beneath the dashboard, into Jesse's palm.

"You were taping all that?" Sally squinted at the antiquated contraption.

Jesse slipped the tape into a plastic case and tucked it in his breast pocket. "I mean to play it at the Cabinet hearing. In your defense."

"You honestly think I have any chance?"

"Why not? You survived what you just told me about, along with everything since."

"Don't ask why. Seems this body just keeps breathing no matter what. Sometimes I think about fixing that."

"*Cut that shit out!*" His fist thumped the dashboard, making her jump. Enraged, he looked twice as huge, skin tightening on his head, neck, and hands so veins bulged. The greenery outside zipped by a little blurrier, making her dizzy 'til she looked down. His upper legs, tense against the seat, looked like great logs wrapped in blue jeans.

She was imagining one of those knees bulldozing someone's chin, when he went on, "Damnit, my best friend and I are sticking our asses on the line trying to keep you alive. *Rob's sticking his ass on the line for you*, whether or not he quits thinking with his dick long enough to notice. And you're talking about suicide! Damn you, I should—"

Sally fumed back, not because it seemed like a particularly good idea, more as an alternative to pissing herself. "Yeah, and you know what? I don't remember asking any of you to do that! Besides, that's not what I—"

"*Bullshit.*" His face twisted like one of Rob's scarier moments, only worse because Jesse seemed so at home with it. *Such a mature monster.* He probably had absolute control over where and when it came out…except now, all of a sudden, for some reason.

"So, why the hell should I be grateful? You're doing it for Rob because he wouldn't go along with you otherwise. Once he thinks I'm off that hook, you're gonna brainwash him so he'll look at me and wanna kill me. Or do to me like those bastards in—" She let out an agonized, clenched-teeth noise.

Jesse snorted 'til he was calmer. "That's not my plan."

"But the others will. Think I don't know how it works?

I'll bet your friend back there is already getting started, whittling him down."

"So you think Rob's gonna change his tune that easy?"

"Not the Rob I know. But there's something else in him too, same way there's something in me other than the Sally I guess he thinks he loves. Except with him, it's not some fucked-up thing that was put there. It's part of what he is naturally, something made of ugliness and hatred that's—" She cut herself off. "Sorry. It's just—Look, I didn't mean—"

"Yeah, you did. That's not my problem." Just like that, there was stoic ol' Jesse again. "Anyway, this thing with you, it doesn't matter whether you were born with it or not. Whatever that ritual turned you into, whatever your parents' torture did after that, it's part of who and what you are now, which is all anyone has to work with. It's all that'll ever matter to Rob."

"But what'll he do when he—"

"You expect me to know something like that? Hell, I just met the kid last night."

Sally blinked at him then laughed weakly. It was too damn weird, talking with Jesse like this. Even Rob wasn't this incongruous with everything Sally had thought she knew about the Crimbone.

According to the oldest stories from the Old World, the feud with the Schomites should only have lasted a few generations. At one point, the Schomites had been just one more race who resisted the spread of the Spirah Empire. Some other races had been willing to compromise for peace, while others weren't.

Only the Schomites fought back with such focused,

venomous hatred, running deeper than territorial disputes, like they hated the gods themselves, meant to *punish* the children of those gods for spreading the divine will. Finally, the Schomite sorcerers performed a ritual of catastrophic reverberation. It had sucked something of the essence from everyone and everything, from the Spirelights, from the Schomites, from the other races and all species, from the very land of the Old World itself. Churned into something else, it was put into Schomite fighters, thus birthing a race of monsters.

After a few centuries of their onslaught, several weaker races were driven to extinction for siding with the Spirelights. So the feud became a crusade, across worlds and ages, one that couldn't end 'til the abomination was eliminated.

Growing up, she guessed she'd believed all that as much as any child of the Secret Police. Then Talino's thugs got ahold of her. At his table, she'd been too incoherent with fear and pain and humiliation to think of childhood stories and how they did or didn't apply to her situation. In the years since, on the road, all she'd ever given a damn about was survival.

The Crimbone were a hazard to be avoided, occasionally to fight and kill. Only now did she think of the old stories, the old doctrines. Because no one before Jesse so deeply contradicted them, not even Rob.

Before long, Jesse turned onto a narrow gravel drive. It got so steep that Sally was surprised the big vehicles made the climb. Trees flanked them like walls, and fog rolled out to meet them.

"Good sign," Jesse murmured, maybe to himself.

SEVEN

Gradually the trees thinned, into what could almost be called a clearing. At the center, there stood a tall, narrow, clapboard cottage.

"We're gonna stay in that for a week?" Rob looked skeptical.

"Outhouse is to the right of it, back just a ways. 'Round back, there should be a stack of firewood for the stove. If you can't make that last, you'll find an axe and a wood splitter in the shed so you can chop more. We keep these reserve spaces furnished, scattered throughout the Crimbone-protected states and provinces. Generally, they're for refugees, like dispossessed civilian Schomites on the run from Earth-line law."

"So what happens when you get back?"

"Assuming things go well—wait, scratch that, assuming things don't get completely fucked to shit—we'll probably take you up north, start your real education. You probably won't be there long, if you are a High Natural. Vermont ain't exactly the place that could use one the most."

Rob still had no idea what a High Natural was, let alone if he was one. Except when Puttergong had said it, it hadn't felt like his first time hearing it. There came that weird familiarity, too solid for *déjà vu* but still shy of a real memory. Either way, he was out of the Jeep before Zane killed the ignition, up next to Sally's window before the van fully stopped. When she climbed out, he could tell she'd been crying. What the hell had Jesse told her?

She didn't say anything, just pressed her face against his chest and squeezed his shoulders. Running his hands through her hair, he couldn't wait 'til Jesse and Zane were gone. All around, the world felt like some ugly, invading predator he couldn't drive away.

Jesse checked out the house. Zane leaned on the Jeep 'til he came out. "Everything set?"

"Mostly. Not as much food as I thought. When was this place last used, anyway?"

"Who knows? There enough food for a week, assuming the kids know how to ration?"

"Probably."

Zane looked to the knives on Rob's belt, then smelled and listened to the forest. "Eh, they'll do fine."

Jesse nodded, feeling ever stranger around Rob. Maybe it was because he'd gotten used to hearing about the guy as his son's best friend for all these years. All Jesse's Earth-line pals from his castoff days were long dead of old age, assuming they'd made it that far. Now here was Rob, where Louis was supposed to be.

Jesse shouted to the kids, "Need any showing around?"

Sally climbed the porch. "I think we can figure things out for ourselves."

There, that hard-soft flash in those reddish-copper eyes… Yeah, Jesse was starting to get it. He caught Rob by the shoulder. "Whatever the hell she is, Spirelight or something else…she's made of something you don't just always find. I'm saying you're one damn lucky little sonofabitch. Take care of her."

As their eyes met, Rob felt the strange sensation of

picking a girl up for a date, facing the scariest future father-in-law in history. *No, you already killed that guy, remember?*

"Hey Jess, give me another minute with the boy, would you?" Zane led Rob back to the Jeep and popped the glove box. Into his massive palm tumbled a chunk of computer paper bound through punched holes. Pink card stock covered either side. "While you're waiting, start catching up on your history."

Rob read the top leaf: *The Schomite Heritage in the New World.* He flipped through it and spotted lots of old photographs, drawings and diagrams photocopied onto the pages, interspersed amongst small-print text. "Anything in here about how I'm supposed to use these?" He tapped a knife handle again. "I mean, y'know, fighting stances, exercises I could do, shit like that?"

Zane bellowed laughter. "Kid, the training you'll go through for that, we don't put down on paper. You'll know why soon enough, don't worry. Besides, from what I hear, you've already figured out some moves of your own. And hey, I thought you were supposed to be a High Natural."

"Think maybe someone could please explain what the hell that means?"

"You haven't remembered yet? Hey, don't worry. If you are, you will soon enough. You anxious to learn to handle those blades? How good are you at handling yourself?"

"What, like in a tight spot? I'm—"

"In life, in love, in hate, in danger or safety, whatever. Over the generations, I guess these lands have taken the Schomites in and made us their own, but that's not enough for a Crimbone. That's the real reason we cast our children to the world, to the Earth-line people, before we teach you anything important of your true heritage. So you'll be forced to absorb a perspective on all of it, its nature, its people, their art, their craft, their song. So at the end of the day, you know you're as much a part of them or anything here as you are of the Crimbone line. I'll let you in on something. Jesse and me, we've been at this together for more decades than you'd believe. If you're smart—not just strong and skilled, but smart enough to use that strength and skill—you might make it that far. You know how good I'd be with those knives of yours if I tried using them?"

"Whoever you were up against, they'd probably be a bunch of dead motherfuckers."

"I'd probably take two swings, slip and cut my own dick off. You know why?"

"Because the blades came to me, because of how I'm fused with them."

"Hey, you *are* smart. But no, not quite. The blades are your soul. Like I said, your choices are nothing but the confirmation of your truest self. A Crimbone finds those choices with three things; the voice of the land, the blood in your own veins, and those blades. Through them—when you decide to use 'em, or when you decide not to use 'em— you work the will of your purest self, against whatever opposes it. Remember, though, a lot of that opposition comes from whatever bullshit you've let the idiots around you fill your head with. And no, not just those Earth-line pussies. That might include me, or Jesse, or your girl back there pretending not to listen in on this conversation. The blades will never fail you, unless you wield them towards ends untrue to yourself."

Considering what Rob had accomplished so far—a mother and daughter jerking and twitching to a stop at the end of his arms— he couldn't find much comfort in Zane's words.

GUESSWORK

Late Sunday morning, the Second Chief Elder of Pennsylvania opened his window on the Pittsburgh skyline and let the winds know that he wished to see two Crimbone.

Kirb Buchner and Terry Lopez's roads led to the tower of black glass that rose from the middle of downtown. Upon spotting each other near the front door, they exchanged smirking grunts. Not much else it could mean, two Crimbone finding their way to this courtyard at once. They entered the lobby and took a stairwell no Earth-line people ever used, then sat in a waiting room on the top floor. Only one phone line worked up here, with no internet or fax machine. The office received a lot of packages and letters, though. For a while, the Second Chief Elder spoke on the phone with Vermont in the next room.

Terry listened in, though you'd never know by looking at him. Nothing about his lazy posture suggested how all his energy was directed into his sense of hearing, or that said sense was focused on penetrating the Elder's office, through walls that weren't thin. His other senses were cold, sterile and distant, like images flickering in the back of his mind.

Finally, he whispered to Kirb, "Something big's happening up in Vermont. Something about a High Natural, and some huge astrophysical disaster that leveled half a town. The Spirelight Secret Police are involved. It has something to do with those dead bus station attendants and last week's apartment slaying." He didn't need to specify further. The dead man had been on parole after a stint for dealing crack, so the cops said his death was gang-related. Needless to say, they'd downplayed the more colorful details for the media.

"Cannibal Spirelights now, huh," said Kirb. "So the Elder thinks they headed to Vermont?"

"Yeah. Sounds like someone's worried about open war, as in the kind the Earth-line people would notice."

"You mean other than puppet-cover?"

"The Vermont Cabinet sure seems to think so. It's the Elder here wants us to look into it, make sure the Vermont Cabinet doesn't screw it up any more than they already have."

An hour later, the Elder called them in and told them about half of what Terry had already overheard. They were to drive to Brattleboro, take the hearts of any Spirelights they found—Secret Police or not—and bring the fledgling to Pittsburgh. Avoid contact with Vermont brethren if possible. If it became unavoidable, inform them they'd been overruled. From what they knew of Vermont, Kirb and Terry didn't see that going well, but they still headed straight for the rusty blue van Terry kept in lockup. Neither man spoke 'til they felt the city's farewell.

"Kirb," said Terry. "You realize we weren't given a choice today, about taking this job?"

Kirb's eyes stayed on the road. "Whatever's going on here, there's no choice left. Can't you feel it? This world's narrowing everyone's trail. It started in Vermont, then narrowed all the way down to the Elder, leaving him no other way but us. If this fledgling's a High Natural, his trail's narrowed tightest of all. Since he's still a fledgling, he doesn't even know how to see that trail, let alone keep to it."

They found Brattleboro in time with Monday's sun. There wasn't much traffic, but before they so much as found their bearings, two cars almost broadsided them. Another nearly rear-ended them. A fourth pulled out sharply, almost too close for Kirb to stomp the brakes in time. All this happened in the space of ten minutes.

"*Motherfucker*," hissed Kirb, "does this place really just not like our looks or what?"

"I don't think it likes Crimbone right now, period. C'mon, let's grab breakfast."

"Fuck that. At this rate, we'll probably get food poisoning."

"Not as likely as if we caught and killed and grilled it ourselves." Terry's eyes narrowed sorrowfully. "I always heard this state favored the Schomites."

"Maybe, but the town's *pissed*. My guess is, that little out-of-control fledgling punk's been busy. Let's figure what we can—about why—from the papers."

They grabbed a local newspaper then found a Friendly's Diner on the outer end of town. The waitress was too perky for this hour. "Just so you know, you guys should get out of town." They both figured she'd really said something like, *Just so you know, we're out of hash browns.*

Over coffee, they divided the paper between them. Kirb read up on the car wreck on Putney Road with the dead hippies in the trunk. Terry got the story about the house full of corpses across the river. They read quickly, then exchanged pages.

When the waitress brought their food, Kirb noticed a cigarette tucked in her ear.

As he read the rest of the article, mentions of the town of Marlboro kept catching his eye. The police sergeant heading the investigation was originally from Marlboro, the article found a few cute little ways to mention. They were investigating possible connections between the massacre across the river with the murders in town. A former Marlboro College student was believed missing. Speculations placed him as either victim or one of several perpetrators.

When the waitress scuttled back over, Kirb spotted her nerves buzzing anxiously. Her cigarette had left her ear, now between two fingers. A glance confirmed it as a Marlboro cigarette.

"What you're looking for isn't here anymore, okay, gentlemen?" *Is everything here okay, gentlemen?*

Kirb said, "Say, how do we find Marlboro College?"

The waitress rattled off directions. Once she left, Terry said, "So you think the High Natural's hiding out at the college?"

"I think the High Natural—if that's what he is—might be the missing former Marlboro student. If he ain't at the campus, he's somewhere on that mountain."

The road to Marlboro led back to the interstate, then up an exit ramp not far from the one into town. As the terrestrial spirit shifted from the spread of civilization to mountainous wilderness, Kirb and Terry felt the ancestral familiarity of something only vaguely pretending to be tamed by Earth-line progress. Even the broad, paved, well-kept road tilted and curved dangerously in its steep climb.

"What are you getting from this place?" asked Kirb.

"It's still feeling us out. It'll be hard for us to get—"

From the right, the brush heaved and tore, and a huge, gaunt moose skidded into the road. Terry had never seen so much stark terror in the eyes of such a big, powerful animal. Metal screeched like a bird of prey as it pulverized the grill and glass showered their faces like raindrops. The moose's head jutted through the windshield like a trophy on a wall. Its muzzle barreled against Kirb's shoulder while an antler transfixed his face. The van spun and screeched. Then they soared, slammed, and rolled downwards. The cliff wasn't incredibly high, but the bottom was enough out of sight that no one above would spot the wreck for a while.

By the time Terry regained some senses, he'd already crawled most of the way out. He wasn't sure how he'd managed to unbuckle his seatbelt, let alone haul himself through the shattered window. His joints rattled in their sockets, his muscles nearly torn from the bones. His weapon—a large hammer molded from a single chunk of the black metal—was already in hand. When his free hand groped to steady himself, he touched the moose's damp, mangled hide. High above sounded the wheezing laugh of the creature that had driven the animal from the forest into their path. Twenty years ago, the laugh's owner had landed Terry in another auto wreck, intending to force him to use his hammer on the angry friends of the biker he'd crashed into.

Terry wiped blood from his eyes and stared up the cliff side. "Puttergong!"

Gurgling growls came from within the van. "Puttergong? Who the fuck's Puttergong?" Kirb's arm flailed from the upturned passenger doorway, ragged sinew hanging from exposed bones.

Puttergong's wheezing laugh sounded louder and madder than ever. Kirb jackknifed out, on the palm of that mangled arm. His weapon of black metal was a crescent-moon sickle that ran a foot and a half out from the handle. He held it ready in his other hand, despite the broken shoulder. His face was a putty sack of jumbled features. One eye dangled next to his mouth. That mouth had gone wider and ragged on one side, showing two rows of shattered teeth.

"Guess this place don't like y'all degenerate ol' *Crimbone-light*," hooted the Familiar's hovering voice.

The bloated shape barreled from the trees towards Kirb's chest. The sickle flailed in what would have once been a flawless killing sweep. The Familiar glided under the blade then sucked itself in tight as it shot between Kirb's legs. Its rear talons opened both his femoral arteries. More blood spurted and splashed the mangled metal surface, and he toppled backwards.

As Terry gripped his hammer, Puttergong flapped down and landed on the red, wet surface where Kirb had just stood. "Hate to say it, ol' Thumper-Stumper, but you disappointed me."

Obviously Puttergong meant for Terry to charge in. No, he'd make Puttergong come to him. He'd probably die like Kirb, but his body was in enough of a single piece that he might take his old Familiar with him.

First, though, he croaked, "Why?"

"'Cause ye just can't cut it, Thumper-Stumper. None o' your Earth-line pussy-whipped generation of Crimbone can. Ye ain't been cuttin' it for I don't wanna think how far back!

Hell, you ain't even got it straight who or what you're supposed to be listenin' to no more. This ol' mountain's been sayin' to back off since before you started climbin' it, 'cause this shit ain't your fight, ain't none of yer damn business. But *nooo*, you fellers just had to keep on *followin' orders* from some pussyass civvy shit Schomite charge back in the armpit of the burgs. So I done decided it's time we went back to the drawin' board an' got shit *back on schedule*."

With that, the Familiar bolted from its perch, wings wider than Terry ever remembered them spanning. He timed his defense by fragments of a second, swung the hammer—

—And plowed empty air. Puttergong hadn't come forward at all, just hopped violently, as though taking flight. Before Terry could right himself, the creature *did* swoop forward, jaws agape, razor teeth aimed right at its former fledgling's throat.

FOOTWORK

ONE

Hours after Jesse and Zane left on Saturday, Rob had found a chipped, stained chunk of glass hanging on the wall, something he guessed was supposed to be a mirror. He dusted it off as best he could, with an old shirt someone had left lying around—probably a little something from the last guests here. Maybe they'd left in a hurry, because the mountain didn't like the smell of them. Maybe it had liked their pursuers better.

Sally had been exploring the loft floor above. She came down the narrow, shady, miniature spiral staircase to find him peeling back the strips of tape from the gauze on his face. She slipped up behind him silently. He didn't flinch when he spotted her in the mirror. She put a hand on his shoulder. Her touch was nice, especially now. He liked her reflection better than the red ruin about to make its first appearance.

A damp antiseptic smell puffed from beneath the bandages. Then there, on his forehead, the first inch of a thin red line, then the one next to it, full of tiny black barb-speckled staples. The surrounding flesh was white and shriveled. How could it look so clean, when the bandage was so brown-red-greenish splotchy? Rob looked at his reflection and let out a dull laugh. Sally's hand slipped from his shoulder. The red, stitch-tracked line forked halfway up his cheek, past either side of his eye. He wasn't surprised when she turned away.

"Hey, you know," he said, "it's not as bad as I expected. Guess it's worse than you bargained for, though. Heh."

She pressed a small fist to her mouth, then looked at him. "What did I say before? Give me more credit."

They both glanced at the mesh of peeled-off bandages, still open in his palm like a rotted-out turtle shell. The dull splotches ran through its center like a forked spine.

"Fine," he said. "What is it, then?"

"*Don't you get it now?* This is what's waiting for us. Over and over, piling up 'til something cuts too deep to leave just a scar."

He glanced in the mirror again. No, he wasn't ugly. He looked more like a bad joke, a painting of some goofy, messed-up kid from the sticks, like someone had strolled by and run a red marker up and down that face to look like a badass Crimbone scar.

"See?" she went on, "My family…They won't stop until we're—"

"They're dead." There, he'd blurted it out. "I killed them." *They're dead by my hand, and you don't have to be afraid of them anymore.*

He wasn't sure which came first, her laughter or sobs. Both grew hysterical, alternating then merging. Then she grabbed him so hard that it hurt, squeezed and kneaded at him, rubbed her face against his chest. Blood pumped beneath the stitches like it meant to break the mending flesh. He ran his hands through her hair, kissed her, pressed the length of his body as full as he could to hers, felt her press and grind back. Her enthusiasm was such a pleasant surprise, it almost weirded him out.

Well, why shouldn't she get excited? We're what we have. I'm what she has, because they're dead, because they couldn't kill me. What else needed to be real?

He growled low and pressed closer, rougher…then all of a sudden, something about her wasn't so warm. He eased back. "What's wrong?"

She sank a little deeper into herself. "Jesus. They're really gone. I mean really dead. Can you believe it?"

"Yeah." *I gutted them myself, remember?* Damnit, why couldn't he feel more of this with her, lift at least some of her burden? After everything they'd shared, that frame of reference was one thing she'd denied him, even when she'd finally told him what those bastards had done to her. "I thought you wanted that."

Finally, she looked at him. "I'm not angry at you, Rob."

He didn't quite believe her. No, she was too far away to be angry, too deep in the core of herself, encased in too much ice, afraid to let herself back into this world without her family as a frame of reference.

"You don't need them to free you," he said. "You never did. You need yourself. You need me. We have a place together, wherever we are."

Still, there'd always be that point where it would get to be too much, when the littlest things would make her see her weaknesses and failings, and the ice would be all she could retreat to…a little deeper each time, always in more danger of getting lost there. Yeah, Rob sure knew how to spot that one. He wouldn't—couldn't—lose her to it.

Then she hit him with, "How did it feel? When you killed them?"

"How do you think? You know how it is. Right? It's just…everything boils down to you and them, and whatever fixes it so you're the one who's still kickin' afterwards. Everything else comes later, when you have time to think about it."

"But you killed them with your black blades."

"Yeah." He saw in her eyes what she was really scared of…what she knew. *He'd thirsted for their deaths, exactly like any Crimbone who'd ever tried to kill her.* She started turning away, but he caught her shoulder. "Like I'll use them on anything that tries to hurt you."

That should be the only answer that mattered, right? So why wasn't it? Maybe she wished it was too. Too many conflicting responses were hitting her at once, along with questions too painful to ask. So she slipped back into that cold place, away from them, away from him.

Now he awoke next to her in the dark, felt cold himself. It must be near dawn. She'd rolled away, taking most of the blanket with her. It'd be nice to just watch her sleep for a while. There wasn't enough moonlight, especially with the one small window looking in on the loft.

A moment ago, in his dream, he'd been holding the knives. They'd been soaked like the temple's floor. The rest of the pack had moved on, for more slaughter and feasting. He'd stood alone, staring down at the book lying on the altar, the same book Zane had given him, open somewhere in the middle. The temple was dark, yet Rob saw the pages just fine, the words on the right, the picture on the left. Except the picture was different than the one he'd seen when he'd sat reading it in the cabin. Both showed the same scene—Magur Sevi emerging before the Schomites from the valley of mist—but he'd seen this one somewhere else. Hadn't he? This one was almost as richly detailed, but it was drawn in pencil.

Almost time to move on, Rob.

"Not really. We still have a week."

A week's not that long. It might be longer than an epoch, though, if that's any consolation. Had Jesse Karn somehow sent Louis to check on things, just to irritate Rob?

Right now, an epoch felt damn short. Days were long. Moments were longer. Lives were short. Even awake in bed, Rob still saw the temple, smelled the gore that soaked it and his body. He couldn't see Louis, so he opened his eyes and touched his stitches. Last time he'd touched his face, they hadn't been there. That had been back in the Spirelight temple. If he'd touched his legs, arms or torso there, he'd have felt the open, coursing wounds. It would probably be a long time before he'd see the temple, see Louis or the Old World again.

It won't be that long. Just until you sleep again, 'til you dream again.

"Yeah," he said. "These days, I can't seem to wait 'til I'm asleep. To start dreaming again, I mean." In the low morning light, he glanced over at Sally.

Yeah, but those aren't exactly dreams, you know.

Rob sat up. Damn, it was cold in here. He wanted to curl back up against Sally, to dream only of her. "I know. They're memories, aren't they?"

He practically saw that slow shrug Louis used to do, his eyes scanning the floor for answers. *Not exactly that, either, but we can call them that if you like.*

When Rob rubbed his temples, his fingertips grazed a prickly line. The flesh around the stitches no longer gave pulling, low-burning protest. They were healing and toughening fast, growing up from tender whiny wounds to cold, deep scars. Beneath them, his brain felt like a knotted tangle. Running uphill, then in the ruined temple, his mind hadn't felt knotted and his skull hadn't felt like a prison. Even his wounds had howled ecstatically, caring nothing for the scars they'd soon become. He couldn't howl now, not with Sally sleeping there next to him. Instead, he tried to whisper himself through the rut.

"It has something to do with this whole High Natural thing. I think I'm…No, they're not my memories. I wasn't one of those Crimbone. Or I might have been a few of them, in a way, in their times, but…It has something to do with the Coscan bloodline. Crimbone bloodlines carry on the power, the prowess of those who've come before, isn't that right?" The book had mentioned something like that. "Most fledglings, it's in 'em, but it sleeps, waits to be passed on, to live in the next generation's dreams. Maybe some of it wakes up once they're seasoned, but not much, not even the tip of the iceberg. Not all bloodlines survive so long. If a Crimbone bloodline survives a certain number of generations, after so many thousands of years, it all builds up enough…" He clenched his fists.

Go on. You're doing fine.

Sally stretched and groaned in her sleep. "Quiet," Rob hissed at Louis. "You might wake her."

Dude, if you're worried about me *waking her up, you really* are *going nuts.*

"Could we go outside? Talk out there?" No answer sounded. Rob took that for a yes.

He found his way down the spiral staircase as quietly as he could in the dark. The black blades lay on the table like uncollected silverware, next to Zane's book. One of Rob's hands fell on the scabbards, while the other leafed through the pages, to a grainy photocopy of an old Schomite painting. Less than a week ago, the early light through the kitchen window would hardly have been enough for him to see it. By now, he could recite the words from memory:

"Out of the deadly, misty valley he came, clad already in his long, dark coat, his blades dripping, his face already its mass of scars, this Crimbone the likes of which we'd not seen, so purely so, he might never have been a fledgling. Already he was mad, for it was a madman's laugh with which he greeted us. With that laugh, the mists of the deadly valley rolled back behind him. When we peered past his shoulders, we saw into the valley, and we saw that he had butchered to the last the abominations that had so long held us to the slope. He ought to have been dead already, many times over, from all his deep wounds. But he could not die, not with a fate unfulfilled, one he owed us and our enemies…"

Rob looked again at the picture. Magur Sevi, the great Crimbone hero of the Old World, returning from the valley, his blades dripping…the first High Natural.

Rob picked up his own two great knives. As always, their touch tingled and sparked at something. There, yes, the memory, of those blades plowing through flesh and bone, the taste of the glow. Now it seemed like his nerves had lived in the metal in that moment. Something had spurted with the blood, alien energy that flowed into him…

It was less cold outside than in. *Why'd you bring those along?*

"These are the same knives from that old drawing of yours, aren't they?"

You've been given the blades that are your soul.

Rob stepped down off the porch and rubbed his feet in wet grass. No crickets or night birds chirped. Too bad this hadn't happened back during the summer. For one thing, Louis had still been alive then. "You could've handled it, Lou…We could've taken it all on together."

Taken on what?

"Will you not play dumb right now?"

No, really. We could've taken on lots of things. There's a lot we did take on, remember?

Rob slid one knife from the scabbard. It started as an idle motion, but there was no idleness once he saw that strange black metal, when he felt its weight unfettered, perfectly balanced in his hand. The blade shimmered in the fading moonlight…shimmered red, shimmered black. It felt more…buoyant in his grasp than he remembered. It occurred to him he'd never cleaned the blades after breaking them in. He held this one out with the flat up and waved it in the moonlight. A silvery bar ran up and down it, hilt to tip, like the slide on a scale. Sure enough, when he touched the metal with his fingertips, it was smooth and clean, as though it had absorbed the enemy's blood…drank it. "This whole world. Like we took on the Old World."

Yeah, but we never took on the Old World, not like you're thinking. As for this world, it's been taking us on, letting us live on its terms for the last ten thousand years at least. C'mon, you've been reading that book.

So far, the book had been mostly about those thousands of years here. It was the glimpses of the Old World that captivated Rob. The red swirl filled his eyes, that billowing mist that tried to take too many shapes at once. The Earth-line world rose, spread, evolved. The Spirelights and the Schomites caught its currents and flowed with it because the lands let them. Bit by bit, they manipulated their way into the Earth-line intrigues, so Earth-line bloodletting became the mask and camouflage for Deschembine bloodletting, sometimes the vehicle and pawn.

All of that happened before you read about it.

"Except it's still going on."

Because now you've read it, so you start to live it. Except you're still living what's going on now, around you, and you're already getting the two mixed up.

"So is that what it means to be a High Natural, or whatever the fuck I'm supposed to be?"

Man, you are so close *to getting it!*

"That's not all it is, though, and you damn well fucking know it. From the sound of things, if the Schomites thrive too well anywhere, we have to worry about the Spirelight Secret Police backing whatever Earth-line war's brewing nearby. So the Crimbone slip in and make sure those wars ruin whatever use the Spirelights could possibly have for those spots, which at least leaves enough natural resources for us to get by on. Except now we have to worry about those Earth-line people permanently ruining the whole damn planet with their *technology* of destruction."

Yeah, I know. I saw all that up close overseas, remember? Pardon me if you're not blowing my mind with whatever grand solution to everything you've figured out after reading a book while hiding out in a cabin on a wooded mountain for a few days.

"Except now it'll all go on through me—has to go on through me—and I can't just fall in and play that game. That ain't what a Crimbone does." Rob bit his lip. "It should've gone on through both of us."

Not when you think about it. Not for much longer. See, there's really nowhere else to go. If there were, we'd be there by now, or at least be able to see whatever it was.

"Bullshit!"

Yeah? Think about everything you've read, all this stuff you're remembering. Look at where the Earth-line people are by now. Do you think our little feuds really matter for them in the end? Not really. So why do you think that is?

Rob ripped the second blade free. The scabbards fell in the grass. "Because we've let ourselves get weak here."

No. We've fought a strong fight, for as long as we could. The lands have blessed our fight, watching for a while what would grow from it. Soon it'll reel us in beneath its own natural ways. Before long, the civilian Schomites here won't need the Crimbone anymore. There'll be no more use for the Spirelight Secret Police…except to join up with the Earth-line police departments, maybe.

"Great, even bigger assholes as cops!" Some abstract panic electrified Rob's limbs. His first blade swung in a whirling arc. His whole body moved into it like a tight-tuned machine, the energy meeting in that single stroke, wide and strong and fluid enough to disembowel three men at once. It retracted just as his other arm shot out in a perfect stabbing motion. He spun on his heels, one blade parrying while the other made a deadlier sweep.

Footwork and body alignment slipped into methods

and movements he'd learned in old martial arts and fencing courses, blended with rougher moves he'd picked up on the street or in bars. Then he found his way into something more refined, natural, instinctual. His feet pivoted, shifted, slid and danced in the grass, arms finding their ways into deadlier, impossibly coordinated attacks. At least he'd have thought it impossible days ago. Every motion felt utterly familiar, yet he'd never thought he could move like this. Hell, a *human body* wasn't supposed to be able to move like this! Strange endorphins, dormant all his life, exploded through his bloodstream. The knots in his brain were gone, the fog evaporated into a pure, high flame. What had come before the flame, before this explosion of ages?

A boy named Rob Coscan and a girl named Sally Wildfire had been brought here for some reason. Rob strained, reached for that boy and girl. Blue bled brighter over the skies, blotting out the night, a star at a time.

Rob slumped to one knee. "Why can't she just fight it a little harder? I…You got any idea how much it can suck, loving her like this? I've heard what she's been through. I see what she's going through. Part of me feels it with her even when we're not in the same place. Not being there for her, through whatever, is the one thing I can't accept. But I can't do anything with this. She won't let me. Why didn't you let me help you, Lou?"

Maybe I could have. Maybe she still can. But what would be the point?

"So that's why you fucking killed yourself?" Rob's stitches strained. "Because you thought there was no more point?"

You know better than that.

"So what good is a Crimbone High Natural, showing up when the lands decide they don't need the Crimbone anymore?"

Who knows?

"It might help if someone finally told me just what the fuck a *High Natural* is."

You tell me. While you're at it, go ahead and tell yourself. No, don't think about it. Just spit it out. See what you find.

Rob drew a deep breath, then said, "A Crimbone who's *actively, consciously awake* to all the memories, all the power and attunement, of every ancestor who lives on within my blood, all at once. Sounds great, right? Except whenever I try to look inside at even a fraction of it, it all hits me at once, so I feel like I gotta *let myself* go crazy, just so my brain doesn't explode!"

So maybe your brain will explode. Or you'll go completely crazy. Or just maybe, you'll figure out how to chill the fuck out, learn to just let it all settle in a bit at a time. Weirder things have happened…like, oh, I don't know, a Crimbone and a Spirelight falling in love. Maybe the coming times are when a Crimbone High Natural will be needed most. Except not to fight for the old hatreds. Maybe it's time the Crimbone truly make the Schomites strong in this world. But not to dominate, and not to survive as refugees…but to finally be truly a part of these lands.

"Just absorbed into it, you mean. Be Earth-line people."

Maybe. Why not?

"Because they're *weak.*" Rob rose, knives poised anew. "They've made *us* weak. Yeah, sure, we call it *blending in, living secretly among them*, but what we've really done is let them fucking domesticate us. They don't hear the voice of these lands. They never have, *and they never will, unless* we *shake them awake*. Otherwise, why should we or the lands care what happens to them? We've never fully harnessed the strength here because we've been too scared, too timid, playing by their rules—not the land's, theirs. Don't you get it, Lou? Why do you think it took us in, in the first place?" The blades spun in twin rainbow arcs, clockwise and counter-clockwise. Rob's body and consciousness were one, ablaze, thirsting.

That's exactly what our ancestors thought, when they got here. There's no more room for that mentality. There's no more room for us, not as we are.

"Oh there's room," Rob growled. "Room for me, room for Sally. I'll make room if I have to. *I'll carve it out with these!*"

One blade stabbed backwards while the other swung forward. The latter edge struck something thick and tough, right as Rob snapped his wrist, hips pivoting with sadistic coordination. Overhead brush tore through itself, and he darted backwards. The heavy branch struck the ground in front of him. His head started to clear. He stood at the end of the yard, at the thick forest's edge. The house sat many yards back.

"Louis?" No answer came. Rob touched his face and saw watery red on his fingertips in the moonlight.

Back on the porch, a white shape stood outlined in the doorway. There was enough light by now that he might have made her out anyway, except she also *glowed*. That was one more thing that would always be there. Where the other Spirelights would incite rampaging bloodlust, though, she filled him with only helpless longing. He started across the yard. She stared at his lowered knives. They slipped from his grasp and let off soggy crunches as the tips stuck in the earth.

"See?" he said. "I'm not gonna hurt you. I never will." That was one thing he'd prove to her somehow, even if he couldn't rid her of her own demons. He climbed the porch and embraced her. He shivered as he held her, felt her warmth. "Please don't hate me, Sally," he whispered. "Please don't ever hate me."

She cupped his face. "Listen to me. I don't hate you. I know you won't hurt me. That's not what I'm afraid of." She touched his stitches. "Come on in. I don't want you out here, making yourself bleed this early in the morning."

Two

Sheldon awoke aware and alert, from deep dreamless sleep, in the bed of Janie's dead brother. There was no clock in here, so he looked at the light through the window. Janie would be at school. Annie had worked late, so she'd still be asleep.

He'd wasted Sunday, hadn't even checked the local news for leads. At least he'd spared Janie more trouble from local punks. The Boys & Girls Club was closed on Sundays. Outside the crack house up Elliot Street, he'd found the one called Russ shooting his mouth off about how he'd get that little bitch Janie and fuck her up for putting his friends in the hospital.

Russ was found hours later, stuffed in a trash can,

blubbering through a shattered jaw, all four limbs broken. The cops might have gotten a better description of the attacker, if the victim hadn't bitten his own tongue in half. Afterwards, Sheldon had caught up with Janie and Annie in Twice Upon A Time Antiques. He hadn't mentioned what he'd been up to. After that, Annie had taken the kids to a movie. Sheldon had never been to a movie theatre before. He hadn't mentioned that, either.

Had Annie known about his duties, she'd probably tease him, say something like *Silly young man, lettin' yourself get spoiled, goin' soft an' lazy.*

Scowling, he slipped out of bed and found his sandals. For all he knew, Sally had already moved on, this time with her beast. No, they'd still be in town, or somewhere nearby. They thought they could relax, that they'd—

—Unless they realized they'd missed one, or the Familiar told them. They'd be on their way to find him…along with Janie and Annie. Sheldon stormed down the hall, then yanked himself to a halt. *Calm down, idiot. Think now. Feel when you're finished.* He took deep, slow breaths. Annie's door was to his right. Within, there sounded a sleeper's faint shifts.

Outside, Sheldon's eyes met the dew-bright morning clear and sharp, limbs hard and steady. That creep Russ had helped to chase the last rust from his brain. Now there was other rust to cleanse. Around back, the machete leaned against the fence where he'd left it. The haft felt as good as before, but the blade looked less sure now. Could it have deteriorated more in two days, or had it just looked better in the mist, to his rattled, anxious brain?

When he swung, the blade whistled. Dewdrops rained

from it, followed by floating specks of rust. The rust was red, but the drops were clear. The next time he shook moisture from the metal, there would be no rust, and the drops would be red. With another swing, he felt the weight, then wiped it against his leg and set it down on some dry boards.

Yesterday, he'd passed a hardware store on Main Street. Now he went there and bought rags, oil, and a small sharpening stone…along with a collection of spray cans, each with a different inactive ingredient from a list in his head. Few people would think to mix the products as he meant to, but it would be worth it once the mixture activated. The last thing he picked up was a tin can of lighter fluid. The hardware store sold machetes, new ones that might be sturdier. No, he'd chosen his weapon, had already started developing the needed familiarity. Before all else, Dad had always said, be familiar with your instruments. The more arduous the task, the more intimate should be your acquaintance with the instrument. Towards that end, Sheldon could think of nothing better than the work ahead. He retrieved the machete from the backyard, kept it low at his side, and headed towards the woods. He needed privacy for this.

Past the graveyard, deep in the trees, the hill banked almost sharply enough to be a cliff. Midway down, Sheldon found a brush-shrouded, hollowed-out ledge. He pushed the brush aside with the flat of the blade, then crawled in and sat with his legs folded beneath him. A road ran by at the bottom of the hill. Hopefully, no one would look up as they drove by, see him through the vines and shadow.

He set to work polishing the blade. The rust didn't run

as deep as he'd feared, and it wasn't long before the red gave way to shimmering gray. By the time the first rag was solidly clay-colored, only speckled pocks and slivers showed in the metal. Sheldon oiled it and went to work with the next rag. Before long, his arm got sore and his fingers cramped up, but he kept working. After an hour, he coated the metal in a layer from each spray can, rubbed them in, then he lathered it in lighter fluid. He found a dry stone, held the blade at arm's length, averted his eyes, and struck once like a guitar pick striking a single perfect, echoing chord. For a few seconds, the blade lit up like a giant matchhead, brighter and hotter than he'd expected. By some miracle, the trees and brush didn't catch on fire. Once the smoke wafted away, he wiped off the thin layer of soot. Now the blade glowed as if white-hot in the sun's glare…a blade properly treated by Spirelight alchemy, fit to withstand the black metal of the Crimbone.

Sheldon picked up the sharpening stone. This he couldn't rush, and he wouldn't be done 'til every inch of edge was perfect. Perfect meant shredding the toughest flesh like wet mud, skulls like grapes, bones like twigs.

After three hours, he slipped the cooling machete through his belt and climbed out of the hollow. Up through the trees, he saw the graveyard, but not the street. He drew the machete and spun it in a figure-eight pattern, the better to learn its weight, to get his arms and the body moving just right with it. He spun in small, contained arcs, moving mostly just his wrist, then in broader motions so his whole arm flexed and spun, relearning its range, 'til his body felt new circulation and coordination. He'd go slow, concentrating on the subtleties of the movements, then fast to test his precision. Always the edge led, cutting the air with no clumsy strokes that might glance off a target or otherwise swing untrue. Always it was his hand, his arm, his body that guided, never letting the swinging steel fly on its own or skew his reflexes. Weeds grew tall and branches hung low, but the blade touched none of them except when he chose. Finally, he swung at a low branch of medium width. The *thunk* reverberated in his back and shoulders. The branch fell, leaving a smooth, white knob near the trunk.

"Hehehehehe."

Sheldon whipped about, eyes darting, waist pivoting, feet shifting through crackling leaves. The blade cut upwards and pointed straight out.

"Keep playin' with that there knife, Cop-Boy, you gonna slip an' whack yer pecker off 'fore you ever get a chance to use it…'less you already been puttin' it to that there lil' injun gal…Damn, you cop-kids get started young, huh?"

"Where's your beast, Familiar? Tell him to come out! Don't think you'll distract me so he can sneak up on me."

"Oh, ye don't think so, huh?"

A high branch shook as something took flight. Wind whistled against gliding wings and a heavy downward-speeding body. The machete struck something plump and yielding, cleaved jelly guts and thin, hollow bones. Sheldon's eyes bulged, teeth bared. Half the body dropped at his feet, the other half yards away. Ratty feathers floated down. The smear on the blade was thin, runny, dark. Without touching it, Sheldon knew it would be cold. He looked down and saw that yes, the cut was clean and smooth. Much of the meat was gone, though. Half the edges were ragged, the guts eaten away so the trunk sagged hollowly.

Sheldon's eyes flashed back up. There were no birds in sight. He'd have looked in the direction the dead pigeon had been thrown from, but of course the Familiar would already have changed spots.

"Well that right there tells me all I need to know. You good to go, lil' Cop-Boy! Okay, much fun as it'd be to sit out here an' fuck with your head all night, better keep this here show movin'. So shut up an' listen." High up, the voice darted everywhere.

"Where's your beast?" Sheldon repeated.

"Smart money says, either givin' your sister another high, hard rabid-dawg hump-a-scrump, or practicin' with them shiny new blades o' his."

"New blades?"

"Yeah, you know, the ones Santa brung him. Same ones he stuck in them late two ladies in your life, same ones he'll stick in them two *new* ladies you been spendin' so much time around, if I decide to talk him into it."

Sheldon squeezed the machete handle 'til his knuckles popped. "That's bullshit. They're Earth-line. He wouldn't—"

"Yeah, just like that headless fucker you found back up the mountain. Biter-Boy don't care what it is he killin', not if he feels like he's got a good enough reason, especially if he gets to use the black blades. Believe you me, it wouldn't take much for me to convince him he's got a damn fine reason, in the interest of his lady love, to do some real Earth-line-style lady-killin'."

Don't feel, Sheldon. Think. Think fast. "So Sally and the beast aren't looking for me?"

"Not yet, they ain't. They ain't even right here in this town no more. But they're still close by, hidin' out. That ain't the point, 'cause I'm here, an' I can fly faster than you can run. You piss me off enough, I can be all the way to your little Janie-Girl, 'fore you can even run back to that crazy ol' Annie-Lady. Yeah, you'll git halfway there just in time for me to throw your little Janie-Slut's hollowed out carcass right in your face, faster'n I did that stupid fuckin' pigeon. *So shut the Hee-Haw-Hell up an' listen.*"

Sheldon drew a deep, shuddering breath. "Okay. I'm listening."

"Right. So here's the deal. You wanna kill Biter-Boy, an' if Biter-Boy knew you was around, he'd be all geared up to come kill you. Accordin' to his new bosses, right now he's supposed to be hidin' out there in the middle of ear-fuck nowhere like a good little fledgling. He's got your sweet lil' older sister to keep him good an' laid, so he's fine with that. Were he to know about you, though…well, I'm pretty sure he'd give all that some second thoughts. Some *sharp* second thoughts."

"So why haven't you told him? Isn't that your job?"

"My job's to get Biter-Boy rollin' with the whole shebang as I see fit. An' there ain't a better way on hand than you, Cop-Boy. 'Cause I figure, shit'd work out ten times better if you got out there to where Biter-Boy an' Sally-Poach is hidin', and got yer shot at 'em. So I'm gonna help you get that fair shot, fair an' square."

"So, let me get this straight. You want Biter—" Sheldon winced. "You want your beast to kill me, so you're setting a trap, leading me to where he can do that. And you're just…telling me all this."

"Yep, pretty much. 'Cause you don't wanna jus' kill Biter-Boy. Naw, what you really want is to kill *your lyin', betrayin', murderin' big ol' beast-fuckin' sister.*"

"That's right."

"An' you ain't got a shot in hell of killin' Biter-Boy, but you'll kill your sister sure enough. Yeah, kill 'er real good. An' once you do, why, Biter-Boy's gonna be so pissed, he'll slice you up thin enough to shingle a roof."

"Right. So, how's that serve your purpose any better than just telling him where I am?"

"It don't matter, Cop-Boy, not to you. 'Cause I can tell just by lookin', you gonna go right along an' try your hardest anyhow. You might even give ol' Biter-Boy a real run for his money, which is even better."

"Where are they?"

"Stayin' in a place, halfway down the other side o' Marlboro Mountain."

"Where's that?"

"*Old Fuckin' Lords!* Guess I'm the whole brains of this here business."

"Just tell me where it is. Could I walk there?"

"You could. By the time you got there, though, you might be too pooped to put up a good fight. An' nah, I want you at your screamin' best when you go up against Biter-Boy. *I wanna see you make him* earn *them black blades!*"

"Okay, then. Where's the best place to hitchhike from?"

"Not so fast. See, for you to get all the way up there, find the right place, an' all the while not fuck it up, you gonna need me there for a few steps. So I gotta go finish sweepin' some bullshit up. Meantime, I reckon you better get some of your own business fixed."

Wings beat the air, and a dark, bulbous shape soared off above the highest branches. Sheldon didn't move 'til he heard feet tread over dry leaves. He lowered his machete and stepped behind a thick, low-forking oak. Along came Annie, down a forest path near the graveyard.

Sheldon drove his machete into the earth and stepped out. "Hi, Annie." He waved.

"Little brave! You been out here all day?" Her mouth smiled. Her eyes didn't.

"I've gone into town some. Sort of killing time."

"No one got weird, seein' a young fellow like you not in school on a Monday?"

"No one said anything." Huh. Maybe that's why he'd gotten odd looks in the hardware store. He'd figured it was because of what he was buying.

"Janikens should be home soon. You hurry, you might get home right in time to meet up with her."

"Okay. Hey, thanks for letting me sleep at your place."

She laughed. "Ain't a damn problem, sweetie. Like I said, I know you've got things to do, and I say you can stay under my roof for as long as you need."

"Right, thanks. Look…Remember what we talked about? I mean that first day?"

"Sure I do."

"Yeah. I think maybe I'm close to finding what I'm looking for."

"Out in these woods?"

"Well…I think that's where it started."

"Been finding that good, quiet place where you finally hear the truth, huh, like I told you to do?"

"You could say that."

She frowned. "So you'll be leaving us soon."

He shuffled in the leaves. "Yeah. Tonight. Sorry."

"Don't be sorry, sweetie. That's what you gotta do, it's what you gotta do. I don't know if you ever plan on comin' back to visit, but…keep the option open."

"What do you mean?"

"I mean keep yourself alive, Sheldon. Keep your eyes open, 'cause what it is I think you're really looking for—not that I know the real what exactly—you're about to run up against the trickiest part of all. You could set yourself in the right direction, or a lot else could get tipped the wrong way, so it ruins everything. Everything for you, and for a lot that's beyond you, everything in the world all that potential you got should've gone to makin' better."

THREE

Janie looked into Larry's old room, saw the unmade bed, and felt weird. Of course, as Mom saw things, it had been her son's room 'til a year ago, and now it was a son's room again. Yeah, after just a few days, Mom was acting like Sheldon was her new son. Oh, she didn't treat him like she would if she'd actually been his mom, wouldn't try to enforce a curfew or ground him for breaking rules…not that Mom spent enough time on Planet Earth for that stuff anymore anyway.

Sheldon understood something about Mom's ways like Janie never had. Then again, he also understood stuff about

Janie that no one else did. No…something deeper than understanding, a common wavelength so basic, she'd never thought to notice its absence in other people, not 'til she met someone who shared it. She'd first noticed it on the way to the tower, how he'd talked about the woods, how he'd listened, the things he'd asked when she told him ghost stories…

Downstairs, the front door groaned open. "Janie? Janie, you here?"

She headed to the end of the hallway. "Sheldon? Yeah, I'm here. What'cha yellin' for?"

He appeared on the landing below, face calm, smiling easily. A second ago, he'd sounded desperate to find her, scared even. Now he met her on the stairs, grabbed her hand and pulled her along.

"Hey, hold on, what's up! Where we goin'?"

"Ah, just outside. Let's walk around, go somewhere."

"Anywhere in particular? Like up to the basketball court?"

"Sure, sounds great."

"Okay then, hold up. Lemme go get the ball." She went and found the one Larry had taught her to shoot hoops with.

When she came back out, Sheldon took a bounding leap off the porch, clearing the steps and three squares of the stone walkway. He slid like an ice skater, turning to face her with a big show-off smile. "So no one bugged you today, did they?"

"Huh? Oh, right. Nah." She dribbled the ball in the street a few times. "That girl you punched in the stomach passed me in the hall and looked away real quick. The only one who didn't have to stay at the hospital. She sorta scooted on over to the other side of the hall and stayed there."

"I didn't get you in any trouble, did I?"

"Nah."

No, he'd just gotten her ear talked off, by everyone from schoolyard friends to a teacher or two. Yeah, that was the Brattleboro rumor mill for you. The strange thing was, no one realized the boy from the fight and her mom's "new foster kid" were the same guy.

"So, what'd you do all day?" she asked.

"Been getting ready for something."

"For what?" She noticed his dirt-stained elbows, knees and ankles. "You're gonna leave soon, aren't you? Hell, of course, why not? If stuff's about to start happening for you, why would you stay in this shitty, boring town?"

"This town's not shitty. Cool people like you live here."

"I'm not that cool. My mom's cool, like you. I can see why you two get along. I'm glad you like me, but I don't know why. I'm just one more of those dumb kids who hangs out at the teen center and doesn't understand shit, can't figure out all the neat stuff people like you and Mom see."

"So, how far are we from the basketball court?"

"Wow, glad you were listening."

"No, I was. It's just I want to hang out, have fun. I don't know when I'll see you again." Wow, he really did sound older…like Larry near the end.

Her lower lip trembled. Ah crap, if she let herself start crying now…"You won't come back."

"I—Okay, yeah, I might not be able to. But I really

want to, and even if I can, I don't know when. So I just wanna hang out and have fun while I can. I don't wanna think about where I have to go or where I'll sleep tonight or any of that shit. Please, Janie, just…C'mon, while there's still time."

"Uh, okay. C'mon. We're almost there."

The Brattleboro Union High basketball court was nice at dusk. Evening was the only time Janie ever liked the school grounds. She dribbled the ball, then took the first shot at three yards. The ball rolled off the rim and bounced. Sheldon caught it. Janie watched, curious how he'd play. He dribbled, eyeing the goal like someone sighting a target down a gun barrel. When he launched the ball, it bounced hard off the backboard. Janie laughed before she could help it. All that physical grace and skill, and he didn't know the first thing about shooting hoops.

Sheldon caught the ball and stood awkwardly. The metal backboard was still humming from the strike. "What?"

"Don't throw so hard. You don't watch much basketball, I guess. Here, watch me shoot a few, the way I hold it, how I throw. Then you try."

Jeez. Here she was giving the poor guy lessons, not exactly a pro herself. She was fine at the shooting part but could barely follow the ins and outs of a game on TV, let alone play. She remembered watching it on TV with Larry, struggling to keep straight in her head which players were supposed to be doing what. When she'd ask questions, he'd tease her about having ADD, which was probably true. When it was just her and a friend or two, though, messing around on the court, she wasn't halfway bad. Soon she made two baskets. When she went for a third, Sheldon leapt in front of her, knocked the ball from her hand, caught it, and scuttled off.

"Hey, no fair! I was about to make that."

"Let me try. I think I get it now."

She doubted it, but stood and watched. He made a clean shot, mimicking her stances and motions almost perfectly. The ball rolled on the rim, looked for a second like it would go in, then tumbled off the outer side.

Janie darted, caught it, and tossed it back. "Toss just a little softer. Let it roll off your fingertips a little more."

Over the next half-hour, hour, hour and a half, whatever, he got better and better. Sometimes they took turns, sometimes dribbled and vied for the ball, sometimes rough-housed over it, giggling all the way. Finally, one of them fumbled, the ball bounced off in some direction or other, and they swayed and ambled, still laughing and grinning. His laughter died off before hers, and he stood up straight and serious.

"It's almost time, isn't it?" She followed his gaze up a set of power lines. All she saw was one really fat pigeon, perched on the wire.

Sheldon looked at it like he saw something else. "Yeah. Come on."

"With you? Where?"

"I mean come on, I'll walk you home."

Right, like he'd been about to invite her along on whatever weird adventure he had planned. Hey, that might be cool. Even if it was insane and scary, maybe that was better than growing up stuck here. Nah, she'd probably end up like one of those nasty old ladies you always saw wandering around town, muttering to themselves, screaming at you if you stepped too close.

"Y'know, Janie," he said as they walked, "you're wrong about yourself. You understand all kinds of neat, magic stuff. Like when you showed me the Bloody Tower, remember?"

"Yeah. That was fun." She walked with the ball tucked under one arm, her free hand squeezing his. At the door, she asked, "You wanna come in? See if Mom's around? She might not have left for work yet."

"I already said goodbye to Annie."

"And now you're saying goodbye to me."

"Well, yeah." Had he just winced?

"I don't think you'll come back, even if you do make it…but I hope you do. Oh, and what Mom asked, when you guys first talked? What she wants you to come back and tell her? Well, I wanna know, too. Yeah. I heard all that. I heard you promise."

She hugged him fiercely, then went to kiss him goodbye on the cheek. She ended up kissing him on the lips instead. Before she could feel embarrassed, she saw him smile brightly. As he walked away, she saw his face shift right back to that weird, calm look he'd worn when they'd first met. She didn't find it creepy anymore. It said he might actually survive whatever he was walking into.

AMENDS IN BLOOD

ONE

The woods seemed twice as deep and thick by night, but Sheldon found his way straight to the machete. As he wiped the tip clean on his trousers, a high, mock-feminine voice sounded above. "*I dawn't think yew'll cum back, Sheldon, but I hope ye dew…Be some fuzz-pie innit for ye when you're older.*"

Sheldon looked up, but still didn't spot the Familiar. "Where to?"

"Hike on over to High Street. Then jus' go up, up, up 'til you hit the bridge. Then stick out yer thumb 'til someone stops, then tell 'em you're headin' to the Wilmington General Store."

"So, where's Wilmington?"

"Don't matter, Cop-Boy, 'cause you ain't never gonna see the place. Think I'd have some stupid fuckin' Earth-liners drive you right to the spot so they could fuck it all up? You just get yourself pointed that way, in whoever's car ye can, and leave the rest to me."

"There's still one problem, though."

"Ain't nothin' I ain't thought of, Cop-Boy."

"Yeah? Then what about—"

Something slid from the branches, so Sheldon darted

backwards. It thudded at his feet. He knelt over it. Sally had carried a backpack when he'd last seen her, not a duffel bag. Still, he sensed something of her in the battered wad of nylon and zippers.

"Where'd you get this?"

"Amazin' what you Spirelights forget an' leave lyin' around when things go batshit."

In the bag was a single folded blanket. Sheldon wrapped the machete in it, then zipped it into the bag and hefted it over his shoulder. "I was gonna get something like that first anyway."

"Suuure. That's the kinda thing you should'a been tendin' to while you was knockin' around, tryin' to get your ball through the net with lil' Janie-Girl. Anyone asks, tell 'em it's your sports gear, that bein' true enough." The wheezing laughter echoed with the beat of wings. "See you at the top, Cop-Boy."

Sheldon guessed he'd gotten used to dealing with the Familiar, forcing his hatred out of the way along with his grief. Now that the creature was gone, a lonesome chill filled him. He left the woods then hurried down South Main. The further he got from Janie and Annie—from a house that would welcome him back, shelter him, let him pretend his duty wasn't out there—the more sure-footed he went. He imagined this town called Wilmington, the person he'd pretend to be, what business he had there. Of course, he wouldn't know 'til he saw whoever picked him up. Then he'd have to assess quickly who he needed to be for them. It had to be as basic as possible, open to constant building and reinvention.

Along High Street, he headed through a more

expensive-looking neighborhood than he'd seen so far in Brattleboro, then along a bridge over the interstate. To his left, cars sped by into West Brattleboro, towards Marlboro Mountain.

When the sidewalk ended, he walked along the edge of a ditch with his hitcher thumb stuck out. The zip and wind-rush of passing traffic felt closer. Finally, an SUV pulled off to the roadside, about twenty feet ahead. As he caught up, a window rolled down on the front passenger side. The stereo blared a weird mix of rap and reggae.

Out peered a young Earth-line man with tousled black hair, a beaky nose, and ice-blue eyes that were deeply, deeply stoned. "Hey bud. Need a ride up to campus or somethin'?"

Sheldon absorbed the voice's rhythm, flowed to it in time with the beak-nosed stoner, and adjusted his posture. "Nah man, I gotta get to Wilmington."

The guy asked the driver, "Where's Wilmington?"

"Man, that's, like, the other side of the mountain." The driver peered past his buddy at Sheldon. "How quick you gotta get there, man?"

"Don't really matter." Sheldon shrugged, tuning his speech rhythms and voice timbre. "Just sometime tonight. Either you guys know where the Wilmington General Store is?"

From the back came a squeaky female voice. "Yeah, sure. It's right at the bottom of the hill as you get into town, less time than it takes to get to Bratt. Like maybe…fifteen minutes?"

"Anyway," said the driver, "it's cold out there. Dude, get in if you want."

As the back door slid open, a harsh ceiling light with

the cover missing clicked on. The girl in the back had gleaming fair skin, frizzy blond hair tied back tight enough to look painful, face baby-puffy and rosy, body plump-petite, short legs stretched out, capped in tiny shoes that bobbed like rabbit ears against the back of the driver's seat. The door shut, the light cut off, and the SUV pulled out. The girl sparked a glass pipe for a deep toke, pulling pure yellow flame from her lighter into a tiny, crackling thicket.

The front passenger looked back. "So dude, we're on our way to a party up at Marlboro. Wanna come chill there a while, then see if you can catch another ride or somethin'?"

Wasn't this Marlboro Mountain they were climbing now? There didn't seem to be much of a town, just lots of woods and pastures, with the occasional sprinkle of barns and farmhouses. That's right, there was a college up here somewhere, too. That explained these folks. "Yeah, that's cool."

"So dude, you, like, what, a high schooler or somethin'?"

"Nah, I've been out of high school for like a year."

"So, you goin' to college anywhere?" asked the driver, a shaggy blond heavy-set guy.

"Nah, but I'm tryin' to save money for that."

"Want a toke?" The girl held out the pipe.

"Nah, I'm cool."

"You ain't a nark, are you?" Obviously the front passenger was joking, but there was a grain of real paranoia there.

"Nah, I just…well…"

"Got people you're meetin' in Wilmington you don't wanna be stoned around?"

"Yeah, kinda."

"Not parents or nothin'? Not cops?"

"Randall, will you shut the fuck up?" The driver looked through the mirror. "Nah, Randall here's cool. We're all just a little shook up over all the fucked-up shit."

"Fucked-up shit?"

"Yeah," said the girl, "you know. The murders in town?"

"Yeah, pretty messed up, right?"

"Who you going to see?" The girl's interest deepened and softened along with her voice.

"My sister and her boyfriend." Thinking fast, Sheldon shrugged. "They always like to meet me around that general store when I get over their way. It's like their hangout or somethin'. They'd come get me tonight, but their car's broken down."

Sheldon spent the ride bantering with these folks, particularly with Billy, the driver. It was the girl, Chelsea, who seemed most interested in him, though. He made a show of attention towards her, guessing that's what they expected.

"Careful, man," said Billy. "She's a little siren, that one."

"Shut up!" Chelsea swatted at the back of Billy's seat. Her hands brushed off his shoulder a couple times. "*I am not!* You stay out of this."

"Hey, hey! No hitting the driver."

Billy's speech told how stoned he was, but his driving was fine. Had Sheldon toked up, not even his voice would have changed, unless he wanted it to. One of the last things Grandpa taught him and Sissy was how to handle Earth-line recreational drugs. If they ever got into that crap on their own—for fun like those decadent Earth-liners—he'd promised to knock them both through three walls with one swat. They might run into the stuff while doing detective work, though, need to sample it to blend in. So at age nine, Sheldon had learned to hold lots of beer, wine, hard liquor, cocaine, and marijuana—but only ever after a medication he was told would coat and protect his developing brain from permanent damage. Grandpa probably hadn't expected him to be on his way to his first fight with a Crimbone at the time.

The SUV pulled up to a large white building that looked sort of like an old-time colonial hotel, a bit like it had been an old barn once. It reminded Sheldon of newer homesteads he'd visited. A dozen cars were parked out front, music pumped loudly within, and more college students stood around on the long porch walkway.

"This it?"

"Yeah, this is Marlboro North," said Randall. "Ain't you ever been up here before?"

"Yeah, I been to the college, but not this place."

"Well," droned Billy, "here's the college."

Sheldon thought he'd messed up big time, but Chelsea leaned close. "This is the one off-campus dorm. Sort of the out-of-the-way place."

"Yeah," added Randall, "so they call it Marlboro North and call the northernmost on-campus dorm Out-of-the-Way. Go figure, right?"

If anyone at this shindig was sober enough to drive, chances were they wouldn't be willing to cart some stranger to the next town. So Sheldon would mingle, drink one beer to blend in—one beer wouldn't hinder him by the time the fighting started—then creep out and hitch another ride. As he followed them up the porch steps, he did his best to catch the ambient energy and reflect it for anyone who might be looking. It was all about blurring the collective impression, so he could deal with individuals one at a time. He was working himself overtime already. This trick was for brief encounters, information-gathering that ended in the old ghostly departure.

The general spirit was simple enough: kids ten or so years older than him, living some prolonged process of proving themselves fit for the adult Earth-line world. For them, it was a stressful, uncertain time, and this was how they escaped that stress, made it livable the rest of the time. Down a long hallway, two girls danced to the grunge rock beat, hands clasped, arms flowing as one, bodies twisting and turning. The waltz turned closer, less formal, a grinding, spinning undulation less concerned with the beat, then the girls toppled kissing and groping against the wall. No one paid much attention, so Sheldon pretended not to. He wanted to keep looking at that perfect moment of careless joy. Even if he hadn't needed to fool these people, he couldn't imagine them learning or accepting his stresses, his *rites of passage*, which in a few hours, would probably kill him.

Something cold touched his arm. It was Chelsea, nudging him with a beer. He took it along with her hand, then spun her into a few dance moves of his own, mimicking what he'd just seen, but with his own graceful precision. When she pressed closer, he felt off balance. Had she seen what the girls had done next? Was that what she wanted?

Of course it is. She looks at you and sees a guy her own age. That was the idea, remember?

"Hey, Sheldon." It was Billy. "Look man, I gotta talk with some people, deal with some shit. Then I'll give you a ride the rest of the way, cool?"

"Hey, thanks."

"Sure you're not too drunk to drive?" asked Chelsea.

"I ain't, but you sure are. I'll be back in a few."

Okay, so there was that problem settled. Billy seemed like a cool dude. That was another thing Sheldon wasn't used to. He liked this bunch. There were probably plenty of other people here he'd like if he got to know them. Not as much as he liked Janie and Annie, but in the same way he'd liked other kids he'd known briefly at the homesteads.

Why, then? He and Sissy had gone in deeper with more interesting Earth-line people than this, and for longer, and he'd always pretended to warm up to them without actually getting lost in his own masks.

Chelsea's palm slid across his arm, startling him…because it felt so nice. "Hey kid, you okay?"

She'd called him a kid. What did that mean? As she looked at his eyes, her face changed. Ah, shit! Sheldon pulled himself together. "Yeah, I'm fine." He chugged a third of his beer in one go. Right away, his stomach and chest started kicking him for it.

"Hey," she said, "I'm gonna check if my roommate's around upstairs…Come along."

Sheldon followed her to the stairwell, suspecting she knew damn well that her roommate wouldn't be in the room. His gulp went all the way to his stomach, where it danced and fluttered.

Halfway upstairs, they ran into Billy. "Hey, Chelsea, you see where Sheldon took off to?"

"He's right—" She looked around.

Sheldon stepped up. "Right here, dude."

"Ah, hey man…Huh. Weird. For a second, I didn't see you right there for some reason. Ready to go?"

"Sure."

Sheldon followed Billy out to the car. The air felt colder beneath his new layer of sweat.

While they drove, Billy said, "I think this is the right road to Wilmington. So you get Chelsea's number?"

"Huh?"

"Yeah, man, looked like you two were seriously mackin' on each other. I sorta expected you to wanna hang around, y'know. Guess your sister and her boyfriend are waiting, though."

"Yep."

"She's nice though, ain't she? Chelsea, I mean."

"Yeah, but I bet my girlfriend wouldn't think so."

"Ah. Gotcha. Y'know, dude, it's funny. I'm always givin' Chelsea shit about goin' for younger guys, callin' her a cougar-in-training an' shit. Then when we first saw you there on the roadside…Look, don't get offended or nothin', okay? I guess it was the light or somethin', but I swear to God, man, I thought it was a ten-year-old out there or some shit. So I pulled over, thinkin' *What's some kid doin' hitchhikin' out here at this time of night*, know what I'm sayin'? Then I saw you up close, an'…How old you say you were again?"

"Twenty-two."

"Hell, wow, you're older than me, actually. Now I *really* feel like an asshole. You look more like, I don't know, maybe eighteen?"

Something ground, dug, went pop, and the SUV went spinning. Billy growled curses and grappled with the wheel. The tires plowed gravel and slid to a stop in soft grass.

"Aw man, I did *not* just have a Goddamn blowout! Man, *shit, shit, shit...*" Billy climbed out and peered back along the road. "Man, what the hell we hit?" He followed the skid marks, muttering, "Aw man, this is fucked, this is fucked, this is—"

Billy must have thought a car had sped around the corner with no headlights, because he was struck with about as much force. His head and shoulders smacked the back windshield, sending blood-flecked spiderwebs through the glass. The frame shrieked and shook, mingling with splintering bones.

Sheldon flung open his door, his other hand grabbing the duffel bag as he rolled into the grass. His forearm was in the bag, gripping the machete handle, before he realized he'd gotten it unzipped. The razor edge slit its wrappings, and Sheldon rose, blade ready. Billy was sucked into the air and vanished in the blackness above. A moment later, his back smashed into the SUV roof. More glass shattered and sprayed. He dangled partway off the back, his neck yawning dark and hollow. The Familiar fluttered down and shoved the body with a taloned foot so it thumped in the grass.

"You piece of shit! I swear I'll kill you!"

"Now don't get all self-righteous at me, Cop-Boy. I done told you, leave the rest to me. What'cha think I had in mind?"

Sheldon swallowed. "Where are they?"

"Right behind you." The thing paused to enjoy

Sheldon's reaction. "Off to your left, that is. There's a dirt road, see? It goes on an' up for like a mile or somethin'. Then…well, just watch for lights in the window, or for a shimmerin' tin roof in the moonlight, an' there you are."

"What are you gonna do now?"

"Find me a good spot to watch from, what else?"

Two

"So, tell me about the Old World."

They lay across the mattress, Sally propped up on pillows and blankets, Rob's head on her breast. When she scratched at his scalp, he stretched out more and his smile broadened.

"How would I know?" she asked.

"You grew up knowing, hearing stories about it, right?" For a second, he wondered if that had been smart to bring up.

"The Old World…Vast! Rob, it was vast. I used to read and hear the stories…"

"And you'd dream about what you imagined."

She curled forward so their noses touched. His hands ran through her hair, and he flexed his neck so their lips met. Then her index finger tapped his nose. "Don't distract me. I'm trying to tell you a story."

He play-snapped at her finger, so she bobbed it at him then sealed his lips with it. He kissed the tip, then closed his eyes and rubbed his unscarred cheek against her palm.

"The Old World…I've dreamed about its giant lakes

that were miles deep, yet so clear…You could dive from the immense cliffs, and the air there was different from anywhere else. You'd just glide down for miles, not too fast, almost flying but not quite. When you splashed, the water was so clear that you could look down through it and see the stone ruins of the ancestors, covered in every color of glowing moss. And the people of the Old World…I hear some of them could actually hold their breath long enough to swim down through all those miles and through the ruins."

Eyes closed, Rob felt the softness of Sally's body, but he saw those ruins. The more she spoke, the further the darkness behind his eyes rolled back. Except when she paused, it kept clearing. "Yeah…and in the ruins, the walls…they told stories. Sally, the walls told stories."

"You read that in your book?"

"No, the book doesn't describe things like that…but when you do, I see it. I still can. I walk the ancient halls, and there are others there, both Schomite and Spirelight. I still know I'm Crimbone, and everyone around me knows too, but it doesn't matter as much, even among the Spirelights, because…I guess it's before the wars and the blood-hate got so strong. The walls tell the stories of everything they've seen, not in paintings or carvings or even writing, but…in the elemental swirl of the matter itself. I don't know, it's…"

"Like if you look at it right, you see all history in the stones of the old halls, and in those sacred places, all time, all things can truly be one to you, if you know how to see it…"

"…And I keep looking further back, keep thinking I'm about to see the beginning of everything, and then…"

"And then?"

When his eyes snapped open, they looked deeper. Everything he'd glimpsed in the ancient halls still flickered there. "It turns back so far, past anything you or I have ever known, past anything we have the slightest idea how to put into words. But I *do* start to recognize it. Then it all flows back to right here, to you and me. Sally, how can we possibly fit into all that? Where do we belong in it, and how do we find our way to that one little spot in everything else, where there's no other path to take?"

"We belong right here, right now, because that's all there ever really is."

He blinked and shivered. Where had he just gone? Yeah, he'd still been here with her, but that had only been a tiny corner of where and when he was, just as Rob Coscan was only a tiny corner of who he was. What greater thing—what *sentience*—was Rob Coscan supposed to dissolve into? Had he just felt a bit of it? Never mind. All he wanted to be right now was Rob, here with Sally. He rolled onto his side, rubbed her shoulders and kissed her.

When the laughter started, Rob sat up sharply, euphoria cooling then heating back up as pounding adrenaline.

"What is it?"

"Can't you hear it?"

"Sounds like a bunch of hicks hootin' an' hollerin'. They're far off."

He shook his head. "You hear that laughter then. Listen closer. It's only one voice."

"Okay, yeah. So?"

In a flash, he was on his feet. "It's that creature. Puttergong. My Familiar."

"So, let it stay out there. You don't have to go to it." That's what Sally told him. The burning pull in his veins spoke stronger. *In the end, Biter-Boy, it's your blood writes the book.*

"No," he growled low. He could resist the blood call, but not the unfinished business with Puttergong. Now the thing's laughter was closer to this cabin...closer to Sally.

Rob thundered down the stairs, out through the cabin's living room and kitchen, onto the porch and into the grass, naked as the night that greeted him. The knives still stood stuck in the grass, side by side like twin pillars. As he wrenched them from the earth, it seemed he felt as they did, set free into motion. Underfoot, the smooth yard became brush and brambles, the open moonlit air a tree-choked darkness that embraced him and pulled him in deep. The flailing blades found all sharp brush and thorns in his path and swept them aside. For every twig or leaf or briar vine that crunched and crackled beneath his bare, callused feet, Puttergong's laughter echoed nearer, like a rattle through struck tin. In that echo was the forest's voice, clear, merciless, and consuming in its love for him. He no longer leapt or ducked or climbed or dodged, so much as flowed, through the depths like blood through veins. So it went, down gullies and up hillsides, only vaguely aware of the tiring soreness in his limbs.

"Hehehehehe. Happy Birthday, Biter-Boy!"

Rob halted atop a low hill, blood pounding so hard in his temples that his eyes burned. His feet were scraped and cut all over, but there were few fresh scratches on the rest of his body. "It's not my birthday."

"So get out'a yer birthday suit 'fore ye go joggin'."

"Don't you get it, birdie?" His teeth clenched, palms pressed to the bone by the knife handles they squeezed. "I'm not gonna listen to your bullshit advice anymore."

"That a fact? You listened to me fine just now."

"Yeah, I came to tell you to fuck off."

"Suuure. You say you ain't gonna listen to me, Biter-Boy. But you still listen to your blood. More important, you still listenin' to the voice of this here forest."

"The forest and my blood tell the truth. You tell me lies."

"I keep sayin', Biter-Boy, shit like that don't matter. Truth, lies, whatever anyone or anything tells ye, all that matters is where you end up when you follow the sound. Why you think a Crimbone High Fuckin' Natural would turn up in this weak time an' place? Your pesky spook buddy already pointed it out. This damn world's gettin' sick of us Deschembine fuckers, ain't got no more use for our old squabblin'."

"So, Louis was right. It's time for the wars to end."

"Yeah, 'cept not with some pussyass whimperin' out. This world's runnin' short on stuff to do with us, 'cause we ain't been gettin' off our asses like maybe this world expected when it let us in. What you gotta do, Biter-Boy, is get off your ass, get the other Crimbone off theirs, an' go live up to the Deschembine half of the bargain, *which is get the fuck rid of them pesky Spirelights ye brung with you.* Yeah, them, with their crazyass dream world where everything belongs to 'em 'cause their wacky gods told 'em so…which is exactly what the real world'll look like if they ever get their way, if the Crimbone don't knock 'em out that dream world but good, an' soon. Before you do, you gotta go show this world which half of the Deschembine refugees got the mojo for it."

"You don't get it, birdie. I don't give a flying fuck about your war anymore. I have my own life, my own strength, and you fuckers can all go rot, you hear me?"

"Wow there, Biter-Boy, them's strong words…Might hurt my lil' feelin's, if I believed it. But I got me a hunch, after tonight, you sure as hell is gonna give a shit. Yeah, I reckon after tonight, goin' out an' endin' this here Spirelight-Schomite war, in the only way makes a lick of sense…Yeah, that's gonna seem like a *mighty fine idea.*"

Puttergong's laughter echoed out again. Rob spun and looked back the way he'd come, as though following the waves of the echo. He knew he'd left the lights on, but he couldn't see them through the trees. His mouth gaped, eyes bulging uselessly in new comprehension.

Rob heard his blood, heard the forest, and their message sent him running back towards the cabin.

THREE

Sally stood on the porch, dressed in the clothes Jesse had given her at the motel, along with the heavy duster coat Rob had dug out of that closet of spare clothes they'd found. It was mostly men's clothes, but some of it fit her close enough. Rob had taken to wearing the duster on their forest walks during the day—at least when he'd been awake. Maybe she shouldn't be surprised he was such a night owl. She frankly wasn't sure what kind of sleep schedule she preferred, 'cause it had been years since she'd been able to keep a reliable one. A couple of times, he'd asked if she wanted to go for a moonlit walk, but she hadn't been into it. It wasn't like she was usually scared of the woods at night, but *these* woods…

Now she tugged his duster close, smelled him on it, and listened harder. The porch light didn't work, and the glow from the doorway and windows didn't shine far. How long had it been since the tearing brush and crunching leaves had grown too far away to hear? There, was that it again, coming back? She started across the yard, but the hedgy, knotted wall of forest halted her before she reached it. What had it said to stop her? She'd never know, at least not consciously, because the forest wouldn't speak in any language a Spirelight could understand. The forest spoke to the Crimbone…to Rob. He wouldn't tell her what it said, but he told her he loved her. He told her a lot of things.

Suppose the forest tells him what to tell you? You can't read the forest, but it reads you like it does everyone. Everything the Crimbone say about the land is true, and you know it, no matter how much your upbringing drilled it into you to call it Schomite blasphemy. The highest Tribunal members know it, too. Why do you think they only fuck with all those Schomite-favoring lands indirectly, through Earth-line politics, as long as they can help it?

In the distance, leaves crunched high, higher, level, level, then lower…closer. What had the forest told Rob not to tell her this time?

"Sally." The voice came from her left, plain and passionless. The boy crossed the grass quieter than ever, now four feet away.

Through the trees, Rob sounded close. His Familiar

had told him where to find her family, that they'd hound him and Sally to their deaths, never let them be free and together. At least that's what he'd told her. He also claimed they were all dead. Now the window's glare fell across Sheldon's blank face.

As his arm cocked back the machete, Sally said breathlessly, "Sheldon?"

She'd never be sure how the word sounded, but she had a split instant to see his eyes wake up, mirroring hers. His reflexes had already taken hold, though. His machete swung at her head.

FOUR

Ahead, the forest trail split to reveal lighted windows, but that wasn't the glow that consumed Rob's senses. It was *two* glows, too close together. He'd felt them long before seeing them. There was Sally…and this young one. Though Rob had never seen it, he recognized it. Strong, fresh…How the hell had he ever tasted such a strong glow on the air and not searched 'til he ran it down, glutted his blades and his soul, sucked every drop into himself then howled it back out for the moon? Never mind, he'd do that now. With a bounding leap, his feet hit the smooth grass.

The boy's machete swung. Sally staggered then fell against a porch beam. She slumped to the earth, the side of her head bloody. The red swirl of rage consumed Rob's vision. The boy stared at her, stared at his machete. Then Rob's shriek cut the night as the first of his black blades plowed towards the kid's face. The boy pivoted so the thrust sang past his ear. The machete barely batting aside Rob's second disemboweling stroke. As the little bastard darted back, Rob nearly flew right at him. Something made them both pause, though, blades still poised, metal still singing from that first clash. They panted and glared at each other. Then their eyes drifted to Sally.

She turned on her side, letting out a pained, incoherent moan. Rob's eyes shot to the smeared spot on the machete blade then back at her. She pulled herself partway onto the porch, then slumped over again. Her glow would have told Rob she was alive either way, flickering once or twice but holding strong. "Rob…Sheldon…"

Rob stalked towards Sally's attacker, his face twisting so his stitches opened and bled. He didn't stop 'til he stood completely between Sally and the boy—Sheldon, huh?

"She's not dead," Sheldon shouted. "The blade, I…it turned in my hand. I tried not to—"

"Think I'm gonna give you another chance to try? *Think I'll kill you any less painfully?*"

Rob couldn't just rush in, though, couldn't underestimate the little shit. He'd gotten the others by surprise, but he'd missed that chance with this brat. It had almost gotten Sally killed. Now the little fucker was trying to look all pitiful, like he expected to be let off with a warning—

Typical fucking Spirelight attitude—

Wait a second, how do I know that? I haven't even—

Never mind. Either way, he's already as dangerous as he'll ever be.

Except his glow wasn't how Rob wanted it…*hadn't*

flared to its tastiest intensity. "Come on, kid, so I can drink you dry. *Come find out what little bastards like you are for.*"

There, yes, Sheldon's eyes changed, flared. Rob sprang, his arms guiding the blades in a single continuous, swirling, tumbling, shooting, rising, falling movement. One blade blocked a swipe while the other sailed at Sheldon's throat. The machete flashed like many lightning bolts, deflecting strike after strike before shooting deadly close to Rob's eyes and neck and stomach, all in an instant. Rob drove harder. So did Sheldon. No combinations of attacks, no pairing of offense and defense broke either fighter's form. Several times, Rob felt the edges and tips of his blades catch cloth and flesh, but Sheldon always countered before the strike could drive home. The machete's edge swung an inch from Rob's groin, the tip nicking his inner thigh. His right blade swung up, knocking the machete wide so the boy's arm flailed. He drove his foot into the boy's gut, sending him rolling through the grass.

Damnit, Rob had missed a clear opening. He didn't have time to think about it because Sheldon got back up and attacked again. This time Rob met him with two sweeping arcs, low and high. Motherfucker, the punk had just taken a shot at his nuts. So that's where Rob would skewer the little bastard, hoist him high on one knife and whack his head off with the other. The tip of one black blade caught at the boy's knee, and *yes, there*—but no, the twinkly little cockstain jumped back just in time. Rob drove him further, blades swinging harder and faster. The boy wasn't attacking anymore, just working that machete hard with both arms, all to keep his head and limbs attached. The machete strained, and Rob had no idea why it hadn't broken yet. Through the clash, he saw the boy's panting face, retreating more desperately.

Another few seconds, just another few seconds…

They'd moved back alongside the house, then towards the trees, the ground dropping off rockier and steeper, both their feet struggling harder for balance. Now if Rob tripped up even a little, he'd fall right on his enemy's weapon. He saw that the kid knew it, was watching for the least chance…

Sheldon danced back into the woods and ducked under a low branch. When Rob's slice cleaved the branch, it undid his aim, faltered his balance. The machete's edge zinged across his ribs. Only a blind reflexive pivot saved him, and a tree trunk shook as he slammed against it. His counter stroke clanged close to the machete's hilt. Rob had no clear sweep through the hanging brush, so he kicked again, sent Sheldon spilling sideways, rolling then tumbling a steep ten feet. The boy thumped and rolled, first in mud, then through dead leaves. Rob spotted the path the boy had plowed down the hillside…but where was the damn boy?

The glow was everywhere, permeating the red swirl that boiled Rob's brain, but the source—*where the fuck was the source?* Damnit, it blazed so full and pure, exactly how he wanted it, and so near…

Rob flailed left and right. The twin blades cut their perfect whistling arcs, controlled by instincts that overrode the moment's mania. The glow rippled, so Rob almost followed the disruption back to the source. Then it was still and steady again. How'd the kid gotten out of sight so fast, without a sound? What kind of twisted abilities did these Spirelight fuckers have? What hadn't Jesse or Zane told him? Never mind. The punk obviously waited somewhere close, probably watching. The instant he moved, Rob would see the glow shift at the source, and he'd open Sheldon Wildfire like a trout. For now, he drew his own energy inward, got his head together and listened to the forest. He lifted one blade and saw spattered wetness. It was too dark to see the crimson, but he almost saw the black metal shimmer from within with its own red. If he touched the blood, he knew it would still be hot.

"You love me?" Rob howled to the night, to the forest. "You embrace me? *Then give him to me.*"

Yes, let this forest give him Sheldon Wildfire, just like the swamp of New Orleans had given him Chuck Sawyer. The swamp had told him Chuck was on his trail, closing in. So he'd asked the swamp, *told* it, *sent his will out through the terrain that had embraced him*, to strike against his enemy. Since his early teens, Rob had known of the land's will, felt it guiding him, and he'd asked for its blessing. Never once had he thought to direct its power with his own will. For one thing, he hadn't thought it was possible, for him or anyone. Not 'til that demented old hippie had tried to put a gun to his head. He hadn't planned it any more than he'd known Chuck would turn up after him that night. The swamp had still let him know what was going on. So he'd *told* the swamp what he wanted, and it had happened. His dominant consciousness never quite believed it, though, not 'til tonight. Now he felt the full magnitude, *that he had directed his own pure will through the land to kill his enemy*. Back then, he hadn't known the feeling of the blades, the taste of an enemy's life, their glow, cut free by his hand, flowing into him.

The land is the master, not the puppet. Don't forget that, 'cause it doesn't change, no matter how many rules you think you rewrite for yourself.

"*Fuck that shit,*" Rob growled with a grin. Tonight, this forest had told him the boy was coming, and now he sent out his response. In it was gratitude, but also a request, a command…a will. Why not? He was a part of it, after all, a *powerful* component. Still, if this mountain favored him even a trace less than New Orleans had…

Rob stood fast and waited.

FIVE

Sheldon pressed as tightly beneath the jutting rock as the inner curve allowed. He peered across the rocky outcropping, through several small bushes. As the beast roared, Sheldon felt every spot on his body where the black blades had touched. A straight seeping line ran from his right knee, nearly to the hip. Deeper cuts streaked his chest, another on his left side. Two torn flaps hung from his shoulder, one of cloth, the other bloody meat. Each wound blazed through him as if the black blades had plowed into his heart. He didn't twist or contort as the pain told him to, not even to shudder from the violation of the evil metal.

Get it together. He'll never go away 'til one of you is dead. So go kill him. Or get killed. Like you planned, remember?

Except none of this was like he'd expected, not from the instant he'd seen his sister's eyes. Time somehow paused when she'd said his name, even while his blade hadn't, couldn't. He'd had time to think, *I just killed the last of my family.*

He couldn't remember the blade turning against her skull, let alone whether he'd done that on purpose. Then came the beast, the Crimbone, the man named Rob Coscan.

Staring at that enraged, beastly face, Sheldon had thought *He really does love her, better than any of us ever did. She loves him, because he'll let her be whoever and whatever she is, not just what he wants her to be. I'm the one who tried to kill my own sister, just like Mom tried to kill her.*

That hadn't stopped him from fighting back when Rob Coscan attacked. By the time they'd reached the woods, Sheldon had no longer seen the man who'd stared horror-struck at a wounded lover, who fought to protect her. A beast had swallowed that man. Those eyes showed neither desire nor ability to defend or love, Sally or anyone else, just the purest rampaging bloodlust, overwhelming Sheldon a sword stroke at a time. Sheldon remembered the Crimbone he'd once watched Dad fight. That creature had been a shadow of the pure elemental madness that now pursued him in the form of Rob Coscan.

The machete was chipped and dented all over. The beast was so vicious and strong…*Damn, was it strong!* Sheldon's arms felt nearly ripped from the sockets, just from deflecting those strikes, like they'd come from bones of solid iron, powered by a ten-cylinder engine instead of a heart.

Above, the beast stalked about, panting and snarling louder. A thick breeze blew through the forest, through Sheldon's hiding place, seeming to come in a rhythm with those snarls. Something poked and wriggled against his back so he stiffened. It gave a low squeak, like some kind of rodent, and he froze deeper. He was still pressed as far as he could go beneath the rock, but there should be plenty of room behind him for such a small animal to crawl out. Yet still it scuttled and pressed along his spine. Its tiny wet nose worried at his back. It reached his collar. Tiny, scratchy paws tickled the back of his neck. Then came the stab of its teeth. The pain was small, concentrated, but it felt like a jolt of electricity through Sheldon's body, so he wanted to flail and roll. Instead, only one hand let go of the machete, shooting back and closing around the furry form. The animal gave the tiniest squeal before he broke its back. Out in the night somewhere, the beast perked up, paused and turned, its bare feet shifting through the brush.

Sheldon dropped the dead rodent. His hand shot back to the machete, and he went still again. The beast's footsteps moved out of twigs, leaves and pine needles, onto bare rock. The slow, low, snarling breaths turned to sharp sniffs.

Make yourself relax, so your muscles go loose. You can't be tensed up like this in the next few seconds…

But I'm too scared—

That doesn't matter. Right now, your emotions can't have anything to do with your physical or mental state.

Why bother if I can't win? What about Sally? Even if I kill the beast, she won't—

That doesn't matter, either. You started the fight. So fight 'til it's over.

The beast prowled the rocks, on level with Sheldon, then lower, down alongside the next short drop. It had been very close for a moment, was now further away, but not far enough. Soon it would search for him beneath the rocky juts.

So get out there and fight it.

Not yet…Not yet…

Another sound reached him, close to his head. He peered up as hard as he could without moving his head, but he still couldn't see. Another animal crept towards him, larger than the last one. In front of him, the small bushes rustled and crinkled with more small approaching life, small enough to be insects come to gnaw at him like maggots. Near his feet came the soft padding of yet another animal, probably the same kind as the one by his head. Sheldon wished he were still safe back in Brattleboro with Janie and Annie. Maybe he'd even prefer it back at the Marlboro party, with Randall, Billy and Chelsea, that Billy was too stoned to drive anywhere, still alive.

Yeah, plenty of wishes ran through his mind…mostly that he hadn't swung his blade at Sally. Only this moment's intent guided him. Slowly and silently, he bent his neck back 'til he saw the creature drawing near. A fatly muscled fox bore down as though on a sleeping rabbit. It paused when Sheldon's eyes locked on it. He forgot the other creature near his feet, until the pain of teeth bloomed in his ankle. He kicked and flailed. The fox in front of him lunged and snapped. The machete whipped about, tearing through the outer bushes. The fox leapt away, but the blade still caught it, severing its front legs and spilling its guts. Musty-slick death-smell flooded the confined space, and he choked back his gorge.

Now the beast turned Sheldon's way, a sinewy opaque shape in the tree-filtered moonlight. The other fox tore at his ankle, as the beast crouched and poised. Sheldon flailed down. This fox was quick enough to avoid the blade. By now, the beast had closed half the distance. Sheldon rolled from his shelter, tearing through mangled bushes, his blade shooting out in an iron thrust.

The beast skidded and swung at the machete as if to hew it like a stalk. Sheldon leapt through the air at his enemy, point down. Both black blades hacked at his exposed flanks. His left hand caught a low branch. As he swung up, he kicked the beast hard in the face. The beast staggered, momentarily blinded. Sheldon looped his legs about the thick branch and scrambled higher. The branch sagged, but still held him high and fast. He needed to reach higher shadows and dive on the beast before it got its head together. The branch shook and shuddered as an impact from its base rode up through Sheldon's grasp. He plummeted. Bare rock smacked his back. For a second, he was sure he'd been paralyzed. Then he found himself kicking and shoving the branch off his body.

"Should've stayed out of my fucking forest, Sheldon." The beast stalked forward. "Can't you tell by now? It loves me and hates you. Accept that now, and this'll hurt less."

Sheldon's head fell to the side. The machete had landed four feet to his right. He whimpered, let his head and shoulders fall back, let his body go limp, defeated. The beast came on grinning, blades poised to strike. Sheldon waited, focused, then threw himself sideways, as the first blade struck like a snake. His hand found the machete, and it seemed to leap up and around, pulling his arm along.

The left black blade clanged against rock. The beast pivoted, the right blade whistling around and up. Sheldon's machete whirled at an angle and clanged between the knife's teeth. Before the beast could retract, he yanked the knife clean out of its hand. While one black blade spun into the brush somewhere, the other shot close to Sheldon's face. He parried, hoping to repeat the disarming motion. Not to be had twice, the beast batted it aside. Again, Sheldon leapt down along the outcropping. On a high ledge, he met the beast and drove it back. The machete caught thick stomach muscle, and Sheldon was sure he was about to set Rob Coscan's guts spilling. Then the remaining knife struck the machete twice, knocking it wild then shattering the blade near the hilt.

Sheldon saw the black blade complete its arc. Then it skewered him.

SIX

Juicy meat and sundered organs swallowed the black metal. Muscles contracted as though trying to push it out but only clenched it in there tighter. Spirelight life flared to a supernova, and Rob felt it all around him. It was time to rip this little bastard open and drink that life, along with the death that followed. Out flowed the glow, along with the blood that splashed all over Rob's hands, blood for Sally—

Rob blinked. There was Sally's face, twisted in agony, right in front of him, through the red swirl—

The Spirelight glow, blinding him the way she did. It wouldn't leave him be 'til he drank it down, sucked it up—

Sally in pain because she—

No, not Sally…The kid who'd tried to kill Sally, this Spirelight brat on his knife. Besides, who the hell was—

Sally Wildfire, dumbass! Y'know, the love of your life, the reason you're fighting?

Rob shivered spastically. Only his knife hand remained steady. He could feel how the tip jutted through the boy's back into empty air, but it might as well have been driven deep like a nail into oak. How long since he'd last seen Sally, slumped half in the grass, half on the porch?

She's back there waiting, hurt, probably needing your help.

No, he was out here for the glow, for the kill, because what was sweeter than—

Sally's face, right here in front of him…

Rob cried out like he was the one who'd been stabbed—like this kid would have cried out, if he'd had the wind for it—and jerked the knife free. He fell to his knees. The boy toppled backwards, vanished over the edge, and thumped somewhere on the earth below. Rob rolled onto his side, pushed himself up and vomited. When he stood up, he was surprised to realize it was still dark outside. Actually, only a few seconds had passed.

Back at the cabin, he found Sally on her feet, still wrapped in his duster. One hand pressed the side of the building, the other to her bloody temple. Her life's glow held steady, the clearest thing to his blurred senses. Before he touched her, he stooped to set down his remaining knife. It wasn't in his hand. Had he dropped it at the scene, or somewhere on the way back?

Tomorrow…tomorrow he'd find his knives. Right now, he and Sally found each other. They embraced feebly, then fell unconscious in the dewy grass together.

SEVEN

Randall Cronenberg considered himself a pretty laid-back guy. Tonight, he was stoned and wanted to feel mellow. So normally, when the night drew on and he was close to passing out and no one had seen Billy in a few hours, he wouldn't have worried. Except Chelsea said Billy had given that weird dude a ride to Wilmington. Oh well, Billy had been hitting it off with the kid. They'd probably met up with that sister and gone for a few drinks or something.

Randall waited tables at the Lucca Bistro, though. Tonight, he'd come in to the news that his coworker Rob Coscan was reported missing. It rattled him so bad that the boss said he could leave early. He'd called Chelsea and Billy. Like true friends, they'd greeted him with weed. Then Billy pulled off and picked up that weird little hitchhiker dude.

Now it was edging towards three in the morning. Randall stood on the front porch of Marlboro North, smoking a cigarette. It was his first taste of tobacco since his dad had died of lung cancer three years ago. A few halfway-sober drivers had gone cruising, to see if Billy had been in a wreck somewhere. Down the highway, someone said, there were lots of skid marks and broken glass next to a field, but no SUV and no Billy.

A door whined open somewhere. Randall turned and saw a short, plump girl-shape, with just enough moonlight behind her to show off Chelsea's golden hair. Randall chucked his cigarette butt in the grass, then remembered that they kept tin cans out here for smokers. His chest was sore and his throat was gummy. God, he'd better not get back into this gross habit. Chelsea rubbed his back. He put an arm around her and they snuggled close.

Off in the trees to their right, something rustled, crashed then came tearing and shambling forward. When Randall jumped, Chelsea hugged him tighter. "God, you're jumpy. Maybe it's time you tried actually sleeping?"

The noise tore from the woods and tumbled helter-skelter towards them. A small hand fell across the porch railing, dark and gleaming.

"Hey, who's that?" Chelsea said.

The hand slid away, leaving a dark smear on the railing.

Randall heard himself call, "Billy?"

When the porch light cut on, Randall thought, *Shit, more people, here to make this bad scene worse.*

But no, Chelsea had just gone and flipped it on. Then they both thundered down the porch ramp. Around the corner, the bloody visitor staggered into the light. It was that guy, the hitchhiker. Only—wait, no, not him at all. This was just a kid, probably ten or something.

Holy Fuck, what the hell had the little dude gotten himself into? They didn't see just how mangled he was 'til he looked at them, then fell facedown, into the light.

Chelsea knew some first aid, so she knelt by the kid. Randall ran inside and called 911.

EPILOGUE:
HEADLIGHTS ON THE
HIGHWAY

ONE

Jesse and Zane got back three days early.

First Jesse had pleaded his own case to the Tribunal, then Rob and Sally's. Zane spoke up during the first part. For the second, he stood by Jesse's side, but kept quiet. Only half the Schomites at the hearing were Crimbone, the ones to whom Jesse spoke most passionately and inventively. Of these, half were truly moved by the tape when he played it, albeit grudgingly. The other half growled, remembering everything a recording device let the others forget. Like where the Spirelights' glow really came from, everything they felt entitled to in its name.

After millennia of fighting back against worse atrocities, whenever any Crimbone encountered a Spirelight and reacted like those guys in New Orleans had, *of course* the Spirelights blubbered like the girl on the tape, painting themselves as the victims, instead of aggressors who'd gotten what was coming to them.

Jesse couldn't dispute the personal experiences that bred such sentiment, but he'd reminded everyone that the girl on the tape had wanted nothing to do with any of that. That she'd displayed such independent strength of spirit to transcend her people's doctrine should earn anyone's respect. Rob, it turned out, came under little attack.

Those men in New Orleans had disgraced only themselves, Jesse argued. Should their victim—even a Spirelight—be further punished for those crimes, all Crimbone would shoulder the dishonor. At this, one of the non-Crimbone objected, stating that the transgressions in New Orleans were subject to a separate investigation.

Jesse saw how his words hit his brethren, though. The civilian Schomites would see it too. The Cabinets hadn't held their age-old employment of the beast race by assuming they'd subjugated it.

Jesse had allowed a week for an answer. Pretty damn generous, considering both he and Zane remembered times when it would be thought indolent to take more than a day of it. If rumors were true about those Pittsburgh boys, that might have sped things up.

"Quit acting anxious," Zane grumbled on the drive back up Marlboro Mountain. "It's messing with your driving."

"I am anxious," said Jesse, "and you drive worse than this in a normal mood, so fuck off."

"Whatever we find, trust me, it's already waiting for us by now." Then not so smug or sure, Zane added, "How you think they'll take the news?"

Jesse didn't answer, just tried not to let his driving get

any worse.

At the cabin, they found the same scared, battered kids in love…except more battered and scared, less like kids. They both talked less and spoke more sharply when they did.

Sally's eyes stared harder, deeper…the eyes of a woman from some colder country, where people drew less close and seldom spoke to each other. A thick, scabby gash ran from her hairline above her left ear, curving to touch her eyebrow. The eye was thickly bloodshot in the outer corner and sagged lazily.

All of Rob's stitches had fallen out. The scar was a thin red upside-down lightning bolt that would soon turn icy pale. It looked more at home on his face, among sharper, sunken angles. Darker circles ringed eyes full of something not quite fire, not quite ice. Against his hips, the Crimbone blades hung comfortably in their scabbards.

Jesse smelled fresh wounds under Rob's clothes…wounds that would leave larger scars.

"Okay…" Rob fought for a steady voice. "What's the deal?"

Zane started to speak, but Jesse took Rob aside.

"*So what's the fucking deal?*" said Rob. Yeah, there was the same scared, wild kid Jesse had pulled out of the Connecticut River.

"For starters," said Jesse, "it looks like you might actually be a High Natural."

"You knew."

"Knew what?"

"That I missed one of them."

"Not for sure. I'll bet you have an answer to at least

one thing I asked you earlier, though."

"Huh?"

"Never mind. You'll do the math eventually."

"Anyway, I won't miss again. So what did they say?"

"They've agreed to place Sally under special protection. She'll live under observation, but she'll never be directly interfered with unless it becomes necessary."

"*Becomes necessary?*"

"They've agreed not to kill her. The Vermont Cabinet is eager to get to know you."

"But not Sally."

"No."

"So where they expect her to go?"

"Where they send her," Jesse corrected. Then, "How would I know?"

Two

He'd be out of the hospital soon. Not because he was fit to leave, but because he'd let them know he was conscious, and he'd given them the number to the nearest homestead.

Before long, agents would arrive, a man and a woman who may or may not be an actual couple. Either way, they'd have some kids in tow to complete the family image. They'd be so relieved to find their runaway son, horror-stricken at his brutalized state. They'd give the hospital his fake identity, after which they'd fabricate billing arrangements. They'd spirit him out that same night, take him to some homestead to heal. That's when the questions would start. He'd have no more answers than Sally had, years ago.

So what about Janie and Annie? Had he found the answers he'd promised them? He hadn't found what he'd gone looking for, neither vengeance nor death in the attempt.

Sally's eyes, though…Sheldon still saw the eyes of the sister who'd pleaded with him years ago. Even Sissy had never figured out that he'd been the one to answer those pleas. Mom and Dad and Sissy couldn't hurt Sally anymore. Neither could Sheldon. Despite everything, he hoped her beast didn't either.

Maybe that was the drugs talking. In their haze, he felt the blade's trail through his midsection, through organs that would take months to heal, probably a year before he'd be back in action. Even then, he'd still feel the burning trail of the black metal, where it had plowed through his guts. He'd feel it for the rest of his life.

"He's a tough one, all right," said a woman who wasn't one of the doctors. "One of the Wildfires, isn't he?"

"One of them, yeah," said the man with her. "From the looks of things, even they weren't as tough as him."

"Yes, except…Well, you read the descriptions of his wounds. So what happened? Did he manage to kill the Crimbone who did this to him?"

"Doesn't look like it." The man whistled. "Left for dead, by a Crimbone…That doesn't happen, you know. Look, can't you already see it, sense the difference in him?"

"Don't remind me." The woman's voice sounded nauseous. "We just have no idea what it means. Not yet, anyway."

THREE

Dusk fell across the Brattleboro bus station. On Putney Road, a few of the cars zipped and chugged by, their headlights already on.

A girl sat on the front steps of the rattletrap trailer that passed for a terminal. She hugged her over-large jean jacket close. The bus she'd been told to take had left an hour ago. Its headlights hadn't been on yet. They would be, on the bus she did take.

At the front desk, she'd exchanged the ticket Jesse had given her for the one she now carried. Her new duffel bag sat at her feet. It was lighter than the one she'd lost.

The ticket envelope had still been sealed when Jesse handed it to her. "Don't tell me where it's to," he'd said.

"So what if I don't go where it says?"

"I can't say what'll happen."

"If I don't follow instructions, do you think it'll be you they send to kill me?"

"Please," he'd said, his eyes trembling paternally. "I don't want to find out."

Now she felt bad, because here she was, about to put him in that position. It was better than life on such terms. Come to think of it, she'd never lived by her own terms, had she? No, just according to everything she'd been running from. It was time to try something new.

From across the lot, back from the restroom, there

came a tall, scruffy-haired young man wearing the duster coat he'd taken from the cabin. By now, it was so dim that she didn't see the fresh scar 'til he was five feet away. Most of her depth perception was back, though her vision still blurred in the right corner, where her little brother had hit her in the face with a damn machete.

Rob sat down and put his arm around Sally. She leaned her head on his shoulder. He rubbed her neck and back, trying to work out some of the tension.

Then her bus pulled in, headlights aglow. Rob and Sally stood up together. She hefted her duffel bag. He walked her over to the bus. It had been hours since either of them had cried. The ghosts of those tears were more visible on her face than his.

People lined up behind them. A moment later, the driver was ready to take tickets. The girl handed hers over. So did the boy. He'd bought his a few minutes ago.

There weren't many people on this bus. Rob and Sally sat towards the back. He kissed her forehead then smiled, comforting as he could manage. She kissed and stroked the scar.

When the bus pulled out, she lay her head on his shoulder and tried to sleep.

They were headed down the East Coast, where there were more neutral territories. She had clothes for them both in her bag. He had a little money, his last savings pulled from the cash machine, plus the security deposit he'd extracted from his landlady hours earlier. Good thing he hadn't run into Darren at the house…too much temptation to go for one last drink together. That wasn't who he was anymore.

Plus, it would have sucked, putting his friend in that sort of awkward position. He'd been itchy enough as it was. Jesse and Zane might have figured out where he'd gone, while Sally waited here.

At least they'd made it onto the bus. Damn, it was surreal how fast Brattleboro dropped away, into the distance behind them. Beneath the duster coat, the twin black blades of Magur Sevi lay comfortably against Rob Coscan's hips.

FOUR

Puttergong watches 'til the bus pulls out, then he takes off high over the town and trees. Out above the highway, he slows down, lets the bus catch up some, and coasts overhead.

Okay, so maybe shit ain't gone quite like it was s'posed to. No, wait, actually, it went damn near spot on. Cop-Boy did his part, Sally-Poach did hers, an' Biter-Boy went batshit-berserk! Yep, that was his part, alright.

There's just three little itsy-bitsy problems: Cop-Boy ain't dead, neither is Sally-Poach, an'...well shit, Puttergong don't quite know what the hell's up with Biter-Boy. That's okay, though. There's all the time in the world to figure it out.

Interestin' days, these is, more interestin' than Puttergong's seen in a right long spell. Ain't they just gettin' more an' more interestin' all the time.

Matt Spencer is the author of five novels, two collections, and numerous novellas and short stories. He's been a journalist, New Orleans restaurant cook, factory worker, radio DJ, and a no-good ramblin' bum. He's also a song lyricist, playwright, actor, and martial artist. He lives in Vermont with his girlfriend and two cats. Check him out online at http://mattspencerauthor.wordpress.com, on Twitter at @MattSpencerFSFH, and on Facebook at Books by Matt Spencer.

Thanks for reading, folks. Hope you enjoyed the ride. Now don't forget to go to let everyone else know what you thought! Be sure to pop over to Amazon, Goodreads, your blog, and whatever social media you frequent, and drop a short review (or a long one, if you feel like it).

9 780578 451459